AND YOUR ENEMIES CLOSER

ROB PARKER

THIRTY MILES TRILOGY
BOOK TWO

RED DOG
UK

Published by RED DOG PRESS 2023

First Edition

Hardback ISBN 978-1-915433-03-9
Paperback ISBN 978-1-915433-19-0

www.reddogpress.co.uk

For my family and friends.

PROLOGUE

MIDNIGHT, AND THE silence couldn't have been louder.

There were six of them in total. Four standing, two on the ground, bound tight in tarpaulin.

Standing over the bodies, a woman and three men stood beside a cliff face that overlooked the dark, rolling peaks of a massive landfill. Four badges between them, one individual suspended. That didn't alter the bond they shared. Trauma was more adhesive than any glue.

'Is this the deepest point?' Madison asked. She was battered and blood-spattered, dressed incongruously in a boxing vest and satin fight shorts.

'I can't see any part that might be deeper,' replied Seabreeze, the slight but wiry man who'd brought them here.

'We don't have long,' Christopher reminded them. Clearly, he was jittering with nerves—the hard-man shaven scalp exposed as a lie.

Brendan Foley—the man who had started it all, the suspended officer—said nothing. He couldn't. His mind had turned blank.

Had he meant to kill the men down there? Yes.

Should he have killed them? No.

But in those fraught moments, when the blood had pumped harder than ever, there hadn't been time to sweat the details.

It was either him, or them.

So, he'd made sure it was them.

Four faces peered over the edge of the landfill, the sound of scavenging gulls drowning out the hiss of the nearby motorway, lights trailing a snake of hazed sodium between two cities.

Manchester, to the east. Liverpool, to the west.

'Let's do this, then.' Seabreeze grabbed the nearest long bundle. Madison reached to help, and together, they managed to heave it over the side.

Together, they watched as the human-shaped oblong spun slowly towards the acres of refuse. The height of the fall gave the object speed, and when it hit the surface of junk and packaging, the body was immediately swallowed and lost. As he peered into the darkness, trying to make out shapes, it took a second to establish that he couldn't make out the other corpse. Both bodies buried.

Crime sealed.

'As far as I'm concerned,' said Madison, 'that's case closed.' She glanced around. 'Any objections?'

'None,' replied Christopher, before spitting off the cliff in an apparent defiant purge of the whole episode's bad taste.

'Not a thing,' said Seabreeze, as he turned away, heading back to the parked cars.

Brendan didn't say anything. He turned on autopilot, and started walking back too.

All of this was watched by a shadowy figure just yards away, buzzing with the illicit.

He now possessed information of seismic importance.

PART 1

LITTLE GODS

CHAPTER 1

THAT TWENTY QUID for the key code had been well worth it. The door to the storage centre silently swung open.

He took stealthy, broad strides to the central elevators. His hat was pulled down low, one of those Russian ones with the flappy ears. He'd tied it under the chin, in a neat bow, but it kept catching on his beard. Given a choice, he'd undo it—but he knew the cameras were everywhere. He didn't dare look up.

Brendan Foley found himself standing before two industrial-size lift shafts, with a stairway on the left, and a handy map on the wall. Room 2272. *Where is that?*

His glance darted across the map. Second floor. He took the stairs, two at a time. At the top, a simple decision. Left or right? He couldn't be seen to hesitate, not with those cameras on him. He moved to the right, picking up pace.

As far as he could see, yellow, steel-padlocked doors lined the corridor, one after the other, scrolling past him on either side. He watched the numbers ticking down as he walked. *2320. 2318…* Nearly there.

Twenty seconds later, he was inspecting the stiff padlock of door 2272. It unnerved him. He wasn't sure what would be enough.

He checked left, and right. Quiet. Empty corridor. Three in the morning would do that for you.

But there were cameras every twenty yards, covering both directions. *Comprehensive, professional bastards.*

He was playing with fire. He looked back down at the painted yellow steel.

He had to get at what was on the other side.

He had to see if it was true.

His heart pummelled his ribcage.

Brendan discreetly unbuttoned his jacket, and took a firm grip of the eighteen-inch bolt cutters in his gloved fists. Turning his back to the nearest camera, he slid the blades over the thick ring of metal, and squeezed the handles together as though in a last meaningful gesture.

The hydraulic assistance in the bolt cutter's mechanism gained ground, and he felt the metal give slowly. He opened the cutters and tried again, trying not to groan with the exertion. He withdrew the blades with a heavy breath and checked his progress.

He'd cut into the bar by only a few millimetres.

But millimetres could add up—if he was quick. He checked both ways, brought up the cutters and squeezed again.

Progress was better this time—he had the right pressure and correct angle—but after a few more pumps, he could feel the lactic acid building up in his shoulders.

No good.

Brendan took deep breaths, suddenly aware of the extra noise he was making, and hoped to god that the security guard was either snoozing on the job, or doing something else entirely. Urgency hit hard.

The resistance started to give. He pumped the handles again until—with a sudden *ping!*—the padlock clattered to the floor. A buzz of elation coursed through him, but it was short-lived.

'I hope you know what you're doing.' The voice was close, gruff, biting.

Brendan swore quietly beneath his breath, then slowly turned. This wasn't a security guard. No uniform in sight. It was a civilian. Big bloke, leather jacket, rugby build, red hair slightly longer on top but right round in a thick beard until it greyed slightly at the point of his chin.

'I'm talking to you,' the man pressed.

'I couldn't find my key,' Brendan replied. 'I had to get in.' All he could think of was the door in front of him, ajar just an inch, the dark beyond looming with sinister promise.

'It's not yours, is it?' said Big Red. All statement, no enquiry.

'Fuck off, mate.' Brendan fought back with bravado.

'Do you know who it belongs to?'

That changed everything. This guy was no Joe Bloggs. A smile played across Big Red's lips, and he took a step closer.

Decision time. The plan had all been about getting in and out, no complications. There had been no provision for whoever this guy was, who was clearly in the know. He swung the bolt cutters up, as hard and as fast as he could, at Big Red's chin.

The bigger man was quick however, and jerked his head away at the last moment, the pincers glancing off his jaw. Then he let out an animal roar of fury and dove headfirst at Brendan, pinning him against the corrugated-iron wall.

Brendan gasped in pain as the back of his head bounced off the wall, but he planted his feet wide apart, and pushed back. It got him nowhere. Big Red grabbed him beneath the jaw and began to lift him higher towards the strip-lit ceiling.

He suddenly couldn't breathe, couldn't swallow even, but Brendan at least had the quick-thinking to walk his feet up the wall behind him to take some of the weight off his throat. Then he pushed off the wall as hard as he could, surprising his opponent and toppling them both so that they fell all too noisily to the floor. Brendan threw his arms out. The other man didn't stand a chance, and landed roughly on his back, beneath Brendan—who scrambled upright, straddling the man to rain blows, his opponent's head rolling from side to side in useless attempts to avoid the punches.

After two strikes, he thought—that's enough.

After three strikes, he thought this was police brutality.

After four strikes, he remembered he wasn't a policeman anymore.

After five, he remembered what Big Red's presumed employers had done to his family.

He stopped counting and kept pulling his fist back to strike again and again. At some point, the man stopped his groans, but Brendan carried on punching, until the man stopped moving, too.

He slumped against the wall and took a couple of breaths. Looked at his leather-clad knuckles, and the blood that spattered them. Wiped them off on his pants. That scuffle, and all the reverberations it caused, was likely to bring someone looking—if there was anyone in here that wasn't being paid off, he realised. He had to move fast.

Brendan leapt up, his body screaming in protest. Beyond the door, it was pitch black. He reached inside and felt about for a light switch.

The room suddenly became starkly visible.

If Brendan hadn't seen the things he'd seen already in his life, his breath might have caught in his throat. Instead, he stayed rooted to the spot as his thoughts raced far ahead of him.

Against the back wall, stacks of plastic boxes, all in a royal blue. It looked like warehouse stock, all arranged neatly, ready for shipping. In front of them, however, was a slumped figure—a dead man, tied to a chair. His neck lolled at an impossible angle and his eyes stared unseeing at the floor. His skin was deathly pale, except for a smattering of dark patches. This wasn't just your usual corpse. Something was off. Something indefinable. Something wrong in the highest.

Finally able to look away from the cadaver's blank grey stare, he saw the man had a piece of carefully folded paper in his lap. Grateful for his gloves, Brendan approached and eased open a corner of the paper.

There was a message, printed in a clean, simple typeset: TOLD YOU WHERE FUNNY BUSINESS WOULD LEAD. STICK TO THE PROGRAMME IN FUTURE.

Brendan's gaze returned to the dead man. He was like a melted waxwork, folding in on himself. *What the hell happened?*

'Jase?' A voice came from the door.

He whisked around to see Big Red stood there, his cheeks bruised, both brows split and a nose off-centre like a bust sundial. Guilt and disbelief flashed through Brendan—he had done that. The man stood framed in the doorway, staggering slightly as he took in the scene.

It was obvious to Brendan. Big Red had known all along about the man in the chair.

The bigger man's eyes returned to Brendan's face for a moment, fear clear, despite the swelling around his eyes. Then, he bolted.

Brendan let him go, listening to the pounding of his feet down the corridor. He turned back to the scene. The real story was in this room. He walked to the nearest stack of blue boxes, and popped the nearest lid. Inside, it looked like birdseed.

In all of Brendan's experience, no one had ever died because of bird seed.

He plunged in a hand and moved the seeds around, pushing lower and lower, up to his elbow, until he felt his fingertips brush against something. Something soft. Something he could grip.

He pulled his hand out of the box and held it at face level, staring at the contents.

'Oh, *shit*,' he whispered to the dead man sat beside him.

CHAPTER 2

EVEN FROM THIS height, and surrounded by darkness, DI Iona Madison could tell the river was in a rum way. Brown, choked by silt and pockmarked by more than one shopping trolley, it was a bad place to end up—dead or otherwise.

A call had come in. A bag in the Mersey. A foot poking out. Madison didn't have to be here, but curiosity had got the better of her—that and duty. This was her patch, although it hadn't been for long. And she was determined to show her worth.

She had left the bright, spinning proclamation of the parked blues on the pavement by the bridge railing, to walk around to the opposite riverbank for a better look. She wore a black puffer jacket to ward off the late chill, brown boots fit for a hike, and her hair was tied back in a ponytail. The youngest DI the northern forces had ever seen, and she was not one for pissing about.

Torch beams swung across the water's surface, catching the black neoprene of the divers' heads. Whoever had first spotted the bag—if it even existed—hadn't stuck around after calling in. They were literally fishing in the dark here. This could be a hoax, or it could be a murder, but they wouldn't leave until they found out which.

She quietly surveyed the scene below her, hands gripping the railing. Anonymous callers usually stuck around for a nosey to watch their handiwork play out, but all she could see now was the empty space where Mr Smith's nightclub had once stood, the absent building even more imposing now. Madison had had her first snog in there, promptly followed by her first alcohol-induced puke.

There was a shout below, but it didn't carry the excited urgency of discovery, more of a check-in. The divers were pointing out underwater obstacles. She tried to imagine the generations of crap that had been chucked in there. A car boot sale emptied out into the filthy water.

Madison's thoughts were interrupted by her phone buzzing. It was gone two in the morning, so it could only be work-related. In fact, it didn't matter what time of day it was; it was only ever work. Work-life balance? She'd need a life to have one of those.

The name on the caller ID caught her cold though. Foley. Her former boss. Ringing at two in the morning. Whatever this was about, it couldn't be good.

'Boss,' she said by way of a greeting.

'Hi Iona—and it's Brendan, please,' came the reply.

'What's happening, mate?'

'Anonymous tip for you.'

Madison pinched her eyes shut. Anonymous tips from Brendan Foley, the copper who was no more. He still couldn't turn the instinct off.

She sighed. 'Okay, but I hope it's come from your line of work. You're still on doors, right?'

'Yeah. And yeah, let's just say it is. Because this has to get sorted.'

'Christ, Brendan…' Madison had followed Foley into the dark once before, and it had ended badly for all involved.

'There's a storage company by LA Bowl, down on Winwick Road.'

'I know it.'

'Check out unit 2272, second floor. And you'll want forensics.'

'What am I to expect?'

'Something worth looking at.'

Madison went quiet. What the hell was her old boss playing at? 'Do you want to give me anything else? We've a busy night of our own.'

'Just get down there, because I'm not sure how much longer it'll all be in place.'

That caught Madison's attention. Held it tight.

A shout buffeted to her on the breeze, and it took her a moment to realise it wasn't in her ear but from down in the river. 'Gaffer!'

'I have to go. But please don't let this be anything stupid.' She hung up before Brendan could say anything else. 'What have you got?' she called into the darkness.

'A bag. A big one!' came the returning shout, echoing off the high walls either side of the water. It took her a moment to place the diver, but the torchlights all connected on him, suddenly turning him into a beacon. He was on his back, treading water. Another diver was helping him, and they hoisted something up. It was red, and popped to the surface, seeming to grow as it emerged. The object had the word *Slazenger* emblazoned up the side in what used to be white.

'And?' she shouted down.

After a quick check of the bag's zip—no mean feat while treading water—the diver peered close, then coughed into the water. The cough became a retch, then his white face peered up at them, like a ghost in the night.

'Body inside.'

CHAPTER 3

DETECTIVE SERGEANT TOM Christopher crept out of bed as quietly as he could, though he knew that the phone going off had probably done enough damage already.

'Where are you going?' asked Emma into the darkness. Christopher turned to her, pulling on the jeans he'd left by his bed. They'd only been in the house a few nights, but he'd dragged his bedtime protocols with him. In this instance, always having a set of clothes ready to go in case the phone went off in the middle of the night.

As it had done.

His boss, DI Madison, was only too aware of Emma's condition—seven weeks pregnant, needing every hour of sleep God would send—so she had given Christopher a dropped call to get him up, followed by an immediate text: NEEDED ASAP. STORAGE CENTRE, LA BOWL. CALL FOR UPDATE EN ROUTE.

'Got a work call. Need to nip out.' He kept his voice soft. It was still months until baby's arrival. He wanted to be a good dad, and he was determined to start on the right foot—and that included now, before baby had even got there.

'Aren't you supposed to be off tonight?' Emma asked. She understood cop conduct and practice more than most. After all, she was one. Sergeant Emma Morgan had been the desk sarge at Warrington nick, when she and DS Christopher had started exchanging glances at each other last summer. Now, a summer later, they were into the first trimester of a pregnancy they'd both agreed on—but neither of them had thought in their wildest dreams it would happen so fast. They'd never had any doubts. When you knew, *you knew*. But the early stages of the pregnancy weren't so simple.

'It's the boss,' he replied, rubbing his shaven scalp in a futile attempt to wake himself up. He hadn't been sleeping well, fretting over the sudden earth-tilting responsibility that was coming. Still, on nights like tonight, he still plummeted. 'She wouldn't call if it wasn't important.'

'Then I hope that next time, she calls someone else,' said Emma, rolling over with effort, shifting the bump from one side of the mattress to the other. Christopher watched, unable to get over the shape of her, and the pride it instilled in him. He would make this *work*. That's what good dads did.

A FEW MINUTES later, he was in the car along with a caffeine drink from the fridge. He started up his VW Golf with a purr of the engine.

Immediately, he took off to the storage lock-up, knowing exactly where he was going. That was the thing about being a copper in a small town—you always knew where things were and where you needed to be. But as instructed, he called Madison via hands-free as he left the cul-de-sac in Cinnamon Brow.

'I'm on my way, boss,' he said, as soon as Madison picked up. 'Five minutes, give or take. What's the story?'

'I've sent a car down there, and they'll meet you. Apparently, there's something in one of the lock-ups that might disappear if we take our time—which is why I've sent the car ahead. But I want a detective on scene, and frankly, I only want it to be you.'

'*Me?* Why?'

'Foley called it in.'

'Foley?' Christopher hadn't heard from his old DI in months, but now he understood why Madison wanted him and only him. Shared history, and all that. 'What's he up to now?'

'I haven't a clue, but I'll be there myself before too long.'

'Okay, what's the holdup?'

'We've just pulled a kid out of the Mersey, body stuffed in a cricket bag.'

'Jesus.'

'See you in the hour.' Madison hung up, as Christopher swung into the car park shared by the industrial units. One of them was Storage Plus, the lock-up in question. As promised, a squad car was already parked in a loading bay, two police constables waiting by the vehicle door.

Within moments, Christopher was with them, introducing himself, showing his warrant card—and learning that they were PCs Fenchurch and McMonagle. He knew McMonagle as Mac from the nick gym, but he didn't recognise the other man.

The automatic doors to the storage unit had been locked open, and they stepped inside the cool embrace of the facility, where they were guided upstairs by an employee in a red polo shirt emblazoned with a big plus sign on the back, giving the accidental impression of a lifeguard.

'Anyone else in?' asked Christopher.

McMonagle answered. 'Not sure. Only got here two minutes ago. Waiting for you as per orders, sir.'

'CCTV?'

'What time frame?'

The centre employee took this one, but he was clearly nervous. 'All night, I think. Front door, the stairs and the upstairs corridors.'

'I'll do what I can.'

As they crested the stairwell and rounded the corner, they were struck by the sight of a man in the distance, examining a door to one of the lock-ups. He appeared to have a padlock in his hand.

They paused, silent, watching the man, who leaned against a door to push it open. 2272, Christopher assumed. Then, the man froze to the spot. Beyond, the corridor peeled off into the distance.

'Are there any other ways out?' he whispered.

'The corridor loops around and comes back here. There's just the lift and then these stairs.'

Christopher turned around to look at the landing to the second floor. The opening for the stairs and industrial lift door were side by side on the far wall. 'Then we have him trapped. Mac, call for a second car. The DI's coming but we'll need some brute force.'

'I think DI Madison would have that covered too, sir,' said McMonagle. DI Madison was northern forces lightweight boxing champion, a belt she'd now held for some time.

'I don't doubt that at all. But she may be a bit preoccupied by the time she gets here.'

The three policemen moved into the corridor.

'Gents,' said Christopher, 'you block the stairs and lift—one each. I'll flush him round the corridor, and down to you. Sound cool?'

'Yeah,' Mac said with relish.

'Okay, then. And if you two drop out of sight, maybe I'll have a chance of convincing him to come quietly.'

The officers did as they were told. Christopher marched down the corridor, as if he was just another weary member of Joe Public who had to go ferret something from his lock-up in the middle of the night. As he approached the man, he twirled his car keys.

A phone pressed to his ear, the man was too preoccupied to even see Christopher. He was speaking urgently down the line. 'We have to shift this lot. Now. And do something about bloody Jason.'

Who was Jason?

Suddenly, the man looked up and locked eyes with Christopher, who started to reach for his warrant card. The man—flushed jowls and a golfer's body—immediately sprinted to the far end of the corridor.

Christopher gave chase, head down, shouting out: 'Police!'

The clatter of rapid footsteps echoed off every surface.

Around the bend, Christopher shouted, 'He's coming right to you!'

But as soon as he turned the corner, Mac came up to deliver a stunning rugby tackle, dumping the man on the concrete floor. Their victim gasped as air exploded out of his lungs.

'Sorry, sir,' Mac said, sitting on the man's chest. Efficiently, he snapped on a pair of cuffs. 'Took the initiative and all that.'

'Well played, mate,' said Christopher, with a pulse of delight. 'Take him downstairs to the car. I'm going to have a look-see. Don't forget to give his rights an airing.'

Within moments, DS Christopher was back at the door of 2272, holding a padlock that had been split roughly. This unit had been the focus of all sorts tonight. And when he opened the door, he saw exactly why.

CHAPTER 4

THE CLUB, FLEXION, was as tired and clichéd as its name suggested. A backstreet nineties relic in St Helens, another one of those bridging towns between the twin hubs of Manchester and Liverpool. Famous for rugby league and glassworks, austerity had given it the customary northern town kicking.

It had just gone half past two when Brendan appeared at the club's main entrance. The door had clearly been the victim of recent vandalism, a spiderwork of cracks decorating the pane-glass window.

Even from here, he could hear the mute thump of bass from inside. He stepped inside and was met by a man with a full extra foot of height over Brendan.

'It's almost kick-out time,' said the doorman, in a baritone with a lilt of Merseyside.

'I know, Dec—but I'm here now.'

'What do you expect me to do about it?'

'Let me catch up?' Brendan buttoned up the black peacoat he'd stashed in the car, all the way to his chin. 'At least help sweep the dregs out?'

'You were supposed to be here at nine thirty,' sighed Declan, easing himself onto a bar stool that had been propped at the bottom of a flight of stairs.

'Family emergency. Couldn't get out of it. I'm sorry.'

'You're lucky it's been a quiet one, then. Tuesday nights always are.' Declan shifted his weight on the stool. 'But left in the lurch is still left in the lurch.' His mouth set in a thin line of judgement.

Brendan didn't have time for this, and said words even he wasn't convinced by. 'It won't happen again.'

'Are you saying that if there was another "family emergency"…'—the doorman produced air quotes so wide you could drive a bus between them—'…you wouldn't do the same?'

Brendan didn't say anything. Didn't know what to.

'Okay, do the rounds upstairs,' said Declan, with a sigh. 'Mark out anyone who might be up for causing trouble when he's told it's home time. And don't expect a full night's pay for this one.'

Brendan nodded, acknowledging silently. Fair enough. But it only fed his humiliation. Detective to club doorman in a matter of months. How was that for a fall from grace? He marched up the stairs to complete the last thirty minutes of a shift he didn't want but paid a wage he sorely needed.

The first thing he found when he got to the top of the darkened stairway was a pile of vomit, and, worse still, it wasn't that fresh. This place really was the arse end of the region's night-life offerings. He stepped over the mess, and pushed through the double doors into the club itself. The lights were pulsing, and some techno bassline was throbbing angrily. No sign of any other staff. He set out on a circuit of the dancefloor.

A jeer rose up from a booth as he walked past. 'Can anyone else smell bacon! Here, piggy piggy!'

Brendan turned and looked into the eyes of the revellers, clocked the pinpricked pupils. The knowledge that marshalling this lot was his life now made him want to add to that pile at the top of the stairway.

'Anything else you lot want to say?' Brendan asked.

'Yeah,' said the tallest, so out of it he looked half-asleep. 'Go buy me a beer.' With that, he threw a handful of notes in Brendan's face. The fivers fluttered at his feet. Brendan held back the shameful urge to collect those notes. What he could do with that extra cash...

He let them fall and reached over the table, spilling every drink to hurl the man out.

'Home time, buddy,' he said, realising that his adrenaline from the storage unit hadn't receded at all.

CHAPTER 5

HARVEY CULPEPPER WAS running the shower as hot as he could stand it, when his wife Charlotte knocked on the door, demanding he get a move on.

He thought on his feet. Instead of vacating the bathroom, could he coax her *in*? What was it, half seven in the morning? Neither of them had to be anywhere soon, and when you were an underworld boss of Harvey Culpepper's magnitude, you made your own rules about where you would be and when.

'Come in,' he called through the en-suite's steam. After a moment, the door opened, sucking out vapour, revealing the shadowy figure of Charlotte. To his semi-trained eye, she looked to be halfway through her make-up routine—maybe three-fifths.

'You coming in?'

'Dorian's been on,' she said. She was beautiful in an intense way. The kind of woman that would allow you the luxury of inspecting the goods—until she popped a stiletto clean through your eye socket. The kind of woman that turned on Harvey Culpepper something rotten. The kind of woman he'd gone out of his way to make his.

'And?'

Dorian often called in the mornings.

His wife's eyes were sharp. 'The bizzies have seized that lock-up.'

Any amorous stirrings dissipated in an instant.

'Fuck me!' He wrenched the shower off. 'What time?' Timing was always important.

'Don't know yet. Dorian hasn't heard from the Mancs.'

'Probably a good sign.' Harvey left the en-suite, slipping his pot-belly past Charlotte's frame, and headed for the mobile on his bedside table. Nothing, aside from the obligatory news notifications and Bloomberg's stock exchange report. That was a good sign, and he began to calm. No text messages, no missed calls.

He turned to his wife. 'Do you know if they got everything?'

'He said it's all been seized,' she said.

Harvey sat on the edge of the bed, naked and still dripping. 'I'm assuming that means the warning has gone too.'

'I'd take that as read.'

Harvey sat quietly, mulling over the implications. He was confident enough to believe that sending a body to a business partner—and not just any body, but someone on said partner's payroll—was a move that would get the message across. But if said body got picked up by the police? Well, it was no longer a warning. It was an error. An error with a murder charge.

'How did they find it?'

Charlotte moved to the dresser. 'He didn't say.'

'Then that's the hole that needs plugging. We start there. Do you want to come along? You're good when it comes to getting answers.'

'I think I'll leave you to this one.' She gazed at herself in the mirror. 'I've yoga and the rounds to do.'

'You get that dolled up for yoga?'

She turned back to him, smiling with something that looked like victory. 'I wouldn't normally, but there's a couple of very fit blokes who've started. Got to keep my hand in.'

Any other husband would have baulked—and any other wife would never have uttered such a brazen thought in the first place. But Harvey knew there was nothing commonplace about either of them. Never had been. 'Sure. Just know I'll cut their bollocks off if it gets serious.'

Charlotte walked purposefully to Harvey. It was clear that she knew already what she'd find. It was a strange quirk of their marriage, but the mere thought of his wife's indiscretions excited him, and when she straddled him, it was immediately evident. 'If they ever thought about getting serious, I'd cut their bollocks off myself. Now shut up. I can spare you five minutes.'

CHAPTER 6

'FORGIVE THE INFORMALITY, DI Madison, but I hadn't anticipated such an exciting morning.'

Dr Mackie, the Home Office pathologist at Warrington Hospital's morgue, stood in full tennis kit—Barbie-pink Lycra from head to toe. She was trim, with many admirers both male and female on the force and at the hospital, but admiration hadn't made her soft. She was still as sharp and intuitive as anybody Madison had ever met in her career to date.

After they'd worked together last year, and Mackie had been appointed to undertake coroner's duties on the case they had been working on, the doctor had elected to stay. She seemed to like the control, enjoyed being a bigger fish in a smaller pond, and enjoyed the mortuary set-up, even though it was one of the weirdest in the country, sat in Warrington Hospital's car park. It had been the ambulance garage originally, but as vehicles had become larger and demand spiked, the garage turned less and less useful. A lick of paint and a few internal walls later, it had been repurposed to house the hospital's less fortunate visitors. It had its pros and cons. The deceased had to be wheeled out behind a series of flimsy screens, which was a pain in the arse, but it meant that there were no complications when it came to bringing bodies in from elsewhere. A driver simply headed round to this end of the hospital grounds and bunged the body out.

Excitement wasn't the word Madison would usually use, as she faced down two bodies, each laid out on metal tables. She had no medical background at all, but even to her untrained eye, their conditions couldn't be more different.

'This place still feels pretty empty,' she said. 'After last year.'

Last year.

When Madison was Detective Sergeant on a case that had punched through the nation's media—twenty-seven bodies found in a patch of Warrington woodland. Each one had ended up here, and Madison had been around to witness the whole episode.

'Well, yes,' replied Mackie. 'I've already done the prelims, so I thought you'd appreciate the catch-up.'

'I do appreciate that.'

'You'll be even more grateful when I tell you what was going on inside *this* one.' Mackie stood at the head of one of the cadavers. It had a strange death pallor, even more so than its fetid companion—the body from the river.

'Attending officers remarked that something was off when they saw him at the scene at the lock-up.'

'*Off?* Off might be something you see a handful of times in your career. What has happened here is nothing short of sensational.'

'What's the story?'

'He was strapped to a chair, but he was dead before then. That was just to hold him in place. How he actually died, I've no idea.' There was genuine wonder in Mackie's voice, and in her features.

'No injuries?'

'Oh yes, absolutely. Riddled with them. His insides look like they've been in a car accident. But he… can't have been.'

Madison gazed at the corpse, tried to make sense of what she'd heard. The body was a strange colour, almost patterned, eggshell white in places, liver purple in others—but nothing she could see made sense of the injuries described. 'Run this by me again. Inside, he's mush. But outside, he's fine?'

'Exactly. But even so, he has a full, intact bone structure. Every single bone is strong, but every single organ—bar the brain—has been pulverised. Which begs the question... what is the level of force required to injure organs whilst bypassing the skeleton? And why no bruising?'

'All this colour is down to internal bruising and ensuing lividity? Nothing at the surface?'

'Do you ever read Agatha Christie, DI Madison?'

Madison thought of all the fantasy novels by her bed, well-thumbed. Gaiman, Pratchett, Tolkien and Martin. She'd never read a Christie. Never even owned one. 'Tell me.'

'Christie was the Queen of the locked room mystery.'

'And that is?'

'A mystery that's impossible to solve. All the ingredients and action has happened in one place. A crime's been committed but there's seemingly no possible answer to how.'

Madison stared at the man on the table and was suddenly very glad she hadn't been present for the cutting and pulling. 'So, this is a locked room mystery—in a human body?'

Mackie smiled grimly. 'You're clearly a DI for a reason, ma'am.'

CHAPTER 7

BRENDAN LAY IN bed, listening to his boys getting up, his wife following soon after from her side of the bed they barely shared anymore.

He stared at the ceiling while he listened to the family hammer through the morning routine of getting washed, fed and out the door in time for preschool, college and work. He wanted to go down and see them, wanted to hug them goodbye, but something wouldn't let him.

Guilt. Shame. Frustration.

A year ago, he'd have been down there helping, but now he found it hard to even look his children in the eye. They left him to it after shifts at the club, reasoning he needed the shuteye, but he couldn't rest at all. All he could do was look at the cracks in the ceiling—a ceiling that he wouldn't be looking at for much longer.

The house was sold, subject to contract. Truth be told, it had been for sale since last winter, but the market had been doornail-dead. They'd had to reduce, and reduce, to coax anything. Finally, they were there, and rented accommodation was their next stop. They hadn't picked it yet, but he was pliable. His only rule? *Anywhere but here.*

Rolling over the mattress, images flooded his mind.

That man, in the chair.

Loose and weird.

An emotion started to emerge. Frustration.

Then another forged its way in. Something he was really unfamiliar with.

Envy.

If he'd still been a copper, he could have begun looking into this. Looking into the question of the discoloured man. How and why something terrible had happened to him. He had his own ideas—he'd been there, after all, having followed his own reasoning and methodology, having followed a distinct trail of illegal breadcrumbs, his powers of deduction as strong as ever— but he didn't have the authority, the weight of resources, nor the legal standing, to do anything about it. That, for the first time since he'd quit the force, pissed him off.

He remembered that Madison was in charge now, and that Madison was more than able to crack on. She could *and would* look into things with her own forensic drive, her intuition and abilities. She could make *this* happen—and bring the Culpeppers down. She would make sure of it.

He rolled over, and breathed out hard.

He was a forward-thinking man, never in stasis, always looking at the future, the tasks at hand—and how he could make them both work. But, with a flash of shame, he admonished himself quickly. So much for being a man of action, when he was festering in bed like this. He leapt up, pulled on his white shirt from the night before and headed down the stairs. Still in his boxers, smelling the sweat left over from his fracas in the storage facility, his shame only amplified with each downward step. But he was moving. Forward. He was going to get coffee, some Weetabix, and a march on. Try to find out what his behaviour—messing up the lock-up, sending for the police— would do to the Culpepper family. The family he'd sacrificed his career and his happiness for.

But to not drive forward the investigation himself? That was *hard*.

He arrived at the bottom of the stairs and turned down the hall into the kitchen, when he heard the front door go. His wife, Mim, strode in.

'Oh, you're up. Well, it was nice of you to come and see the kids off,' she said, grabbing her handbag from the banister. 'And me for that matter.'

Brendan felt guilt surge. 'I'm sorry, darling, I—'

'Just leave it, Brendan.'

She was tall, about the same height as he was, but taller in her work heels. She carried that immaculate presentation of a woman on a business mission. Her hair had grown out from the bob he'd always known her for. Now, she had long ringlets that reflected copper in whatever light touched them. She wore a pristine white blouse, black pencil skirt, a single gold band on her left wrist.

And she was leaving.

He adored her.

And couldn't stop letting her down.

The door closed and he found himself alone, staring into the space where his wife had stood only moments ago, cursing himself once again for being the person who made her feel that way.

Somehow, he wasn't the same man anymore, no matter how much he wanted to be—but he could get back there again. He had to believe it.

Put the Culpeppers away, then fix himself, and, in turn, his family.

Emboldened, he went back upstairs to get dressed. This wouldn't beat him. Nobody and nothing would.

CHAPTER 8

MACKIE AND MADISON moved to another morgue slab, another body.

This was where the smell came from.

'This one's more simple—happily,' said Mackie.

Madison admired her humour. There was nothing happy about what lay on the metal table.

'A male teenager,' Mackie continued. 'Sixteen... seventeen at a push.'

It was a horrible sight. A mottled boy.

'We've had to move quickly with him because water and decomposition are intimate bedfellows. The liquid environment can slow down the rate of deterioration, but once the corpse is introduced to air again, speed ramps up. So, our lad here already looks quite a bit different from when he came in just a few hours ago.'

Madison could see what she meant. But when the bag had been pulled up, the boy's body still inside, the forensic decision had been to leave him in there. The bag was evidence, plain and simple. She'd get to that in a moment.

'We have the usual vascular marbling associated with being in the water for a significant length of time, but aside from that, it'll be hard to ascertain precisely how long he's been there— aside from the obvious that it must have been a long while.'

'Why is time so hard to determine?'

'What is it they say, detective? It's grim up north. It's grim alright. Bloody freezing half the time. And this fellow came from the Mersey. The river might even have frozen over at Christmas time. That slows decomposition right down.'

'So, we're still none the wiser? Could be any time in recent history?'

'Not quite. I'd start with the bag. See what you can get from that. But the bag also protected him from scavengers. Nothing could have a nibble. Obviously, that didn't stop the various microorganisms that live in our crystalline northern rivers… But still, can't have everything.'

Madison felt a rush of bile, light-headedness circling with it. 'Anything at all you'd remark? Did he drown like this?' The idea of being stuffed in a bag then tossed into a river was abhorrent.

'No—because he has a bloody big hole in his heart, and a knife wound to go with it. Didn't I mention that?'

'No.'

Mackie continued as her eyes cast along the body. 'Well, his heart was punctured, then he was folded into the bag and dumped into the drink.'

'The attack itself?'

'Single knife wound. Clean as a whistle. No sign of struggle.'

'So, it would be fair to say it was a surprise, determined attack. Most likely premeditated.'

'You're the detective.'

'And if I asked for your take on it?'

Silence. Then…

'If I was off the record and this was you and I chatting over a couple of Babychams in our local social club, I'd say this was a calm attack that relied on the element of surprise. The killer was very sure, very precise, and the poor lad never had time to know what hit him.'

'How long would it have taken him to die?'

'Lights will have gone out in under a minute.'

Madison stared at the body. 'He was naked in the bag, wasn't he?'

'That's right.'

'Anything else you can tell me?'

'Well, the murder weapon wasn't in the bag—like I said, you can't have everything, Detective.'

Madison smiled at her companion cheerlessly, and moved across to the bag, propped up on two evidence trays on the counter by the wall. It was huge, as sports bags go. Four feet long and thick enough for all sorts of kit. A cricket bag, a quick web search had revealed. Madison thought it looked a decent bag for taking on holiday. Wheels and everything.

There were all sorts of obstacles here, not just in identifying the boy but in finding the perpetrator. The bag would have to be examined thoroughly, but there was a reason why secrets were thrown in deep, wet places—water had a habit of wiping things clean. The amino acids in a fingerprint would be dissolved by the constant wash, and from the state of the bag, it had clearly been down there for several months. The chances of finding a concrete lead were remote at best. The murderer must have known all of this.

This bag, the body... They were the only pieces of evidence.

'Can this be sent to forensics please?' Madison asked.

'It was next on my list,' Mackie replied.

'Thank you. Do you have any tricks for getting this smell out of my nose?'

'Thirty years hard graft in the job, detective,' Mackie replied with a pinched smile, opening the mortuary door for Madison to pass through. 'That, and gin. Lots of gin.'

Madison found herself already out in the cool, tiled corridor, which was always dark no matter how many health and safety evaluations suggested even a strip light would make a difference. She took a moment.

This wasn't a talking to, or an urgent putting oneself back together. It was a second for one deep breath of reset.

Two bodies. On her patch.

This was it. Time for this DI to stake her claim. Prove that Brendan Foley's recommendation of her for the job had been the right choice. No matter what Foley had decided to do with his life, he had been an exceptional police officer and a dogged detective. His opinion mattered, and he'd given her this role on a plate, pointing her out to their collective superiors. *She's the one, she's the horse you back.*

She was determined to prove her old boss right.

But that train of thought only brought her old boss back to mind, and his role in all this, whatever *this* was.

What in the hell had Brendan Foley got himself into here?

CHAPTER 9

GARLAND ROURKE WAS a relic. The last of his kind, almost.

As he stood by the pool table in Pendleton Mission, he felt as though extinction couldn't come soon enough.

'And Jason was definitely dead?' he asked now.

'Hundred per cent. And dead in a bad way,' said Fintan Boyd.

'Well, holy fucking shit, the Scousers outdid themselves this time.' Garland removed the bandana that kept his tangled mane at bay, and mopped his brow. He'd been cleaning since sun-up for two reasons. One? The place was a tip. And two? Early activity tended to get the hangover out of the way early. But the topic of conversation was threatening to bring it back.

'And the boxes?' He didn't even glance at Fintan.

'The old bill have the lot. Brynn, too.'

This last made Garland turn. 'Brynn?'

'I couldn't go back in. Not after my face ended up like this. So, I sent Brynn in to see what was what. They nicked him.'

Garland thought about Brynn and what his resistance to pressure might be. He quickly assessed that loyalty wasn't the issue; he didn't keep people around who had any waver in that department. But being grilled by experienced coppers was different. He hoped, for all their sakes, that Brynn was a man of integrity.

'And you?' Garland pointed at Fintan. Despite the beard, it was obvious he had been in a violent altercation. Bruises shaded both eyes, and his jaw was swollen.

'The bloke who saw me. Pretty sure he was a copper. Looked it. But never identified himself. I asked him what he was doing. Turns out, he was trying to break in.'

'So, he knew what was in there?'

Fintan seemed to think for a moment. He absent-mindedly took the white ball from the table, turning it in his hands like a gemstone.

'Fin?' Garland pressed.

'I saw him in the lock-up, before I scarpered. He looked surprised. By the seed, and what was in it obviously.'

'He saw that, did he?'

'Yeah. But I don't think he knew what he was looking for.'

Garland took the cue ball from Fintan, polished it on his jeans, and rolled it into the middle pocket. It clunked and trundled as the table digested, before spitting it out in the tray below.

'And he didn't identify himself? Police are bound by law to do that, you know?'

'Positive. Like I say, he carried himself like a cop, but never once said he was one.' Fintan stood straighter.

'The police still got there in the end, then.'

'Someone must have called it in.'

'What time did they get there?'

'I sent Brynn in at 2.45. So it's our problem.'

'Yeah. It was always going to be our problem.' Garland thought about the terms of the arrangement he and those bastard Culpeppers had made. The Scousers dropped off at the unit before 2 a.m. The Mancs picked it up any time after.

On one hand, the handover was a faultless plan, and one that would bridge the supply gaps in Manchester quite nicely. The Culpeppers had the product, after all. Europe was their personal narcotics factory when it came to getting the good stuff. The

Scousers knew how to import and export like nobody else, the dockside rats. Getting it over to Manchester had been tougher, but with a bit of negotiation and some upward thinking from Garland, the two cities could play together.

The loss of Jason was just one part of the disaster. Garland now had no product, although he had paid for it and was now massively out of pocket. And the market they'd so successfully managed to grow and harness since the previous year—well, he risked losing them. The thing with drug addicts, they didn't tend to wait patiently for their next hit. They'd go elsewhere, undoing all of Garland's careful progress.

He went over to the counter of the Mission, in the back left corner of the room. It was all a cover, a ruse—a giant money-laundering unit with a philanthropic mask—but it served so many purposes for Garland. His customers came to him. He could deal here on his premises, discreetly. Kept his ear to the ground when it came to news, because nobody was more in the know than the people who lived on the streets. This was a clubhouse of sorts for the Devil's Defects, the biker crew he'd been the top dog of for close to two decades.

There was a dual purpose here, however. He cared about this place.

He cared about the people who came in here, and how he could help them. The little man was always shat on. He had always seen himself as a leather-clad Robin Hood, ready to roll at a moment's notice, to stick it to the man and give to the poor—narcotics, meals, the lot.

But now, this might ruin everything. With the loss of the drugs, he was two hundred grand out of pocket, and had the Culpeppers on his back. Hadn't they just killed one of his own?

Garland remembered something.

Jason.

'Did Jason have his jacket with him?' he asked, reaching over the counter to drag out a bottle of Beefeater's Gin.

'He didn't, Garland.'

'Fucking hell.' He could only assume that taking the jacket from the lock-up had been a reason to rub salt into the wounds. A biker's leather jacket was his soul, his life story and his skin all at once. Each patch added was a symbol of the wearer's history—his legacy. To take a biker's jacket was a middle finger to the crew he was part of. 'We need to get that back.'

'I'm not sure—' Fintan began, but Garland shot in with heat.

'Fuck the Culpeppers. That's the code. The jacket is everything. It stays with the member. We get it back.'

'Are you sure? Want me to reach out to the Culpeppers? See if they'll hand it over with minimum fuss?'

Minimum fuss, seethed Garland. Nothing about this was causing *minimum fuss*. He swigged from the bottle. *Fuck hangovers, and fuck this.* 'Have a go. Then find out who this sorta-copper is. He's stuck his nose in where it doesn't belong, and we need to chop it off.'

There was a pause, then: 'Gotcha gaffer.'

That's all he needed to hear.

CHAPTER 10

MADISON DIDN'T SO much as breeze between the front doors of Warrington nick, as batter through them with gale force.

Every minute—every second—counted. Her patch come close to chaos in the space of a single night. She didn't care what people thought about her personally, but she did care what they thought of her professional ability. She'd not scrapped like thunder to get where she was, only to see her hard-won efforts crumble around her.

She checked with the desk sergeant, an interim promotion now that Emma Morgan was on maternity leave. Her temporary replacement was Narinder Patel; much stricter than Morgan had ever been. 'Monroe wants you in at nine, DI Madison.'

'Would he mind if I went in early?' Best foot forward and all that.

'I'd wait, if I were you.'

Madison paused. Patel lowered her eyes, as if sensing she may have overstepped with her tone. Madison knew that a gaze from her could do that—bring ice and fire in one go. 'He's on to GMP, I think.'

Madison nodded her thanks. Always good to keep your desk sergeant on side, because they were the ones that kept the wheels of the station greased and moving, and they always had a fair handle on all the info. 'I'm going to get a coffee, then. How do you take yours?'

Patel softened visibly, a smile appearing. 'White, one sugar.'

WARRINGTON POLICE STATION was a chaotic hub that somehow still managed to work. A Victorian swimming baths set for destruction, it had been saved at the last moment by someone at the town hall with a spreadsheet and numbers. A new police force had just been established for the town. Over a hundred bodies suddenly needed a roof over their heads and the space to work. And power, preferably, although that had been somewhat of an afterthought, judging by the cables that snaked thick and ugly round every bend.

Madison took the dank central corridor, which still carried a note of chlorine. She opened the doors, and was hit by heat, noise and echo. *Christ*, she thought. It wasn't even nine, and the station was brimming.

The opaque skylight windows gave all the illumination needed. The room was high, cavernous and deep—thanks to the huge swimming pool that sat right in the middle, six feet deep at the near end, tapering gradually to double that at the far side. It was empty of water, yet full of people. Uniforms, non-uniforms, CID—they were all down there, sections partitioned by moveable felt screens. It wasn't ideal, but somehow, it worked. In the middle, towards the near end, was the coffee station—the central watering hole for any nick worth its name.

She took the stone steps down into the pool, and made that coffee for Patel. After dropping off Patel's, she weaved back through to her office—nothing more than an eight-by-eight partitioned square. Not great when sensitive information needed more than a notice board to keep a lid on it.

She had a desk, a phone, a computer and a small waste-paper bin—that was it. She kept her coat on against the chill that still lingered in the early mornings. The heating pipes were over by the walls, up and out of the depths of the pool. Post-it notes were stuck to the side of her desk. Eight of them, each a message from the team. She swore under her breath as she rifled through them.

Mackie. Please call. She'd only just left her, what could that be about?

Monroe. Nine AM. Yeah, yeah, she knew.

Gavigan. Scene cleared for release, nothing else found. He was head SOCO, there last night at the river when the body was pulled out. It was at least something that they hadn't found any other surprises.

Christopher. Seeing a man about a dog. That was written in a scrawl from her DS. Clearly, he'd been here before her and had curiously nipped off again. She wondered where to, but knowing Tom Christopher like she did, any supposed dereliction of duty would only ever be worthwhile and necessary.

Blundell. Suspect's legal rep has arrived. Ready when you are. Blundell was the station custody officer. The suspect Christopher caught at the lock-up was ready for interview. Madison felt the buzz of progress.

She checked the remaining three—nothing that required immediate attention—so she left them there and binned the unimportant ones.

Leaving her cubicle, she turned immediately left, and glanced into the next one. This was the office shared by her own CID unit, which comprised Christopher, DS Karthik—and DC Isabelle Broom, drafted in late last year to fill the gap left by disgraced Detective Hoyt. The mere thought of Hoyt's departure threatened a red mist. The old adage to keep your friends close and your enemies closer sometimes still wasn't enough. Sometimes you still didn't learn, no matter how many times you heard it.

Their office comprised a desk on either side, directly facing the screens, and a round table in the middle which served as her

CID unit's meeting place. Broom was at her desk in the far corner, and must have immediately sensed Madison's arrival because she turned to face her. She was younger than Madison, who, in the recruitment process, had been keen to offer the same opportunities that her old boss Brendan Foley had granted her.

'Yes, boss?' Her eyes were wide, brown hair shoulder-length.

'Morning,' Madison replied. 'Any idea where Christopher has got to?'

'He just said man about a dog. I didn't think anything of it.'

'Me neither. It's been a big night. Need bringing up to speed?'

'I got the gist off Christopher before he left. Body from the river, no ID so far. Big do at that storage place off Norman Street. Bloke in custody.'

'Want to back me up in a chat with said bloke?'

Immediately, Broom's features opened with excitement. 'Too right, I do.'

Madison saw the third desk, empty and spotless. 'I assume Karthik's not in yet?'

'Not yet, but I'd expect him in bang on nine.'

'He is a punctual bugger, I'll give him that.'

'We off now to the custody suite?'

'No, hold your horses. Got to check in with the sheriff first. But get up to speed with Christopher's report.'

'Gotcha, boss.'

Madison marched straight out of the pool, grabbing her coffee as she went. Five to nine. She wanted to show she was right there, on the button. Two bodies in Warrington overnight, in totally different circumstances. But as bad as that sounded, it wasn't as bad as what her predecessor went through when the Warrington 27 had been found last year.

Nothing, Madison thought, could ever be that bad again.

CHAPTER 11

THE OFFICE PARK was banal. It was one of those pop-up work hubs for temporary companies, where people with bright ideas seemed to cobble together a business idea, finding the cash for a month-by-month lease. Within hours, they'd be handed the keys to a hundred-square-foot shoebox serving as their new venture's centre of commerce—and away they went. If the business failed, it failed, and back to the ideas farm they went. If it went well, they'd soon jump across the hall to a fifteen-by-fifteen, with a second desk, then maybe even a twenty-five-by-twenty-five. Then, they were really cooking.

Everything about these places was short-term—apart from the management company that was happy to take your cash. Some would say that they provided a service, offering young entrepreneurs a leg up. Others—more cynical perhaps—might think there was more than a touch of taking advantage of the bright-eyed.

Mim hadn't made her mind up yet which camp she fell in. But today, as the sun had risen strong and bright, she hadn't even made it inside.

She sat in the car, the black Audi A3 hatchback that was her runaround, whilst the dash clock blinked 8.56 a.m. in an orange glow. That gave her four minutes to calm down, reapply her mascara, and get upstairs to Effortless Design LLC. It was a fledgling design agency that had liked her experience—despite the career gap of ten years for mummy stuff—but, clearly, they hadn't been able to afford anyone else.

Miriam Foley was now the family breadwinner.

She'd give it one more minute, convinced she could get up into the office in three.

Parting with Mick was always hard—the way his little hands reached for her as she handed him over to the crèche assistant, the word—*Mama!*—shakily leaking from his sobs. But that wasn't what had prompted her tears this morning. She had her husband to thank for that.

Dammit, Brendan, she thought, pulling a bag of make-up-remover wipes from the car's glove compartment. She decided to start all over again with a blank canvas. Easier to cover up the puffiness that way. With a folded wipe, she attacked her face.

8.57 a.m. Damn, damn, *damn*.

Brendan was getting worse, no doubt about it. His descent had begun suddenly, with unexpected bouts of sleeplessness. His moods had dipped, and darkness seemed to weigh on him heavier every day. She knew it was to be expected. His father had been stabbed at the nick, his heart punctured by one of Brendan's own workforce. There'd been an attempt on his brother's life too, which had resulted in the deaths of four friends, prompting his brother Ross to go into hiding. Since then, no one had seen or heard of him—and Brendan had quit his job.

She couldn't be sure what had happened. One minute, Brendan had been a driven, high-flying detective—the youngest DI the region had ever seen. This hadn't been a surprise to anybody, given his aptitude and dedication to the role.

But still, he'd given it all up—and she still didn't fully understand why.

If he wanted to bring those responsible for the attacks on his father and brother to account, surely staying in his role with the police would have been the best way? But now, he seemed to have lost any motivation.

8.58 a.m. Clean face, foundation in hand, all ready. This would be a record.

She was amazed with what Brendan had chosen to do with his time—doorman. But who was she to judge? They'd quickly fallen into a 'ships in the night' routine. He'd get in late, sleep. She'd get up, leave him to it. They'd have a couple of hours between her getting home at six and him leaving for work at eight. Rinse and repeat.

She missed him. She missed her husband.

8.59 a.m., and the cannonball of understanding hit her hard in the stomach. Brendan was no longer the man she'd married.

She was almost back up and running in the make-up department, when her eyes started to leak again. She tried to prevent the tears from escaping. No good. Just as her husband's name came to mind one last time, her eyes leaked, staining her mascara.

She gave up, and sobbed.

Effortless Design LLC would have to wait.

CHAPTER 12

BRENDAN FOLEY WALKED up the three steps to the front door of the block of flats, pausing to carefully step over a dog shit so old it was frosted with petrification.

The glass door was streaked with greasy fingerprints. He could barely see his own reflection, but he didn't want to. Looking back at him, would be a man he had trouble recognising anymore.

He rang the bell, which sounded plaintively like a lost electronic sheep.

'Hello?' scratched a voice through the intercom.

'Seabreeze, it's your old mate—Brendan.' He glanced around the neighbourhood. It was a cold, late afternoon in Orford, brickwork as tired as the tarmac streets. It looked like a hurricane could press delete on the whole place.

'Foley?'

'Just Brendan now, pal.'

'Ugh, yeah. Give me a sec. I'll buzz you in.'

'Cheers.'

Brendan took a step backwards. He was stood before a two-storey tenement. What the fuck was Seabreeze doing here? He was as sharp and on the ball as anyone Brendan had encountered during his time on the force, always dressed with polish and precision. Why would he live in a place where you had to play dog-shit hopscotch?

A buzz rang out, followed by a click as the lock released. Brendan swung open the door, and entered. Just as he stepped inside, one of the ground-floor entrances opened.

The figure of Seabreeze emerged, outlined in the open doorway. He was in a dressing gown the colour of Hugh Hefner's carpet, and looking just as stained. More surprises. His hair was longer, held back from his forehead by thick-framed glasses perched on his brow. Dark chest hair gave the impression that he was both hirsute and nude beneath the robe. He looked bashful.

'Sorry to catch you on your day off,' Brendan murmured.

'No probs, mate,' came the reply. He didn't back into the room, so Brendan forced the issue.

'I'll need to come in pal—sorry for the imposition.'

Seabreeze lowered his gaze. 'Of course.'

Brendan followed Seabreeze down a dark hallway that was lined with cheaply framed art prints, although on closer inspection, they weren't art prints at all. They were stills from old movies, dinosaurs and minotaurs raging. The pictures spanned the length of the hallway, punctuated by doors either side. At the end of the corridor, he glimpsed an open-plan kitchen and living space. The scent of burnt toast floated on the air. On a Tabasco-orange leather sofa, eating a piece of toast, was the most beautiful woman Brendan had ever seen. She wore a robe too, but with just enough bronzed skin on show to suggest little else beneath the silky fabric.

'A coffee?' asked Seabreeze, already in the kitchen space.

'No thanks, mate. I'll keep it brief. I'm already disturbing you enough.'

'It's no trouble, boss.'

An uneasy silence descended for a moment, before Seabreeze caught on. He turned to his wife, partner—what was she, exactly? 'Fiona, could you give us two shakes? It's a work thing. Confidentiality, and all that.'

The woman rose to her feet. 'Course. I'll get a shower, and when I come out, you're going to tell me what we're doing today. Get thinking.'

Brendan realised where he'd seen her before. The telly. She was a soap actress, on one of the half-hour slots around tea time. Bloody Seabreeze—ever the ladies' man.

'Thank you,' Brendan said, as she drifted past him. 'I won't keep him long.' As soon as the coast was clear, he turned back to his pal. 'How are you, mate?'

'Surviving.' Seabreeze's smile was meek as weak tea.

'Me too. I hear you're going fast track?' Brendan was referring to the rumour he'd heard, that Seabreeze, the tech whiz of Warrington Constabulary, was halfway through the accelerated inspector programme.

Seabreeze's smile grew heavy. 'I was, but I got bumped off halfway through. Failed the maths exam.'

'You?' Brendan was shocked.

'Yeah.' Seabreeze shrugged. 'Something about if I bought a car in 1999 for x amount of yen, what would it be worth now in Hungarian Florints?'

Brendan shook his head. 'Because that always came up on cases I was involved with.'

They both laughed at that. Time to get straight to the point.

'Mate, I'm after a favour, if possible.'

'Shoot!' Seabreeze took an end of the sofa. Brendan did the same.

'I need to find someone,' he began.

Seabreeze didn't answer immediately. 'Go on.'

'My brother.'

Brendan's brother and his whereabouts were tangled in all sorts of legal issues. At best guess, he should be arrested on sight. At worst, he needed to be apprehended and questioned. And if that quandary wasn't making Brendan uneasy enough, dragging a serving police employee into it was something else entirely. But what choice did he have? Give up entirely?

'The brother that went missing?' Seabreeze asked.

'I only have one brother, and—yeah—that's him.'

Seabreeze didn't answer. Brendan knew this was pushing the boundaries of legality, and the limits of their friendship.

'All I know is, he was never found. But evidence at the scene on the East Lancs suggested he got away.'

Seabreeze shifted on the sofa. 'Brendan, I don't want to be the one to tell you this…' He looked awkward. 'But, the reason he may not have been found is because they might have taken him somewhere else, then done… Y'know?'

Brendan did know, and had thought about it so much he'd gone at it from all angles. His brother, Ross, had been driving along the East Lancs motorway in a westerly direction en route to Liverpool, accompanied by four friends. All of them small-time crims. Brendan had never gone into the family business. What their intentions had been was anybody's guess, but clearly they'd never made their destination. Eyewitnesses at the time had reported two motorbikes pincering the car on either side, and peppering it with automatic gunfire.

Capture hadn't been part of the agenda. Every one of the people in that car had been supposed to die on the spot. Worse than that, Brendan knew what the criminals behind this were like. Grim. If the Culpeppers had a Foley in their possession, they'd have made damn sure that Brendan knew all the grizzly details of his brother's end.

Which meant that Brendan was convinced his brother had escaped. 'He had to have got out, Jordan. I feel sure he did.'

'Using my first name?' said Seabreeze, raising his eyebrows. 'Trying to show how serious this is?'

Brendan spread his hands. 'Please, mate. Help me find my brother. I wouldn't know where to begin on my own. Don't make me beg. No one else has your skills.'

'Or the access, right?'

Brendan felt the heat rise to his cheeks. Seabreeze was an active technician for the police, which gave him a plethora of databases and resources. Anybody could do a Google search, but not everybody had facial recognition software, ViCap and HOLMES at their fingertips. Still, it was humiliating—to have to ask.

Seabreeze seemed to relax, having asked the question. 'Don't sweat it, mate. I understand. He's your brother.'

All Brendan could do was nod slowly.

His friend reached by the side of the sofa, and pulled out a laptop, flipping it open. 'His Facebook still active?'

Brendan felt a flutter of excitement. Seabreeze was in. He leant forwards. 'I haven't been contacted as next of kin to shut it down, if that's what you're asking.'

'Good. I can scrape some pictures from there, then.'

Brendan shuffled along, so he could see what Seabreeze was doing. 'He was a pretty dedicated Instagram user, but under a pseudonym.'

The laptop's screen started to whizz by, but it was all codes and HTML. 'That'll work, too. There's always a strong correlation and plenty of clues between a Facebook profile and a supposedly anonymous Insta account. Any areas in the country I should focus on? Places he's been known to go to in the past when things are rough?' As he spoke, his eyes never left the screen, and his fingers raced across the keys.

Brendan stood up, pacing. 'He's a Warrington lad—born and bred. We holidayed in tents in North Wales growing up, and he seemed to like it there.'

'Cool, cool. He'll be pissed off though, won't he?'

'If I know my brother, he will.' Having just lost his son and father to cold-blooded criminal killers—and his wife to the realisation that their marriage was based on a child that was no longer there…

Yeah, Brendan thought. *Pissed off would cover it.*

'So, he won't have gone far. Doesn't want to bump into anybody at Tescos, but close enough that he can still keep an eye on what's what.' Seabreeze's gaze flickered back and forth in the blue screen light.

'I'd go along with that.' Brendan, if he was right, would go one further. His guess was that Ross had been heading into Liverpool that night to confront his son's killers. After losing his father and his friends to those same killers, he imagined his brother's desire for revenge would be incandescent. 'And I think he knew where to go if shit ever really went sour.'

'Then we have something to go off,' said Seabreeze, leaning back from his laptop. 'Leave it with me. I'm putting these parameters into a scraping tool, something you probably wouldn't get over the counter at PC World. It'll scour the web top to bottom. It needs time to do its thing. I'm back in tomorrow. We can talk, then.'

'Thank you, mate. However I can square it with you, let me know. And sorry if I've ruined your plans for the day.' He nodded towards the back of the flat.

Seabreeze grinned, and finally looked up from the screen. 'You've actually saved my bacon. Just next time you go rogue, call someone else. Okay?'

CHAPTER 13

MADISON ARRIVED AT Monroe's door with three minutes to spare. The superintendent emerged in a white *Cheadle Harriers* T-shirt and tracksuit pants. A towel draped over his neck, and a water bottle, completed the look.

'Chat whilst I row?' he said, without any preamble.

'Yes, sir.' What choice did she have?

She followed him into a side room that masqueraded as the station gym. It was a changing room—barely fit for purpose—lockers ripped out and cardiovascular equipment dragged in.

Monroe was a tall, broad man, softened by lifestyle and the years. But, he was loyal. When the shit had been halfway through the fan last year, he'd backed his CID units—given them time and space to sort things out. When it had come to the crunch, he'd pulled out all the stops. That brought a respect that money couldn't buy.

'Let's start with the body in the bag,' he said, sitting astride the Concept 2 rowing machine. Madison was no stranger to the unit. Few things replicated the full-body workout of boxing training, never mind its intensity, but the rower went a long way to attack that crown. She watched him pick a five-kilometre programme and get to work with long, steady strokes that made use of every inch of his height. 'I've read your report,' he began between breaths. 'What else is there between the lines?'

Madison perched on the seat of a reclined exercise bike. 'I've included everything up to about six a.m., but then I went to see Mackie.'

'Ah yes, I did lean on her a bit when two bodies came in. We're lucky to have her.' Mackie was originally the Home Office pathologist, who had taken a liking to Warrington after the career-making Warrington 27 case last year. Here, she had reach to all the big cases in Liverpool, Manchester, in between and beyond. She had decided to stick around in the Wire.

'Yeah, was good to see her.'

'And the body? You inspected it yourself?'

'Yeah, I did.' While it was strange to be thinking along such lines, she found it hard not to think about the other body—the one from the lock-up. That was the one that held all sorts of mysteries. She fought to push it out of her thoughts, if only for the time being. 'The body from the bag was a young male, mid–late teens.'

'ID?' Monroe asked over the roar of the machine's pistons as he continued to pull back in regular motions. He hadn't even broken a sweat.

'Face in advanced putrefaction. I don't think we'll get much from there, although dental work appears intact.'

'Obvious other identifiers?'

'A lopsided gym routine, which focused on the show muscles, and a stab wound to the heart.'

'So a murder case, then?'

'Yes.' It always looked that way, but without sight of the obvious wound beforehand, it was hard to confirm—despite how unlikely it was the lad had somehow zipped himself into a bag and thrown himself into the river. Now there was evidence of a mortal wound, a murder investigation could properly start. 'The bag is with forensics. Should hear within the day if there's anything to point us in the right direction.'

'And I assume you're going to run through the usual means of establishing missing persons that fit the victim's description?'

'Yes, I'm about to put Karthik onto ViCAP, Holmes, all the main databases. See what hits we get.'

'Excellent work.' It was only then that Madison realised her boss hadn't even needed to speed up his breathing with the exercise. She was impressed. 'So, how about this fracas at the storage lock-up?'

This was where Madison got nervous. 'Have you read Christopher's report?'

'Yes. Doesn't answer my main question, though.'

Shit, she thought. He'd gone straight for it—as, she supposed, he should. There was a glaring omission in Christopher's report. 'I have a number of questions myself, sir,' she said.

'Christopher's write-up suggested he was following your instruction to attend the scene.'

'That's correct, sir.'

'How did you know about what was happening before the emergency services did? And stop calling me sir.'

She could have kicked herself—that was a sure sign she was nervous. 'I received a tip-off.'

'A helpful member of the public with a direct line to a DI. That's very lucky, I'd say.'

She couldn't lie. She wasn't duty bound to Foley through anything but historical loyalty. 'It was Brendan Foley, sir.'

She expected a volley, but Monroe smiled instead. 'I expected as much. Don't worry, Iona. I know how hard it is when your phone rings and there's information, no matter where it comes from.'

She felt a rush of relief and the glow of camaraderie and approval. She worked so hard for moments like these, and for the Super to recognise the job's grey areas and to sympathise… it made her proud and happy.

'The next question then,' said Monroe, 'is how did Foley know?'

'I don't know.'

'He's sticking his nose in somewhere that involves all his usual points of interest. Drugs, organised crime, dead bodies appearing out of nowhere...'

Madison stayed quiet and let the Super talk.

'Have you been in much contact since he left us?'

Madison thought back to the day Foley left the force for good. The memorial for the twenty-seven souls lost. The unveiling of that monument to tragedy, which held more than a few shades of virtue signalling. The town had to be seen to do something. It was in the nation's eyeline, a case with acute loss of life in the grimmest of circumstances. It didn't matter if all those people in that hole had committed crimes of their own. A grand gesture was needed, and the town hall had obliged in spades.

On that day, Foley had given her his job. She would always be grateful. In the events leading up to that exchange, she'd saved his life and he'd saved hers.

He'd already lost his father, his nephew, a missing brother. He was a brilliant detective, an asset to any force that would have him, but it seemed that now his mind had robbed him of that too. Madison knew Monroe had tried to keep him, but he'd insisted on leaving.

'We swap the odd text from time to time,' Madison said eventually. 'Nothing more than the perfunctory. Last night was the first time we've spoken in a long time.'

'How do you think he's holding up?'

'Very hard to say.'

'He's refused every service support the police has offered him. Counselling, desk work, even the pension.'

'It seems he wanted a clean break.'

'It seems he's turned his back on the force. Except for last night. When he needed it.'

Madison nodded slowly. The thought had occurred to her. She didn't think that Brendan was actively using her *per se*, but that is exactly how it seemed now in the cold light of day. He'd done something daft, and used his old police connections to clean up after him.

'What about the contents of the lock-up?' Monroe asked. Sweat was finally pearling his brow.

'Mackie says the body is in a state she's never seen before. No ID as yet, but we'll get one. His face and head were intact.'

'At least that's something. And the narcotics in the bird seed? The note?'

'High street value, with the heavy footfall surrounding the short time the product was there, along with the whiffs of payoffs to lock-up staff. It looks like a dead drop scaled right up. All the way up. That was there for someone to collect.'

'So a major drug deal.'

'Yes. And the note suggests that wasn't the first.'

'And the body suggests something went wrong.'

'Yes.'

They didn't speak for a moment, the only sound the steady, rhythmical whirr of the rower's drum.

'Major drug deals on our patch again. Foley involved somehow. That other name is going to come up again, isn't it?'

Madison wouldn't say the name. The one she now associated with fear and guilt.

Monroe wasn't so circumspect. 'Culpepper.' Their long-fought adversary.

There was nothing else left to say. Madison stood up off the exercise bicycle. 'Leave it with me. Sir.'

CHAPTER 14

CHRISTOPHER WASN'T USED to this lack of control, the helpless trust and hope he was forced to place in others. If he needed something to happen, he made it happen, no matter the scrap and fight it took. But here, now, in the congested ultrasound suite at Warrington Hospital, all he could do was cling to blind faith.

And hope that massive fucking needle went nowhere near his unborn son.

Finding the boy had been fine, even if he was only the size of a half-decent grape. He was sat there on the monochrome screen, etched in shades of ethereal white, in a familiar foetal pose. He was already perfect, a little mass in steady bloom.

'Okay, the local should be taking effect now, Emma,' said one of the doctors—the one Christopher took to be the main one, because he wasn't wearing a white coat.

Emma looked at Christopher from her place on the bed. Her body was surrounded by nurses, technicians and doctors—including the one holding that needle.

'Keep those eyes on me, darling,' said Christopher, dragging a thumb across the back of Emma's hand. 'Just look at me.'

Emma blew air out marginally quicker than a sigh, the truest sign Christopher had seen yet that her bravery and strength were being tested.

'Have you done it yet?' she said, her eyes turning to stare at the ceiling.

'Not yet, Emma, but it'll all be done soon,' came the gentle reply from somewhere around her midriff.

'You're doing really well,' Christopher said, looking for the right words. He could just about do the *I love you*s now. But the release of feeling those three words uncorked was all so new to him. He'd never said or felt anything like it.

Growing up how he had, his parents had shown scant interest in their children. They were a means to a benefit end. Free cash and not much talk of love.

Now, he was determined that his son would never go through that. Would never be made to feel anything less than loved. As long as Christopher was there, his son would never want for anything in the affection department. But it wasn't easy, not after all these years. Not when life had taught you to hide your feelings for fear of a backhander.

'Shall we talk about names?' Emma said, before suddenly gasping. 'Brackets, I think the needle's in there now.'

Bless her, thought Christopher, smiling at her use of the word 'brackets'. The needle was nowhere near her. It was still in the doctor's hands. Christ, it was big. He flashed a glance at the doctor, who gave a small nod. Then he smiled and told a white lie. 'Yeah, must be nearly over by now.'

'We can't have Christopher, of course.'

'I'd have thought that would go without saying.'

'What about Junior? Tom Christopher Junior?'

'No, too American.' The needle was coming down, and Christopher found he urgently wanted to change the subject. Couldn't give the little raspberry a name while a needle plunged so close to him.

'I quite like—'

'Deep breath now, Emma,' the doctor interrupted.

'Why?' Then, she suddenly let out a howl, eyes squeezed shut.

'It's okay, darling. It's okay,' Christopher hushed, as he moved his hand up to Emma's shoulder. Her knuckles turned bone white as she gripped the bed sheet. The scream swept into a single sob. 'I've got you,' he said. 'Look at me, I've got you.'

She howled again, causing Christopher to look at the source of her pain—and immediately wished he hadn't. It was a sight that would never leave him. Emma, the girl he'd fallen for, harder than he'd ever thought he'd be capable of, with a thick needle pushed into her abdomen a few inches below her belly button. It turned his stomach, but not nearly as much as what he saw on the screen. His son, small and half-formed—and near, too near, was the column of the needle.

One slip, one judder, and his son would be impaled. Split, jumbled. He forced the thought from his mind, as he watched his son's tiny feet dance by the needle tip. He looked at Emma. 'Hold still, baby.'

Please, for God's sake, don't slip. Please God, let me have this moment. Let me have this boy.

Christopher hadn't realised how much fatherhood meant to him—not until this moment.

I want this. I want so much to be a dad. I want my son.

Another scream from Emma. Christopher grabbed her shoulders. If she thrashed, it would be disastrous—but she relaxed, her brow drooping, her shoulders unravelling.

'We're done, Emma,' said the doctor.

'Well done, my love,' said a nurse.

'How did it go?' asked Christopher.

The doctor was walking the needle to the units, above the biowaste bin in the corner of the room. 'We got the sample. And I'm sure there'll be enough to get an accurate test result.' Christopher blew out the pent-up pressure. First hurdle down. The results would be the next big thing, but you had to take each hurdle one at a time. The CVS treatment was a worrying one, because of how invasive it was. Now, it was a waiting game. Would they be able to keep the baby? There were risks in his family, real risks. The baby had a chance of carrying certain genetic hand-me-downs that would make life miserable for the child, that would be cruel to force him to live through.

But those were big moments, and even bigger decisions, further down the road.

'Phew,' Christopher said, deflating himself now. Emma was smiling up at him.

'The needle wasn't in, was it?' she said, with a relieved smile.

'No, but I—'

'You're a crap liar, Tom Christopher.'

CHAPTER 15

MONROE HAD AGREED to handle the press—it was a task he was always more than happy to take on, meeting his adoring public. Madison didn't mind, though—freed her up to get on with the real work.

Phone in hand, she left the station. There was an obvious first port of call. *Foley.*

Whatever he knew, Madison had to know, too. Now. If he cared at all about the force he'd left behind, he'd have to talk. Madison was prepared to make that very clear.

The conversation couldn't take place anywhere near the flapping ears at the station.

She hit Brendan's name from her call register, and listened to it ring through and out, whilst she watched the day get started on the road outside. The station reception faced the Golden Square shopping centre, one of its many glass entrances immediately opposite. As the first shoppers arrived, she envied their merry ignorance to the challenges she and the police force were facing.

The phone rang out. It had been a late night, but she knew that Brendan slept badly and would likely be awake. What was he up to? His unpredictability unsettled her.

Her phone rang, and she felt a rush of relief. Maybe Brendan had simply missed the call? But the name on the screen caught her by surprise.

'Gavigan?'

Why was he calling again? She'd received his message that the scene had been released, made public again. He was a great forensic, but wildly fastidious he was not, so it wasn't like him to check back in.

The static on the line felt heavy with foreboding, this his voice came through. 'Something else, I'm afraid. The bag you sent over from the mortuary—the big cricket bag? We've started to go through it.'

'Okay…' Again, Madison had no idea why that needed a formal report.

'It's a big one, so we've got three on it.'

'Alright.'

There was a deep breath. 'We've found a thumbprint on a label.'

The buzz in Madison's head again. 'The label at the bottom of the bag? Behind the plastic strip?'

'Yeah, that's the one.'

'Okay, great. But why the call, Gavigan?'

That pregnant static again. 'Because, well… We've already got a hit.'

'That fast? How?' Madison couldn't hide her surprise. Usually, it would take a couple of days to get a result, and that was if the print's owner was on file already. 'I take it we already had the perp in the system?'

'No. I mean, we do, but… I didn't need to check the system.'

'Why not?' She was suddenly buzzing.

'I've been in forensics twenty-two years, so I know my way around a fingerprint, okay? I'd recognise this one anywhere. I stared at it enough last winter.'

Winter. What happened last winter?

'I've double checked it now, too.'

'And?'

'And it looks like our old friend, Mal Jevons, is the guy who killed the kid in the bag, and put him in there.'

The name hit Madison's knees like a bag of bricks. She had to immediately sink down to sit on the station's wet front step. 'What?'

'Malcolm Jevons. The owner of that chop shop over in Bootle. I was there when we went through that place.' He paused. 'I'll never forget it.'

Malcom fucking Jevons. AWOL murderer. One of the real killers of the Warrington 27, who slaughtered and bagged up his victims in the back room of a derelict trophy shop in a dockside Liverpool suburb.

'Madison?' Gavigan asked, clearly perturbed by her silence.

'I'm here,' she reassured him quickly—but she really wasn't. She was miles away, floating where fears and regrets whirled. She was back at the landfill site in Birchwood. With Seabreeze, Christopher and Foley. Back where they had thrown Mal's body into the deepest point they could find—along with his accomplice, Gerry Toyne. It had all taken place after a blood-spurting confrontation; their attempts to kill Brendan Foley had been averted, but with fatal consequences.

The rest of the world thought they were missing, presumably in Europe. Madison had been happy to let that charade play out. But now? Even though Mal and Get were dead—the ghosts, the secrets—they all came flooding back.

And along with them, a searing, heavy-handed panic.

CHAPTER 16

BRENDAN CAME HERE often, although he didn't like to broadcast it. He didn't announce he was going to walk the dog, largely because they didn't have one. Didn't announce he was nipping out for a breather, didn't tell anyone he needed to clear his head. He didn't have a grave to visit for his father, nor would he go if there was one.

The blood that bound them had run to cold sewer water by the time of the old man's death.

He couldn't visit any grave for his brother, because as far as they knew, he wasn't dead. And he'd be damned if he was going to that monstrosity in the centre of town that had been all too quickly thrown up to memorialize each member of the Warrington 27—even though every last one was a criminal.

These were all the reasons why he now found himself on this patch of land in Peel Hall Woods.

Again.

He traced the shape with steady steps, hands tucked into his jeans pockets. He wore a jumper; tree coverage kept the forest floor cool in the mornings.

It had been freezing that day too, but since then, things had changed. The ground had all been turned over and re-seeded. Fresh deciduous fall had added an established, natural feel. The crime scene, once taped, was long gone, no forgotten strands left. There wasn't a single footprint disturbing the place that had once been overrun by cops and SOCOs only a matter of months ago, dragging twenty-seven bodies from the earth.

Nobody came here anymore, except for him. Dog walkers avoided it. Only teenagers dared each other to come out here for selfies and TikToks. It occupied a space no one spoke of. Brendan didn't do superstition, didn't do creepy. But this place, the atmosphere... it was all wrong, living up to its new reputation.

A mass grave.

And yet, he couldn't stop coming. Here was where his life's path had forked. Pulling those bodies up, establishing links to the wider criminal picture of the north-west, then tying it all back round to his own father. Eventually, he had been framed for it all. Overnight, Brendan became the son of a prolific serial killer.

This was the place where the old Brendan had died.

And for that person, he mourned.

A noise suddenly broke the quiet. Soft, but enough to hear.

The scrape of boot against mud.

Brendan looked up, alert.

'I come here too, you know,' said a voice. It was Chief Superintendent Monroe. His suit stood out incongruously against the surroundings. He looked slick—far too slick—but then again, he always did. 'But usually when I see you here, I back off.'

'Sir,' Brendan said, then carefully started to walk back around the outline of the mass grave towards Monroe. No matter how much time elapsed, how many tons of dirt had been filled back in, he didn't think he could ever again walk across that yawning trench.

'Call me Terry.' The Super's eyes shone with understanding.

Brendan was taken aback. 'I don't think I could.'

Monroe shrugged. 'We're just two chaps dealing with the ghosts of the past. I think, when it comes to our p's and q's, we can relax.'

The two of them stood side by side, their gazes resting on the site.

'Do you think we can ever put it to rest?' said Monroe, after a moment.

Brendan thought. 'I don't honestly know.'

'You're struggling to let go.' It wasn't a question.

'Let go of which part?' Brendan replied, dark and stubborn.

'What you went through—the bollocks you showed. It doesn't bear thinking about. There's no way ordinary folk could carry on after that.'

You don't know the half of it, thought Brendan.

'But there comes a time,' Monroe said, 'to move forward. Look after yourself. And your family.'

The word 'family' touched an open sore. 'What do you mean my *family*?'

'I've been in the police for forty years now. You can't help but notice details. See why they happen time and again. Being a cop isn't easy for families, it never is. Christ, I'm on my third wife and I'm still paying for the first two. But you... you're not a cop anymore. You can make that side of things right.'

'Are you here as my old gaffer?'

'I'm here as your friend—or as close to that as old coppers get.'

Brendan felt discomfort at this brush with the personal. 'Then I'll take it under advisement.'

Monroe made a point of ignoring his tone. 'Stop running around in the night. Move forwards. I've seen the job swallow too many people. Don't let it happen to you, too.'

Brendan didn't reply. Couldn't. He had to be stupid to assume that his grand plan, the reason he left the police in the first place—to go off after the Culpeppers himself—wouldn't be noticed. To bring them to account his own way and bring these bastards to justice. If he could just use whatever he found, at whatever cost, he could point cops in the right direction. Anonymously, if necessary. They'd get there eventually.

'We're not thick, Brendan. But some of these pictures are just too big for one man on his own. You are a brilliant detective. You've never needed a warrant card to prove that. But there is only so much I can turn a blind eye to. I'll say playing vigilante detective is certainly at that limit.'

Brendan felt a burst of frustration. 'I can't just let them get away with it!' There. Even saying those few words had blown whatever cover he had already. He wasn't in the right mood for this. How had Monroe known he'd be here?

'I'm not telling you to. I'm asking you to let us handle it.'

'You wouldn't be anywhere near handling it if it weren't for me.'

Monroe turned slightly, and his shadow in the moonlight cast a physical shadow over Brendan. 'You are very lucky. I'm saying your part in last night is being ignored. But it won't—*can't*—be overlooked again. Is that understood?'

Brendan felt no option, because past the stubbornness and drive for recompense, the rational side of him was in full agreement. He couldn't career off doing whatever he wanted. It made a mockery of the system he'd served, the system he needed to put faith in for the Culpeppers to meet justice. Undermining it would do no good, only complicate the issue. His legal head said that the last thing they needed was a question of admissibility in court. He couldn't bear it if the Culpeppers, finally in the dock, had to be set free because of a technicality caused by *him*.

'Got it, boss,' Brendan said, at last.

'Terry.' Monroe turned to walk back. 'Come on. Let's get wandering. It looks like I've two crime organisations I need to bring down.'

Brendan followed, head brimming with questions, but knowing not to push his luck. But Monroe—the sharp bugger—had already read his mind.

'And don't even try to get involved.' He paused. 'Just check the news in the morning.'

CHAPTER 17

WINSTON WILSON WAS, by all accounts, an oddball.

He lived alone—and sure—there was nothing wrong with that. But it was the manner of his existence which was weird.

When his mum had died, she'd left her the house in Gorse Covert, a smattering of houses and cul-de-sacs that reached off Birchwood's infernal industrial quarter. He'd left his flat, the place he'd had since he'd moved out at seventeen, grabbing a bin bag of belongings that he'd later placed down in his mum's hall. There it had stayed for four years; after a while, he simply didn't see it anymore. And he changed *nothing*.

His hoarding wasn't simply about the items; it was his collection. When he'd moved in, he hadn't thrown a thing away. Not a thing. It was all too precious. In a way, he was sad that his own mother couldn't be part of the collection.

He was sitting at the third kitchen table. The house was big. Kitchen tables one and two stood to one side, covered with packets, packaging, emblazoned in all those warnings, advice and words that had been deliberated over with so much care. Who was he to throw away such effort? These were his investments.

Things lived on with him. Including this table, which gave him a small space to eat his chicken and mushroom pot noodle, and watch the telly. On the small flatscreen—which he'd rescued from the tip—the 24-hour news channel rolled on in endless fifteen-minutes. But today a major story was breaking. A face was on the screen, a face he recognised in an instant.

No. It couldn't be.

He watched the story with fascination, excitement building into a relentless charge through his body. The more he saw the face on screen, the more sure he felt.

It was him.

He'd have to check to be sure, but it was *him*.

He leapt up, washed his fork in the sink, and put it upright in a coffee cup to dry. He was no monster, no heathen, he kept the place right. And today, one of his treasures looked to have fully justified its rescue.

His investment was about to pay off.

CHAPTER 18

ONE OF THE biggest things that separated Manchester from Liverpool—to Fintan's mind, at least—was the seagulls. You knew you were in Scouseland when those massive, squawking sea pigeons wheeled overhead.

And it only got worse, deeper into the city.

There, they'd steal sandwiches straight out of your hand, peck your eyes out for your chips.

To Fin's mind—a born-and-bred Manc with all the East Lancs prejudices and shoulder chips that went with it—those birds were a reflection of the city's other inhabitants. The Scousers. But then, he remembered the feral pigeons of Manchester. Winged rats with filthy feathers and crackhead pin eyes. Maybe he should reign in the stereotypes. The Manc–Scouse divide was a chasm deep across those short thirty miles, and it went both ways.

He parked his Bonneville under the awning of a dockside car wash, off to one side, and gave the lot owner twenty quid.

'Don't touch it, and don't let anyone else either,' he said. His pride and earthly joy, his 1987 Triumph Bonneville with the metallic aqua detailing, was not going to get spattered with seagull shit. Not on his watch.

The attendant nodded. Fin walked out of the lot, past the cars queued up for a spruce. The dockside buildings loomed high, and were packed so densely, he couldn't see the sea, even though he could smell its brine.

He knew where he was going—a place he'd never visited before.

He was excited. The relationship between the Devil's Defects and the Culpepper family was a new one, and had already proved lucrative, until recent misunderstandings had threatened to derail things—and got Jase killed. He was here to see if they could do the right thing. See what could be salvaged. If Jason's jacket had been taken in an act of spite, chances were, it would be here.

He turned down one of the side roads, into an empty cobbled street, brick walls rising high on each side. A hundred or so metres down on the right, there was a chain-link gate. Eight by twelve. He arrived beside the gate and peered through to what looked like yet another dockside yard in the grip of renovation. Diggers, portacabins, piles of masonry and sacks of builders' sand. The only detail missing was the buzz of activity.

Cautiously, Fin raised a hand to the gate. It might be electrified. There were stories about this place. Portside Dockyard, a Culpepper spot. He'd heard of people coming here for off-the-books boxing matches to settle rivalries. Straighteners, they were called. He'd heard that if you needed to squash a beef with someone, you could get the match held here. They'd even lay on coaches.

He'd also heard of people coming here and never coming back out. Certain floors in these abandoned buildings that were chop shops.

The gate was solid; he didn't think he could even drive a car through it. There was no buzz of electricity, but even so, he dropped his hand and opened his mouth to call for someone. But before he could send out a shout, a man appeared. He was walking straight towards Fin from the closest of the two warehouses, dressed in jeans and a black work jacket, carrying a white hard hat in one hand. He looked at Fin, as if assessing him, then abandoned the hard hat, placing it on a stray pile of sacks.

Fin wasn't green to the tricks of all sorts of trades, dark or otherwise. The hat was only to keep the ruse up. He knew, and this guy knew, that there was no need to keep up appearances.

As the guy approached the gate, Fin measured him up. Pound for pound, he was heavy and thick, but Fin fancied his chances. The jacket was tight, but only around the paunch. A dark goatee stood stark against the man's pale cheeks. He clearly hadn't seen much sunlight of late.

He looked Fin up and down, lingering on Fin's own jacket. 'A biker,' said the man, in a strong Scouse accent.

'I'm not here for any trouble.' Fin held his palms up. 'I know something went on, although I don't know why. I'll let our big 'uns sort all that out. I just want to get the lad's jacket.'

Goatee's eyebrows arched in mock disbelief. 'You've come for a coat?'

'The lad's going to need burying. He'll be wanting his jacket.'

'If I saw that grave, I'd spit in it. Right in front of his ma.'

Fin would quite like to have this bloke's throat out, but he'd never done any proper wet work before. Besides, there was a steel barrier between the two of them.

'I just want the kid's jacket.'

'You ain't getting no fucking coat. Get back on your tricycle and fuck off back up the road.'

It was a job staying reasonable in the face of this. 'Can you make a call?'

'Who to?'

'Word is the Big Cheese is often on site. If he's in, would you give him a buzz?'

Goatee turned and looked at the top of the nearest building. That was another rumour about this place—that Harvey

Culpepper had an office here, deep in the centre of his own operations. The longer the man gazed up, the longer it felt as though the rumour was true. The man eventually turned back and smiled thinly. 'I don't think I'm gonna be doing anything like that.'

Fin felt his body tense. 'Why not?'

'I'd get going if I were you, or I'll have to get the bizzies down because of a trespasser.'

'You wouldn't be getting the police down here for love nor money.'

'I think you've the wrong impression.'

'I don't think so.'

'I'll be clear as fresh piss. Fuck off—before I make calls you don't want me to make.'

'Why, need some help? Don't think you could take me alone? Bless.' Fin turned his back as Goatee's cheeks flushed. 'Tell your boss I tried to be reasonable. It was you that fucked it up.'

Happy to have had the last word—a frightening one at that—Fin moved away. He didn't look back once. He'd held his own, his heart hopping at the buzz of it.

But then, he still didn't have that jacket. That was a problem.

CHAPTER 19

THE LIFT MADE its usual clanking ascent. The noise, an early warning that company was imminent.

Harvey Culpepper walked from the Chesterfield sofas beneath the window facing the Atlantic to the leather-topped desk that sat in front of the facing window that looked over the city.

A king in an anonymous castle, astride an invisible throne.

The cage doors of the industrial lift opened, and in walked Dorian—Harvey's head gofer, right-hand man and dockyard manager. He strode across the cavernous space towards the office area. The open expanse of floor was covered in restored parquet—a luxury on this floor only. The other parts of the warehouse were kept strictly for function, not form.

'You had a visitor,' said Culpepper.

'A biker,' replied Dorian. 'Brave little fucker.'

Culpepper spun on his desk chair, and glowered out of the window, elbows on knees. 'I didn't expect them to reach out this quickly. I trust you handled it appropriately?'

'With a smacked arse, and a tail between the legs.'

'Good. They need to show they've got the message and are onside.'

'He wasn't for saying sorry.'

Harvey spun slowly back around to face Dorian. 'What did he want?'

'A coat or something.'

Harvey rolled his eyes. 'These bloody bikers and their traditions. What a load of bollocks.'

'I told him to forget the jacket.'

Harvey went very still. 'They won't like that.'

'Fuck 'em.'

'We'll see.'

Neither man said anything for a moment. Then Harvey abruptly stood and walked briskly to a dark section of the room. A black Lamborghini crouched like a panther. 'I'm nipping out for a bit.'

'Yes, boss.'

Harvey slowed, and turned back with a squeak of a polished heel. 'How many doors do we have in this city?'

'All of them.'

'Yes, but how many hands does that give us, on the ground?'

His right-hand man took a moment to think. 'Over a thousand pubs... A couple hands each who are definitely on payroll or on fees. So, two thousand at a guess.'

'And on payroll, not on doors?'

'Anywhere between seventy and a hundred.'

'And favours owed in Europe?'

Dorian seemed to catch on, excitement lighting his eyes. 'I think we could get another couple of hundred over, no problem.'

'So, approaching two-and-a-half-thousand hands. But let's half that number for cry-offs and shithouses.'

'Still over a thousand. Enough for a show of strength.'

Harvey turned back to the car, twirling the keys around a finger. He called back over his shoulder. 'Let's hope it doesn't come to that yet.'

Within moments, he was in the vehicle's leather-upholstered seat, firing up the engine with an orgasmic, primal growl that rang around the warehouse. He gunned the car at an absurd pace across the thirty metres to the lift, where Dorian had already gone to open the doors.

Harvey loved that thirty metres.

It gave him the same thrill, no matter how many times he covered the same small space. One wrong move and the best part of a-hundred-and-fifty grand would be a write-off—but by now he knew this routine by heart, exactly when to hit the brakes.

Dorian dragged closed the elevator doors behind the Lambo's spoiler with practised obedience, and hit the ancient lever to send the lift battering back down. Harvey sat in the Lambo, smoothly riding out the descent, thanks to the vehicle's immaculate suspension.

His confidence bloomed. Harvey Culpepper was protected by wealth and power, able to ride out any storm or disturbance, ready to take on all comers with his big brass balls.

CHAPTER 20

THE MAN IN custody had supplied his name.

Steven Brinson.

His picture was doing the rounds at the station in the hope that someone might recognise him, have a little info that wasn't on any of the databases.

Madison could feel the anticipation and nervous energy vibrating off Broom, sat next to her at the small chipboard table. The room was as unglamorous as blank interview rooms got,

Broom hadn't said anything yet, but her entire posture and countenance screamed, *Up for it*! It made Madison smile.

Well, it would have, if she wasn't somewhat otherwise occupied.

'There's a simple question and I think it would benefit us all if you answered,' Madison said. She spread her hands in a gesture of appeal.

Brinson and his solicitor were left unmoved. Brinson hadn't said a word since coming in, aside from confirming his name and giving an address in Salford. Brinson looked smug, tanned—and Teflon.

'How did you come to be at unit 2272 at Storage Plus, last night?'

Nod from the solicitor, prompting Brinson to speak. 'I've a unit of my own up there. 2276. I was passing.'

'So, who were you chatting to on your phone, while having a good look in 2272?'

His solicitor immediately intervened. When he held up his hand, Madison expected him to instruct a 'no comment' response. Instead, the solicitor spoke himself: 'What would you do if you walked past an open door, and happened to see a body inside?'

'Ah, yes. The body. Thank you for reminding me, Mr Tuttle.'

The solicitor, whose brown suit was the colour of an under-fibrous bowel movement, looked up scornfully.

'We are having trouble identifying the deceased,' Madison persisted. 'Do you think you could help?'

'My client doesn't know him.'

'Can your client speak for himself, please?'

Brinson leaned forwards with a sigh. 'Didn't know him.'

'Are you sure?'

'Didn't know him.' Brinson repeated.

Madison removed a printout from the file on the desk. 'So, you'll find it a surprise and an outrage if I refer to the arresting officer's report last night, who... Oh, would you look at that? He's in my own CID unit. Gosh, he's an honest one isn't he, DC Broom?'

Broom said nothing, but her eyes burned into Brinson. 'Anyway, DS Tom Christopher—who I would trust to guard my pension with—states that you "wanted to shift this lot"—the lot being whatever was in that lock-up unit. Also, that "we needed to do something about Jason".'

'He was mistaken.'

'But you were on the phone.'

'I was about to call 999, when your man started chasing me.'

'Ah, so you're a conscientious witness, as opposed to a guiltily interested party?'

Madison loved the dance of police interviews, especially when the upper hand was hers. It felt like the verbal equivalent of boxing—another thing she loved. Life was all about picking your moments, timing your attacks, knowing when to get your guard up and when to throw the knockout blow.

Brinson didn't say a word.

'If I could interject, Ma'am?' Broom pulled her chair forwards with a scrape.

'Of course, DC Broom.' Madison leant back. She had instructed Broom to step in at any time once the preliminaries were out of the way, using her own judgement.

'I thought it might be helpful to tell Mr Brinson a bit of detail. Whilst he is clearly hugely inconvenienced by this interview, it might help him understand our urgency if we explain a little bit about the body. Jason, we'll call him, because God knows we don't have a better name to hand, so we might as well stick with the one DS Christopher apparently misheard. Anyway, this *Jason...*' Broom threw elaborate air quotes over her head. '... is in such a state that the medical team say they've never seen anything like it before.'

Brinson held Broom's gaze.

'He looked all right from the outside, just a bit weird. Well, that's the word they kept using. You've seen it, haven't you, ma'am?'

'I have,' Madison said, enjoying this. 'It was weird.'

'Except inside him, every single organ was bruised, misshapen... *battered.* It will have been excruciating. Persistently excruciating. And he won't have died quickly, no, not at all. He will have died slowly—one piece at a time—as his organs yielded to these attacks. It will, we shouldn't kid ourselves, have been one of the nastiest ways to go *ever.* Pure nightmare fuel. I get cold whenever I think about it. But, like I said, the exterior of his body was fine, art was there for all to see. Tattoos, Mr Brinson—that's what I'm talking about.'

Brinson's eyes flickered.

'Jason had a few real beauties. And a couple that were very distinctive. Some would say tribal, but not in a design sense—I'm talking of the more anthropological variety. I'm thinking brotherhood, Mr Brinson. You see, looking at you, I couldn't completely work it out. But these pictures I have here—these images of Jason's body—started to point me in the right direction.'

Brinson glanced fleetingly at the photographs in Broom's hand.

'You, Mr Brinson, look like you've just done eighteen holes on a nice summer morning. But I look at *this* picture… and I think your tan is too harsh. Sun for sure, but windburn, too. I think the panda whites around your eyes aren't because of some fancy-dan golfing shades, but from motorbike goggles. And I think there's a strong chance you wouldn't know whether to get out of the deep rough with a sand iron or a curling iron. And when I saw Jason's tattoos, this one caught my eye.'

She tossed the photos onto the table.

The top one featured a particular shape inked under the body's right arm. It depicted what looked like a loop of rope on the ground, its end snapped, beneath a wooden beam.

'That is a broken noose. Not many people have these tattoos. But they denote belonging to the Devil's Defects, a motorcycle chapter. Local, I believe. So, when I look at you Mr Brinson, I think there's a strong chance that if you lift up that golf shirt, the one that's never seen grass never mind a golf course, you'll have the same tattoo as Jason here…' She paused. 'Would you care to show us?'

CHAPTER 21

AS SHE LEFT, Fiona flung out an apology.

Seabreeze had assured her time and again that she never needed to. He understood the tightrope she faced on a daily basis. It was part of their routine, to take all appropriate precautions.

Why wouldn't they?

He was under no illusion that the danger added a spark to their affair. On paper, everything worked Hollywood. Her, the beautiful soap actress. Him, the brilliant cyber-crimes cop. Though movie execs would probably baulk at the scenery needed for the love nest—they persisted in meeting at the cop's down-at-heel council flat in a forgotten Warrington suburb. But it wasn't always about surface appearances. His block of flats had the quickest Internet speed in the entire region, and that was important to Seabreeze—very important.

Her phone had beeped to let her know that her trusted driver was waiting. Within moments, she'd disappeared, any apology hanging in the air.

Now, Seabreeze had booted up his tech, made another coffee, and come up with a plan. How to peel back the layers, looking for clues. Wanting to find Ross Foley.

A soft blue glow from the keyboard and bespoke computer tower indicated he was nearly up and running. Foley had been right to come to him. If he wanted to find his brother, off the books and without the national legwork, Seabreeze didn't think there was anyone better placed than him. Not that he was entirely comfortable with the undertaking.

The young Mauritian had been trained in audio-visual manipulation, comprehensive database analysis, metadata interpretation that was bordering on Sherlockian and—thanks to a little extra-curricular study layered on top—was a growing whizz at digital warfare tactics and traceless hacking. Plus, he had access. All of it. Both official and otherwise.

But these things always came with risks. You wandered unwelcome into the big databases. You'd better be sure not to leave breadcrumbs.

He had a coffee mug in front of him as big as a spittoon, and had put four tablespoons of instant in it. It would probably have him sprinting to the toilet in about an hour, but until then he would be like greased lightning with a coke-infused cattle prod up his arse.

Screen live, cursor angled, modified to a hot red dot.

He pulled his pad close, and gave a quick look at the brainstorm he'd scratched down whilst Fiona had got ready earlier. CCTV. Google Earth. ATM cameras. Chain of logic. Finding someone, he could do.

Everything depended on whether or not Ross Foley had already fled the country. Then, things would get interesting. Tracking someone down across all of mainland Europe—now that would be a challenge.

There were facts he already knew. Passports, credit cards, debit cards—none of these had been used. That suggested prior planning, and an amassing of funds. So simple start, to go back to when Ross survived the attempt on his life on the East Lancs road last October. See what needed to have happened next.

He'd have needed getaway cash, and a place to stay. These days, the only places that didn't require ID on check-in were camp sites and roadside hotel chains. Anything over fifty quid a night was after booking via credit card or cash with passport or driving license. A roadside hotel for a short-term fix might have worked, but it would only be exactly that. The length of time Foley had been missing, without supposed trace, suggested something more permanent, and more thought out—which required planning and cash. Currency always left a memory.

Yeah, he'd find him. No doubt. He gulped down the blisteringly strong coffee, jumped up, did ten press-ups, ten sit-ups. For every half hour at his screen, that's what he did. He was happy enough being the stereotypical hacker, but he would not be happy being a hacker with a triple XL wardrobe. Plus, the break helped him think. He sat down again, raring to go.

He started with information offered—Facebook. He could never get over just how much information was freely granted on social media. He didn't have an account himself, merely a placeholder for access to the service and its search engines. Ross's account had been deactivated, but it didn't take him long to find its archive.

Once he'd found that, he downloaded it as a zip file, then fed that directly into a dark web scraper tool that scoured it for every shred of information, from times and dates of posts, the location of those posts and every time he'd even logged in and browsed the app… the content of posts created, and the people featuring in those posts.

The search spat out an .xml spreadsheet file. He then fed that into a Google maps application that he'd built himself, which transposed geographical data directly onto a mirror of its maps.

And then there—across a map of the UK—lay a second map of all Ross Foley's movements since he'd started using Facebook in the mid-noughties. Seabreeze felt a thrill of excitement as his eyes darted around the screen. This person had clearly been a

prolific user; the map was extensive. Anomalies were obvious—
and these oddities held the key.

So, to add more information to his map of activity, he did
the same with Ross's supposedly secret Instagram account—
secret in the sense that he'd not put his own name to the
account. An account that he'd clearly used to send dick pics to
models. Same login criteria as his Facebook account. Same with
eBay, and recent purchases. Same with Amazon.

Nothing.

Nothing on Twitter, but he managed to get a bit from short-
lived stints on MySpace and Tumblr.

The map of Ross's movements became more intricate with
each new set of information; Seabreeze examined it with a
trained eye.

Using the filter tool, he instructed the map to show him
location data only. There were a number of hotspots north-west
of the country.

Seabreeze could discount this area as a bolthole straight
away. Unless the bloke was weighed down with cojones of epic
proportions, nobody went into hiding in their front garden. And
nobody went into hiding where they regularly went on holiday.

So, it was time to look for sore thumbs further afield. Those
places that had a few visits, but not a lot.

Abruptly, he leapt from his desk. Ten press-ups, ten sit-ups.

Back in the seat. No messing about.

At his screen, he deselected those places on the map with
regular appearances. The screen grew lighter in an instant.
Already much better.

There'd be a few for business reasons, that had to be a given.

Then, he deselected one-time visits and limited number of
visits to five.

The map whittled again, and in those strict parameters, an array of locations were left illuminated, but the number was narrowing.

This was where Brendan's suggestion came in, that Ross had enjoyed camping and the outdoors as a kid. A rural stop-off would fit the profile, so Seabreeze immediately deselected urban areas.

The number dropped sharply. Only a handful of places now.

If this was all supposedly a secret, then there'd be no pictures, so he instructed the map to show him photographs taken by Ross at these rural locations. One by one, he went through them, and if a picture had been taken there and posted online, he got rid of those too, because nobody in their right mind would share pictures of a secret hideaway spot.

Four possible locations remained.

So again, one at a time, he took out any of these locations that had any pattern to their visits. Seabreeze watched with excitement as that left one location on the map.

The village of Stanhope, County Durham.

He zoomed in, and looked at the app usage location data.

Ross Foley had never posted anything to social media on his four visits to Stanhope, but he had used the apps a number of times for browsing, which in turn had cached his location data—and revealed he'd even had an overnight stay, just the once.

Testing it out, thought Seabreeze.

Zooming in again, he saw where Ross had mostly been active on his visits to Stanhope. There was a clear winner.

A caravan park, at the top of a farm track, overlooking the village on the eastern facing hillside of the valley.

Opening a browser window, he typed in the name of the park—Heather View—and looked at the site details.

First off, it didn't allow camping in tents. Which might mean that Foley had bought a caravan. But the location had site security, and a campsite pub—both of which usually meant cameras.

Because of the remoteness, he could pinpoint to the digit the IP address of the site's intranet, and thanks to those hacker skills afforded to him by Her Majesty's Police Force, he was able to get in to the camp site's private intranet like a spectre in slippers. The system was functional and basic, exactly as it should be, and in under ten seconds he'd found the CCTV logs for the bar.

They were on a data refresh, with last month's footage saved.

Seabreeze figured that he'd start with last night. Why not?

And there Foley was. Propping up the bar, drinking alone. Looking like pounded shit. Fitting every cliché of the man on the run.

Unmistakable.

Ross Foley and a pint of Guinness.

It had only been forty five minutes since Seabreeze had sat down at his desk, yet he was almost disappointed to arrive at his aim so quickly.

He worked up a couple of printouts, kicked back for a moment while the machine whirred in the corner and opened up a web browser. Instead of a single website, he used a news digest app to give him a flavour of the bigger picture, rather than be force-fed the news certain outlets wanted him to see. A number of sites were running the same story, which set his own in-built keyword alarms ringing.

No, it couldn't be.

But it was. Malcolm Jevons. His face all over the news. Wanted in connection with a murder.

His stomach dropped. At last, he could visit the loo.

CHAPTER 22

BRENDAN HAD TRIED to take on board what Monroe had advised—to leave the official machines to churn out their own results. But that was easier said than done when the local news was full of Malcolm Jevons.

It made his skin crawl. He had to speak to Madison. Find out what she knew.

Domesticity had come for him hard when he'd stopped being the main breadwinner. Now, he was the one to do the weekly shop. So, when he'd felt at his most impotent, he'd headed to the big Asda in Leigh, the next county over. It afforded him the anonymity he craved even today.

Weekday mornings were always quiet. Brendan liked this time of day to visit—to not get in anyone's way. These places were mazes. He was constantly getting to the end of an aisle and then his list, realising he'd forgotten something that was back at the start.

As he worked his way back and forth between aisles, his mind drew similar patterns, weaving back to the events of last night, and the major drug deal he had foiled. He hoped that the drugs seized would be destroyed or used to coax others to reveal themselves. And that Jason, whoever he was, had died for something more than a deal gone wrong.

He was in the kiddie aisle, having finally worked out that infants' snacks were in the baby products' section. He was trying to work out the difference between Yo Yo Bears and Bear Paws, when a voice emerged next to him.

'Retirement is wonderful, isn't it?'

Brendan's stomach contracted at the voice's gravel, the delivery. The sick joy in every syllable.

'I didn't know you'd retired,' he said, turning.

There he stood, bronzed and toned, sixty years of living the finest a man could. Hair, grey and swept back.

Harvey Culpepper.

In Leigh Asda, with a boxed bottle of single malt under his arm.

'Man of my age, it's good to wind down. Take things easy.' He held up the bottle. Lagavulin. 'Cheapest place to get it.'

Harvey smiled, whereas Brendan was finding it excruciating just to stay in control.

Last winter, Culpepper had declared war on the Foley family, after killing Brendan's father and attempting to assassinate his brother. Now, here he stood, by the fucking nappies—the man who'd caused all his pain, all his hurt, all the death.

'How'd you find me?' he asked.

'Leigh Asda, once a week, the family shop? It doesn't take much to keep an eye.'

'I assume you're not alone?'

Harvey grinned wider. 'Nah. No powers of arrest, have you, son? You're no threat to me anymore.'

Brendan felt a pulse throb in his temple. 'Are you right about that?'

'I am. There's nothing you can do. When you left the police, you became a nobody. You're one of us now.'

'But there are other ways for the next man to make a difference, aren't there? Troublesome ways.' Brendan couldn't stop himself from glaring.

Culpepper's own eyes ignited. 'Yes, I did have some trouble. Last night, in fact.'

'What a shame.'

'You say that with the utmost sincerity. Want to claim responsibility?'

'I'm a concerned citizen now, aren't I?'

A woman inched her way between them to get at the shelves. 'Sorry, love,' she said to Brendan. 'I need a packet of pull-ups.'

Brendan pulled his trolley to the side.

As soon as the woman had moved along, the crime boss began speaking again.

'It's why I came here. To see if you've been poking your nose where it isn't wanted. Because we both know that didn't work too well for you last time, did it?'

It was a struggle not to set him straight. The smugness, the arrogance of this oiled snakeskin of a man—it set Brendan on a righteous spiral he found it hard to control.

'I'd keep your threats to yourself,' he said. 'Because we've had these conversations before, and I'm still here.'

Culpepper looked him up and down. 'You are still here... Because I let you, poor lad. Now, I like to cut to the chase, so clear as day I'm asking you—did you have anything to do with a business problem I had last night? Big Brucey-bonus clue. It was in Warrington, your old patch.'

'I have no idea what you're talking about,' Brendan said, although he wanted for all the world to tell the truth. Brendan had gone from nightclub to nightclub in Liverpool, on an undercover operation answering only to himself. He'd heard about Liverpool's new relationship with a Manc biker gang and bribed a disillusioned bar man to spill the details of a lock-up and the deals that went on there. It was Brendan who'd staked it out, and it was Brendan who, royally, had fucked it up.

He wanted to smile. Never mind just upsetting the apple cart, he'd managed to damage the Culpepper business so much that the main man had come to seek him out. How was that for getting things done?

They stared each other down.

'Now, if you'll excuse me,' Brendan said, 'I've stuff to do.'

'I'd expect a busy few days ahead,' Culpepper warned.

'Good job I'm retired then, isn't it?'

Culpepper turned and left. Brendan wanted to throttle his enemy on sight, but that would lead to arrest.

He still felt like jelly though, as he picked up the Yo-Yo Bears. However removed from the police he now was, Harvey Culpepper still, and probably always would, have an iron grip on Brendan Foley. But he'd never seen Culpepper like this. So quietly *angry*—which would be a very bad thing indeed.

Brendan would have to watch his back, more now than ever before.

HARVEY CULPEPPER HADN'T even got back to his car, before his phone was out. He walked with rageful purpose. As the dial played out, it took a full second to calm himself. Maintaining an aura of cool, no matter how wild the winds buffeted you—that was how you showed your metal. That's how you instilled fear.

That was how you got to be Harvey-fucking-Culpepper.

He altered course to stuff some notes into a charity box, held aloft by a teenage girl who grinned with surprise when she saw how much cash he stuffed in. Culpepper gave her a wink.

The phone picked up.

'It was him. Here's how we'll play it. The price is a million quid. Put it out there, usual channels, turn the volume up. A million on Brendan Foley's head.'

The voice on the other end spoke carefully. 'Are you sure?'

Culpepper stopped in front of the food bank donations bin and dropped the box of Lagavulin in amongst the tinned peas and pot noodles. 'And I'll throw in an extra five hundred K—for his family.'

PART 2

THE LEFT BEHIND

.

CHAPTER 23

YOU COULDN'T REALLY say Brinson had sung as such, but he'd cleared his throat just enough to help.

Madison went straight back to the CID office in the pool, Broom in tow. Kharthik and Christopher were there, eager for a summary.

'Thanks to incredible interviewing by our own DC Broom, we have identified the biker gang involved last night. It's not too far of a stretch to see that this is a deal that went wrong, with a motorcycle chapter called the Devil's Defects coming off worse.' She looked around. 'The details of the transaction suggest that the Devil's had tried to change the terms of the deal at the last minute. They got a major slap on the wrist, in the shape of Jason Limborough. We need to know how long this has been going on for. Get this case airtight.'

Another glance, to make sure that everyone was listening. 'Kharthik, I need you to get to the storage warehouse—find out how many times this place has been used as a dead drop. Someone there is dirty.'

'Yes, boss,' Kharthik replied, standing to take his jacket off the back of a chair. Tall and slender, with more confidence in his rangy posture with every day, he was clearly blossoming under Madison's lead.

She turned to another team member. 'Broom, please deep dive into the Devil's Defects. I want all the main players—all their records, everything we have.'

'Yes, ma'am,' said Broom, her back turning straight as she swivelled back to her computer. Didn't need telling twice.

'Christopher, I'm heading out,' Madison announced. 'Walk and talk.'

'Yes, boss.'

They weaved through the mess area to the front, and Madison leaned in, her voice low. 'Foley was on to something, clear as day—but I don't know how he got the info. It looks like Culpepper is all over it. This body, there's something wrong, and I need you to look directly into it. Only you. If it's anywhere near that name Culpepper, I don't want anybody else on it.'

'Yes, boss... of course.'

They were alone in the corridor's dark. But there would be cameras, so Madison pretended to itch her nose. 'You seen the news?'

'No,' Christopher replied, mirroring the gesture.

'The print, from the bag the kid was in—it was Mal Jevons.'

'Shit!' Christopher almost froze to the spot, but Madison gave his arm a slight tug to keep him moving.

'Yeah. His face is already all over the news.'

'Jesus.'

'I'm sure it'll blow over, but it's a heads up. Culpepper links coming up on both these cases? If it's a coincidence, it's a big one.'

'What do we do?'

'I need you to get to the mortuary. Follow up with Mackie on both these bodies, whist keeping Culpepper in mind. If we can nail this bastard, do a tight jig of our own... we might be able to put it to bed.'

'Does that mean the lad in the bag could be Darren Moston?'

Three young men, all part of a cash machine heist on a patch they weren't supposed to be on—killed by Mal Jevons immediately before his own death. Yet only one wasn't accounted for—until maybe now.

'I think you'd be right, but make sure.'

'Got it, boss.'

By now, they'd arrived at the front desk. Madison nodded a greeting to Patel, and headed for the front door. On the steps, she grabbed Christopher's elbow. Their careers were once again in the balance, thanks to old decisions they couldn't unmake.

'Be careful, Tom. We both know Culpepper's not to be messed with. But if this is him, involved in the drug deal, we have to get him bang to rights this time. And maybe, if we do… our own problems go away.'

Clearly, Christopher didn't need reminding. 'Got it.' She let go of his arm. 'Where are you off to?'

'Foley. I need to find out what he's been up to.'

They parted ways, with Christopher heading straight off into the centre of town, and Madison turning left to the path around the side of the station.

Madison was halfway to her car when she heard a voice call out.

'Detective Inspector Iona Madison?'

'Hello?' She couldn't see anybody. The cars shone bright as toys, their bonnets bouncing glare, but there was no one in sight.

'Detective Inspector Iona Madison?' The voice came again, and this time she could at least pinpoint its source. She turned to the cars parked tight to the station wall.

'Who is that?'

A figure emerged from between a red Fiesta and a black pickup. He was dressed as brightly as the vehicles, a shiny polyester jacket with a faded Seattle Seahawks logo. His hair was a stringy mess. Wraparound shades in brash orange frames.

'How can I help you, sir?' Madison didn't move any closer.

'I'm here about the bodies you and your friends threw into the landfill in Birchwood.'

Madison's lungs could have emptied there and then. She glanced around automatically to see if anyone was in earshot.

'I don't understand what you're talking about.'

And yet, her knees suddenly felt as though they couldn't hold her up for much longer.

'I thought you wouldn't.'

'Sir, this is a private car park for the police service only. I think it's best if you move along.'

She couldn't stop her eyes from darting to the streetlamps framing the corners of the car park, each with a bunch of small, cylindrical security cameras attached a couple of feet below the bulb.

'They've already seen us,' the man said, registering her panicked glance. 'No audio, as far as I can tell, but it's still evidence that we've met. Everything on record. Isn't that the way you like it?'

Madison lowered her face. 'I don't know what you're talking about.' But deep inside, she knew—had always known. That what had happened that night in Huyton, and then in Birchwood, would come back to bite hard one day. She just hadn't expected it to look quite like this.

'One man's trash is another man's treasure,' said the man.

'What is that supposed to mean?'

'People are always throwing things away. Things they shouldn't. Things that are worth something.'

Madison could see that he was enjoying this. 'Can I have a name?'

'You want to know my name?'

'When I'm faced with an unpleasant visit, I find it helps to know who I'm dealing with.'

Her opponent smiled. 'Something to hide?'

Madison raced through the options available to her, and boiled them down to two.

Arrest him? She'd have to take him inside, and give a reason. Could she lie so freely? She didn't think she could.

Ignore him? The best bet. Would grant thinking time, and allow her a chance to come up with something. Or better yet, this stranger could cut his losses. Maybe he didn't know what information he had? Maybe he wasn't in such a position of strength as he thought. This could all be a bluff, after all.

'Goodbye,' she said, resuming a brisk walk to her car. She could feel his oily smile on her back.

'You can call me Stig. And I'll be seeing you soon, DI Iona Madison.'

She had to leave. Now. She knew he was watching her every step.

She couldn't even bring herself to throw a glance his way, as she sped out of the car park, and into the afternoon sunshine. But, deep in her heart, she knew that this man—Stig—was grinning.

CHAPTER 24

CUL-DE-SACS were dead ends. That's why Garland liked them.

He'd lived for years in the middle house of five in a horseshoe, at the furthermost point of the cul-de-sac's pit. He sat there now, overseeing his manor, on the house's front porch. He knew this manor. He could do this.

He gripped a roll-up in his left hand. The chair dragged out onto the porch was more suited to a fireside, with worn patchwork upholstery—a budget throne.

But still, he sat on home turf.

That's all that counted.

Big fish and hand-me-down thrones were what this whole game was about. The Berg had been Manchester's biggest criminal enterprise for generations, headed by their old monarch, Felix Davison. He'd been deposed, his family fractured and disbanded years back. The hole left behind had been intimidating, hard to fill. It had taken Garland Rourke all this time. In quiet moments, sat overlooking his manor, he'd felt content.

Until today.

The events of the night before—losing a man and all that went with it—had been jarring. There was a funeral to attend, palms to grease, a wake to survive. That was all bad enough... but pissing off the Culpeppers was an additional issue they could really do without.

Jase was dead. They still didn't know why.

Garland had to acknowledge that there were elements of the Devil's Defects that he was not privy to. He must have done something to upset them. The Culpeppers weren't known for their forgiveness, and it alarmed him. He knew they could be violent, but they rarely acted without provocation. So what had he done wrong?

His android sat just out of reach. He knew what he should do. Call Culpepper directly. Cut out any middle party; let the big dogs chat. Request a meeting. But a call would only show his desperation. Culpepper would love that.

Still, the longer he left this, the deeper the stagnation. He picked up the phone, and cycled through his secret contacts.

He arrived at where he'd saved Culpepper's underling, under the title *That Scouse Fella*, and moved his thumb to the green call button. Only then, he was suddenly interrupted by an engine's roar.

A visitor.

Slick vehicle, at a guess. Two litre, three litre? Definitely a V8. Speed. He could usually tell from the speed how confident the visitor was, and in this instance? Yeah, this person was rich in the swagger department.

There was the sharp, sleek inward turn of a silver BMW at the top of the road. Recent model, a registration plate read CH22 LOT beneath vivid blue running lights. The engine took a hot leap in decibels. Then, it did something cars in the circle rarely did—and zoomed straight down the cul-de-sac.

The speed of its approach made Garland's stomach rise, his hands gripping the chair's arms, but he was determined to hold solid. He could already see that his Defects—maybe twenty of them in total—were chasing the vehicle down into the belly of the cul-de-sac. Some on bikes, some not, the air full of roaring engines and diesel fumes.

Not enough. Too late.

I'll tighten this up in future, thought Garland. If this person wanted to kill him, they'd already gone through the first obstacle with embarrassing ease.

Garland could clearly see the car's front grille—a Beemer. He felt his jaw rise. The driver was behaving suicidally in Renshaw Circle. Even as he thought this, the vehicle rolled and the driver's door opened.

A Lycra-clad woman stepped out.

She wore a grey hooded top over leggings so pink it made his corneas pop. Her ponytail was high and dancing, make-up immaculate, but even from this distance he could see a soft flush to her cheeks that betrayed exertion.

She raised her face to the house and looked straight at Garland. Then, with the slightest of smiles, turned to the incoming Defects, who all stopped a respectful handful of metres away. Their confusion was obvious. What to do now?

She arched her back in a way that made all the men pause. Leaned into the car. She could be going for anything.

'Hold still!' he called over.

But the woman had already straightened up, holding something. She slammed shut the car door to reveal a black shape, dangling tantalizingly from a single finger. Whatever it was, it was emblazoned with patches.

Jason's leathers.

A puzzle piece fell hard in Garland's mind.

'You're Culpepper's wife,' he said, as he watched her walk up the driveway to the porch step.

'Charlotte,' she replied, calmly. 'And you can put those dogs back in their kennels.' Her voice was a lightning strike of Merseyside. She gestured back towards the Defects, gathered around her car.

'Dangerous game,' Garland said. There was no way he'd take orders. 'These boys, they don't see much of your like round here.'

Delicately, she placed the jacket on the porch railing. 'I think that says more about you lot than it does about anything else, don't you think?'

A dangerous game, but Christ… she played it well.

Garland pointed at the jacket. 'What did he do?'

'I don't know.'

'So why are you here?'

'Some of us know the right way to go about things. How respect works.'

Impressive.

'So, this is a peace offering, girl?'

'I don't know what prompted the jacket's owner to lose his life, but I know it won't have been for nothing.'

'Then why did you order his murder?'

'I didn't. But I can see an error when it's made. I also know when a gesture is right.'

Garland fell quiet. He saw faces pressed into the windows of the surrounding houses. Watching what he would do. Then he spoke. 'His family will be grateful.' He nodded his thanks, the slightest of motions—nothing more. Not for her. 'I'll make sure they'll know it's you who made it happen.'

'I'm not here for credit.' She turned to walk back down the drive, car keys jangling. Try as Garland might, he found the bounce of that ponytail hypnotic. As she got to the car she threw the door open, and called to the Defects. 'Move it, lads. Lady drivers and all that.'

After a second's piss-weak resistance, they slowly parted, bikes reversing.

Charlotte Culpepper didn't even pause to watch their retreat. She shut the car door behind her, and brought the engine back to life, springing the car into reverse. She wound down the window, and waggled her fingers at Garland in a mocking farewell.

What would Garland call her gesture? A fuck-you *toodle-oo*.

CHAPTER 25

CHRISTOPHER PULLED INTO the car park and wasted no time heading inside. In cases gone by, he'd found the nag of trepidation always seemed to come for him whenever he turned up here, but time had dissipated that. Not to mention the fact that this case, or more accurately—these cases –had seen Culpepper rearing up again.

They all knew he was there, in the background. It wasn't like he'd gone away. But after Brendan Foley's retirement, he'd thought that things would cool down.

He'd been wrong.

The shark hadn't swum away. It had just been waiting, in the shallows. Watching everything.

Once inside, he checked in and headed down to Mackie's end of the facility. A soft glow through a glass door ahead pulled him towards Mackie's office.

He knocked, and was called in by a shout of: 'Enter!'

The office was small but well-organised, the back windows discreetly covered by Venetian blinds. Beyond those, lay the mortuary.

Mackie sat at the desk, her legs up, gym wear blazing incongruously as she ate a sandwich. A video was playing that Christopher immediately had to turn away from. Mackie caught a piece of chicken, and sat forward to switch off the screen.

'I've an ID for you. Well, two we think,' he said.

'Excellent—and I've some toxicology for you. But you go first.'

'Kid in the bag—we think it's Darren Moston. He's been missing since he was assumed part of a cash point robbery last year. Part of a three-man crew, the other two already accounted for.'

'Ah, Messers Foley and Fitzmorris. Excellent. That fits rather nicely.' She licked mustard off a finger.

'The other one, the dead guy with his insides busted up—the name we have is Jason Limborough. Affiliation to biker gang, the Devil's Defects. Info came up through interview.'

Mackie paused to consider. 'DS Madison's good at that, isn't she?'

'I believe the credit belongs to DC Broom, Ma'am.'

'Oh, I don't think I've met her. Well, I'll pencil the names in, and get them prepped for formal identification. Or, as best I can do.'

'Could we do dental records? Spare the families?'

'I'm sure we could try. But it'll take more time, so it depends how quick you want a definite answer.'

As quick as bloody possible, thought Christopher.

'So, toxicology is back on our mushed-up insides man,' she said. 'Bag boy should be later.'

'And what do we have?'

She leant forwards and clicked through her computer. 'It's interesting.' She squinted at the screen. 'Two things have really stood out. Internally, our victim had a nice prolonged booze-buzz on. Partied for a couple of days straight, by the looks of things. And he enjoyed a little bit of reefer while he was at it. Sounds a lovely little do, if you ask me. But it's this chap's epidermis that let slip a couple of revelations.'

Epidermis, epidermis… thought Christopher, before senior school biology stepped in from a long-forgotten recess. 'His skin?'

'Skin, eye, nose and mouth swabs revealed two unexpected chemical compounds present—namely, ferric oxide and hydrogen sulphide.'

'Okay, this is where you're really going to lose me.'

'Ferric oxide is rust. Trace elements in this case, but enough to suggest a committed exposure.'

'And that means?'

'It was all over him.'

'How the hell would that happen?'

'He died in an environment where rust was present. Might have been airborne, but the coverage here suggests... I don't know, really. Like he was rolling in it, but tried to wipe himself down after.' She must have caught the expression on his face. 'Remember, I just give the facts—it's your job to play-dough them into something half-workable.'

'And what about the big revelation?'

'Well, this one would explain the smell. He was a stinky bugger, and I was wondering why, because putrefaction hadn't started yet. I wonder if his bowels were perforated and there was some porous leakage of some description, but there was nothing I could find to suggest that—aside from the damage the bowel had taken alongside all the other organs.'

Christopher tried to connect the dots but they weren't in the same book, never mind the same page.

Mackie carried on. 'Hydrogen sulphide is the compound that makes things smell bad. Like rotten eggs, and wastage.'

Christopher felt his face turn blank. 'He'd been rolling about in rust and rubbish?'

'Looking at this, that is about a good an explanation as anything. The qualities again suggest that it was found all over his body, but not completely coated in it. Maybe they'd tried to wash him down, I don't know. But I'd say he was in contact with garbage.'

'This is mad,' said Christopher.

'I must admit, it's a new one on me. And if you throw that in with the state of his internal organs, then you've properly got me stumped.'

'Any ideas? A working hypothesis?'

'It's not my job to guess and point you in any direction. But when you get to the bottom of this, I'd really love to know— please keep me in the loop.'

No proper answer; not that he'd expected.

Christopher was at a loss. The growing snowball on the mountain had just bounced off onto not just another slope, but another damn mountain.

CHAPTER 26

ALVIN LEOPOLD CHANGED lanes for yet the third time—and still, it made no difference.

The navy Beemer was still behind him.

But worse, the vehicle was now making no attempt to hide its pursuit. It was so obvious. Those headlights were all too menacing.

If someone was following him, who the hell were they?

His line of work was, well... Not really a line of work. It was a side-earner. Damn lucrative—and, bearing that in mind, the driver behind him (whoever it was) wasn't about to straddle the fence of legality. This was someone from the criminal murk, come up for a gander.

Alvin swiftly changed lanes, moved to the outside, and dropped gear to pick up speed. If he'd been barrelling along in something that wasn't a fifteen-year-old Fiat Punto, it might have been more convincing as an escape.

Yet, Alvin was far from a slouch behind the wheel, and the sudden move across traffic soon bought him an extra fifty yards when the tailing saloon was blocked by a white van that was racing up, come what may. What the Punto lacked in horsepower, it made up for in deftness, and Alvin dropped back into the slower left-hand lane in front of a bus, before turning off the carriageway all together.

Thrilled with his move, chest bubbling with exhilaration, he took another swift left into a housing estate of two-up two-down red squares. He knew a safe spot down here, a place he could park up and let an hour tick by before resuming his journey into town.

Fuck you.

Beside him, Greenway was an eyesore. A single-storey pub that looked little more than a club house, covered in torn posters. He pulled in, parked tight to its urine-stained wall and ran inside.

Alvin tried to keep his breathing down, but he was jacked with excitement at his getaway, and he damn-near hopped to the bar.

'Your top-selling lager, mate,' he said to a barman. 'Pint.'

The beer was pulled as Alvin took in the place. He'd been here a few times before but wouldn't class himself as a local, thank god. This was where the dregs ended up, and the smell only served to confirm it. It was dark, and he could spot only one other patron—a man so decrepit he looked like he must have been reanimated. He was curating a raft of betting slips with worn fingers, separating them into piles.

Alvin looked out onto the street, and could feel himself relax with every second—a sensation which only increased as the beer landed on the bar in front of him, the colour of off-brand piss.

'Can you sort the head out on that, mate? It's flatter than Chernobyl.'

The barman replied in a low rumble. 'You asked for the top seller. Lines need cleaning.'

Before he had a chance to reply, he saw beyond the window that a sleek dark car had pulled up on the curb.

The Beemer.

'Is there a back exit?' Alvin stammered.

'You haven't even paid yet, Mr Flatter-Than-Chernobyl.'

Alvin pulled his pockets inside out to find some change. But when the pub door flung open, he was frozen in his tracks.

Too late.

'Don't worry, I'll get it,' said a voice. Female. Curiosity snagged, he couldn't help himself from turning.

A woman entered, wearing dark shirt and jeans. Long, peroxide hair, held back in a sleek black clip.

'Can I get you one?' he found himself asking.

'Don't flatter yourself, Alvin,' the woman replied. 'Though that said, if you were George Clooney offering me a pint of *that*, I'd still decline. No offence.'

That last part of the speech was clearly aimed at the barman.

'Lines need cleaning,' he said again, suddenly busying himself.

'A gin and tonic, then?' Alvin tried to ramp up his chutzpah.

She was no older than mid-twenties. He wasn't going to let anyone like that get one over him.

'How's about *Fuck off*,' she replied, then pointed to a table in the empty pub. Alvin walked over and took a seat. He was from a family of strong women; he knew when to zip it.

'I've one word for you, only I'm not going to say it. It's on this card.' From the inside of a jeans pocket, the woman withdrew a small white business card, and placed it on the table. 'You give that card to you-know-who, and tell them to call the number. They'll understand.'

'The word?'

'They'll know all about it.'

'And what about me?'

'You're a CI, Alvin, and have been for years, yet nothing half-decent has come from it. Half your family is inside, banged up for their grubby fingers, yet you still know nowt.' She nodded at the card. 'Give that to the right person, and you'll finally have done something to justify the blind eye you've been getting from us lot. And let's face it—the blind eye has been there because you're hardly Tony fucking Montana. You're barely worth the effort.'

Alvin was dented by her words, his parade pissed on, but was secretly proud that this posh bit of stuff needed help from him.

'Aw, sweetheart. The lady, she doth protest too much.' He looked at the barman for backup, but all it got him in return was a disgusted scowl. Another card slid across the table to him. It was a warrant card, and it showed she was a big deal, before she pocketed it again. He felt his balls try to climb back up into his body.

'Listen up, you fucking peabrain,' said Madison. 'You're a tadpole. A minging little tadpole, in a stinking pond. But if you take that to you-know-who, you might be spared when its drained.'

He looked at the oblong of card, and read a surname. One that he'd heard before.

'You know who to take it to?'

'Yeah, I've an idea.'

'I'm not after an idea. Do you know who to take it to?'

He looked at her and attempted defiance, but he knew that he couldn't reach it. 'Yes,' he mumbled.

'Good. And if I have to come looking for you again, there might be some local name-dropping as to the identity of useless CIs in the neighbourhood.'

He didn't reply.

She stood up. 'Chop chop,' she said, then turned to the barman. 'Sorry for the intrusion.'

The barman grunted. 'You're the nicest woman we've had in all year, and that's saying something.'

She left, and Alvin was left with the worst pint of all time. But then he thought of something he had of value. Something that had come in on his phone just a little earlier. Something that would definitely matter to the police.

'Wait!'

The detective turned around.

'I do have something you'll be interested in,' he said.

She came back and he found himself telling her about the price. The price that had just been put on Brendan Foley's head.

CHAPTER 27

BRENDAN CURSED HOW much of a sly turncoat pride could be.

Sometimes, men got so drunk on machismo, that it walked them down a dark alley of avoidable decisions, leaving them with the bitter taste of regret, and a bad dose of the jitters. Playing Billy Big Bollocks with Harvey Culpepper hadn't been a smart game.

He was starving. Halfway back from Asda, he pulled off the East Lancs, and into the KFC drive-through. One of those spicy box meal things, and a load of gravy to mop it up with. That'd settle his stomach. He sat in the queue for a moment, and leaned back, as other cars joined him. He was only about four cars back, so he wound down the window in anticipation, thinking all the while.

He had to bring Culpepper down. That much was obvious. But what more could he do? He'd given Madison all the tools, all the information he could—though not where he'd got it. He'd interfered just enough to jeopardise an ongoing investigation, if there even was one prior to last night. Did the police know that there were major drug deals taking place under their noses? One thing he knew for sure, was that his dad had gone down in history as the killer of the Warrington 27, not the Culpeppers.

The line moved slowly, but finally he was able to place an order. He might drive somewhere secluded to eat in peace, somewhere where the only interruption would be his own internal wrangling. The box was handed to him, and he felt the heat from it, his nose catching that southern fried aroma, mouth filling with saliva. But before he could pull away, a car pulled up beside to him onto the slip road. He found it an odd place to stop, and glanced across as he put his box on the passenger seat.

The driver was wearing a balaclava. And he was getting out. The car doors behind him opened in unison. Three other men getting out, three other balaclavas.

Shit!

Brendan tried to throw the car in gear, but the car in front was reversing right up to him—in on it. He caught a flash of the driver's black mask as the car came closer. He was pinned, and there was a scream of terror from the drive-through's hatch, as the young woman at the window saw what was happening. Lucky her, to even have time to scream.

He didn't have that luxury.

He tried his door, but he was too close to the hatch of the drive-through, as his passenger door was thrown open. The men had surrounded the car, one climbing inside. He lashed out with his fists and feet. The man fell out of the car. Brendan unbuckled his seatbelt and jumped out of his open window—straight at the drive-through hatch. He banged his hip on the frame, the hatch far smaller than he anticipated—but he was through!—landing hard on a chrome counter, sending out an explosion of paper cups, spraying soft drinks. There were shouts from outside, bad men changing plan on the fly, and yet more screams from inside. He rolled off the counter, and landed on his shoulder, which immediately sang with pain.

'Call the police!' he shouted, to whoever was listening.

'On it!' came a reply. Bless the great British public.

He pulled himself to his feet, and turned to the crowded restaurant.

This was really, *really* bad.

And those men? They were already coming around to the entrance.

'Where's the back door?' Brendan turned to the kitchens and the maze of grills, but the shouting had already started again—more furious now. He caught sight of a black shadow before he was bowled over, winded. The life was forced out of him, his back and shoulders screaming with pain, his skull cracked against the floor.

Someone shouted. 'Got him!'

'Get him out of here,' came another voice.

Everything about this was bad.

The staff had scattered, leaving the two men on the floor, Brendan pinned to the floor by one of them, who had his arms and was trying to roll him over.

Cable ties appeared.

Oh, god.

Brendan wrestled and bucked, managed to get an arm free. He reached to the nearest countertop and managed to hoist himself up slightly. Reasoning that his head was already fucked, he launched a headbutt straight into his assailant's face.

Christ, it hurt. Near-biblical pain shot in a fiery crescent around his skull, but the impact gave him a second. He scrambled with his fingers, touched something, hoped it was what he thought it was, gripped and pulled it in an arc onto the head of his attacker. His own hand scorched with heat. It was a frying cage from a deep fat fryer, and suddenly, Brendan didn't feel so bad about all his secret visits for a box meal, because a memory of watching fillets sizzle had come back and paid off on a grand scale. Half-cooked hash browns and sizzling oil drenched his attacker's face and upper body. A high-pitched scream. The man's eyes were deep frying inside his own head.

Brendan quickly rolled away, hands scrabbling for purchase. The screaming intensified, and there was a screech of chair legs, as the word *Gun!* volleyed about.

He rolled low, scrambling between the fryers and grills to the back of the restaurant unit, but he didn't know where he was going. Half-blind, he dodged staff members crouching for safety.

Gunfire started. Semi-automatic, one at a time, down towards the back of the restaurant—following him. As he ran, Brendan thought that the weapon must preclude them from being professionals—but a gun was a gun. It didn't give two shits how it was fired. Everyone was in danger.

'Everybody get down!' he bellowed to those who hadn't caught on—but most were already cowering.

In a dice-roll of improbably bad luck, he found himself at the foot of a row of cooking units that ended beside a huge, chrome freezer. Dead end. He couldn't be trapped down here, so he turned and started back, picturing the crew vaulting over the front counter to follow him deeper into the kitchen. As he got to the end of the row, he couldn't stop himself from snatching a glance back to the main restaurant space.

They'd spotted him.

Bullets started to rain in a chaotic round of gunfire. His assailants had clearly abandoned any plan, and were desperate now. Ricochets clanged off appliances. He sprinted towards the back of the kitchen, then was forced to turn left, and—*there!*—a back door appeared, a strip of sunlight promising escape like a finish-line ribbon.

He hurled himself towards it, pleading that nobody had been hurt, and felt the guilt tear at the back of his mind. It was him they wanted, and he was doing the right thing—leading them away by making his escape.

Brendan pulled the door open, and sunlight hit his face—along with a black, unforgiving cosh—which cracked him right in his hairline. He fell at the booted feet of another masked man, cursing his luck. His head felt loose, and blood started chasing in hot trails down his cheek.

He heard the familiar high-pitched zip of cable ties. There was a sudden tightness across his shoulders and chest as his arms were pinned behind his back.

He was hauled to his feet. They'd all caught up with him now, and he could hear their excited voices. His kidney exploded in pain, starbright, as someone hit him right on the button.

'That's for my fuckin' eyes,' came a voice. It was deep Lancashire, which, considering he'd just pissed off the Scouse Culpeppers, surprised him. 'Christ this *hurts*,' the man moaned.

He was forced to stand up, to face the man who'd caught him at the back door.

'You've made us very happy and very well off, you—'

A car backfired somewhere nearby—or at least, that's what it sounded like. There was a pause and then a thin track of blood rolled down from beneath the balaclava and between the man's abruptly blank eyes. He dropped.

Some instinct in Brendan told him to do the same, and he felt his legs buckle beneath him as he dropped to the deck, just as bullets cracked against the rear of the restaurant. Everyone else ran for cover.

By now, one thing was abundantly clear—there were two parties involved here. One inside the joint, and one here in the car park. His hands still bound, he squat-sprinted around the side of the building towards his car. Horns were blaring, the sun was hotter than ever and people were screaming in panic.

As soon as he rounded the corner of the building, he paused, crouched over, and tried to point his bound hands as high to the sky as he could, behind his back. When he could reach no more, he pulled his wrists apart and then brought his bound fists crashing down into the base of his spine. Basic training these days included all the various methods to get out of zip ties. The zip tie snapped. He thanked god that, even though he was no longer a cop, his memory of crucial survival information hadn't gone with it.

He ran along the side of the cars to his own, abandoned by the drive-through hatch. A bullet grazed the brickwork behind his head, sending out a dust cloud of masonry. What was happening? He dropped to his knees. He could hear his engine still running, and the sound filled him with hope. If he could survive this, surely he could survive anything? He moved along the flanks of parked cars, and screamed, 'Get down!' But the shout only brought more gunfire. He ducked again, next to the car behind his. His eyes met those of a young woman at the wheel, as glass smashed and her neck seemed to pop. Blood funnelled, staining her T-shirt crimson. Next to her, in the front seat, a baby sat fast in a car seat, screaming.

The horror threatened to swallow him whole.

There was nothing he could do for the woman, whose head dropped forward onto the horn, blaring, plaintive call for assistance, blood pouring into the footwell. The baby would be found soon enough. All he could do was run.

He tore himself away. He climbed in the rear door of his own idling car, clambered over the seats into the front. Acid rose in his throat in a hot wave. He hit the accelerator and started to ram into the abandoned car that blocked the exit of the drive-through, violently shoving it out of his path.

In a spurt of emotion, he realised he was crying. *What have I done? What have I started?*

Brendan accelerated through the gap he'd just forced—out of the drive-through, across the car park, and onto the grass that separated the roadside eatery from the dual carriageway. Escape was close—but still, the thought of the woman with the severed throat, and the screaming baby, almost caused him to black out. He gagged, but it came out as a sob.

'I'm sorry,' he mumbled. 'I'm so sorry.'

Everything about this was wrong. His nausea and fear were what separated him from *them*—what separated good from evil, what separated Foley from Culpepper. Well, this Foley at least.

He sped up to hit the hard shoulder. He needed a sanctuary. There was only one person who he could call on, who he could trust.

DS Iona Madison.

He swung back onto the thirty-mile strip of the East Lancs, his head swimming with visions of blood, ears full of a baby's screams. With trembling hands, he dialled the only number that mattered.

CHAPTER 28

WHEN MADISON RECEIVED the call, her first thought was, *Thank God*.

But as she prepared to bollock him for failing to return her five previous missed calls, her words dried up at the sounds coming down the line.

A shaky voice, ragged breath. Nothing about this was right.

'Iona… someone… two lots… They've just tried to kill me.'

'Where are you?' Her mind was aflame.

'East Lancs.'

'Get off the main roads, now. My flat. You know it?'

Brendan blew out harshly. 'Yes.'

'Go there now.'

'I… I think I know why.'

Madison cut him off. 'We'll talk when you get here, just drive.'

She knew why, too.

It took her ten minutes to get to her place. When she arrived, she couldn't see his car outside the red-brick apartment block, so she went upstairs to wait for him. It was only then that she found him, sat back against her front door.

His skull was covered in blood. The first thing she thought, maybe prompted by the earlier conversation with the weirdo at the nick, was that the property's security cameras must have seen the bloodied man wandering up the stairs.

'Jesus, Foley,' she said, leaning over him to key open the front door. He attempted to drag himself up, but needed help.

'It looks worse than it is,' he said, shakily.

She wasn't so sure.

'Get inside,' she said, shoving him.

'Is it on the news yet?' he said.

'I'll check in a minute.' But Madison knew it already was. As soon as Foley had called, she'd turned the radio on and tuned in to those first lurid reports.

'The kitchen sink, come on.' She angled him towards the far side of the living room, where a kitchen island separated the open living space, then asked him to wait a moment while she lifted all the dirty pans and dishes out, stacking them on the hob.

'Living well, I see,' said Brendan.

'I don't get many visitors,' she replied sharply. 'And when I do, they tend to give me a little warning.'

Cold water running, she helped him lean over the sink then rolled up her sleeves to clean the blood from his scalp.

There was a knock at the door, and Madison felt Brendan stiffen in her arms. Honestly, she'd never seen him on edge as much as this. 'Don't worry,' she said. 'I called reinforcements.'

'It's Christopher,' came a muffled shout.

'Come in,' she shouted, remembering she'd left it unlocked in their hurry to get Foley inside. The door thunked twice, open and shut. DS Christopher entered the flat, closely followed by Jordan 'Seabreeze' Seabaruth.

'Nice reunion,' said Brendan, sluggishly.

Madison sympathised. This quad never brought anything but bad news. Still, it had been her decision to call them.

'We need them here,' she explained, helping Brendan to his feet.

'What's happened?' Christopher rushed over to look at the head wound. 'Phwoar, that's nasty.'

'Nice to see you too, mate,' Brendan said, drying his hands before shaking them with Christopher and then, behind him, Seabreeze.

Brendan sank into a chair, and shared a potted history of the last hour. The chat with Culpepper in the supermarket. The bloody events at KFC.

Once he'd finished, Madison chimed in.

'I spoke with a CI. He said a price had been put on Foley's head, and that it had gone out big in the underworld.'

'We need to get your family safe,' announced Christopher. 'We know what this lot are like.'

Foley went still, his face granite. 'I have to get them,' he said, but Madison had already placed a restraining hand on his shoulder.

'You can't go anywhere,' she said. 'That will draw fire.' She glanced at the others. 'How do we make Brendan and his family safe?'

They paused for a second. 'We keep his location quiet. Us four need to know—no one else. We move them all.'

'Is there a safe house we can use?' Seabreeze said.

'There must be,' said Madison. 'But I have to be careful who I ask.'

Her own words caused her to pause. It was impossible to consider trust in the police without thinking about DC Hoyt—the dark, brooding ex-officer now doing twenty years for the murder of Art Foley. He'd been a mole, buttered up by the other side. Before his imprisonment, Madison had been sleeping with him—she wasn't proud of the fact—entirely in the dark to his ulterior motivations. Just thinking about him made her teeth itch.

'Monroe would be the first port of call,' said Christopher. 'He could sort anything like this.'

Madison turned to Brendan, knowing this involved calling his ex-boss. 'You happy with that?'

'Yes.'

'Give me the locations of your family,' said Christopher, his gaze drilling into Brendan. 'I'll go and pick them up.'

'And I'll speak to Monroe,' added Madison.

'Will they let us do that?' Brendan asked. 'I'm not a cop anymore.'

Christopher stood. 'There's a threat on life here—we wouldn't be much as cops if we didn't try.' He turned to Madison. 'When you have a location, let me know where.' His glance skittered back to Brendan. 'I'll get them there safely, mate. You stay here in the meantime.' It wasn't a question.

Christopher turned to leave, but Madison stopped him.

'There's something else.' Everyone looked at her. 'I was approached by someone. Member of the public. Bit of an oddball, if I'm honest. He called himself Stig. He asked about the bodies me and my friends threw in the landfill.'

'You're joking,' Brendan said, after a moment.

'Wish I was.'

'What the hell did you do?' Seabreeze leant back against one of the barstools.

'I said I didn't know what he was talking about.'

'And how did he respond?'

'He said he'd be seeing me again soon.'

The group stiffened; there was no avoiding the seriousness of this.

'Looks like the early offings of a blackmail attempt,' said Brendan, eventually.

The four of them, in this room—their lives could all be torn to shreds, be publicly hung, drawn and quartered. The story behind what happened didn't matter—would never matter. The next hours here were crucial.

'I had to tell you,' Madison said, quietly. She was right.

Another pause, as they all took in the significance of what had just been shared. Significant for all of them.

'What are we going to do?' said Christopher, eventually. He'd slumped onto the sofa.

'Seabreeze, he was on the station car park cameras. About an hour ago. You can get a look at him, and his arrival. Stig's his name, I don't know whether he goes by any other aliases. We need to find out who he is—'

'Then what?' interrupted Brendan. 'We silence him?' The implications were clear. Crime begot crime; it was self-perpetuating.

'Maybe we can find something to use against him. To make him keep quiet,' said Seabreeze.

'Maybe. But it's dangerous. It's admitting that we did something we shouldn't have.'

Christopher stood again. 'We have to get something on him, find out what he really knows. Find out what damage this can do. If it's a guess, we can brush it away.'

'Some guess,' said Brendan.

'You know what I mean. If it's vague, we can work with that. Get what you can, Seabreeze.'

The Mauritian nodded.

'Where's your family?' Christopher asked Brendan, who immediately told him where his wife worked. Mim could direct him from there. 'Phones on,' he said, leaving.

'I'll call Monroe.' Madison walked across to the bedroom, and pushed the door to—but as she closed it, through the narrowing gap, she noticed Seabreeze approach Brendan, and hand him an envelope.

What the hell? It could have been anything—a birthday card or a bookie slip. But given what a shit magnet Brendan was, she didn't fancy the chances of that piece of paper being a good thing.

CHAPTER 29

DC KHARTHIK WAS oddly looking forward to this.

Whether DI Madison was aware of it or not, she had a major trust issue when it came to doling out the tasks when cases came knocking. More often than not, DS Christopher was stuck with all the heavy lifting.

Kharthik didn't mind that as such—there was a whole difference in rank after all, and such delegation was largely to be expected—but he knew he was capable of more. He was worthy of that same level of trust, had proved it when Madison and he had been together in a high-pressure situation only last year. Kharthik's then boss had had his head split like a breakfast fruit by a high-powered sniper rifle. At the time, Kharthik and Madison had been on the ground under fire from that same shooter. He'd known she was capable. She'd known he was capable. It had only been a matter of time before he'd got a half-decent gig.

And now it was here.

He pulled into Storage Plus by LA Bowl, where all this madness had started, and parked up away from the loading doors. Funny places, storage centres. Big sheds for rent. Mad, really. But he understood exactly why this would work as a dead drop. In a storage unit, you could swap a lot—unseen. Reverse your truck right up under the awning, and you were out of sight, out of mind. And this location—again, Warrington, with its mad geography and personality—provided the perfect spot for a grand deal with a big dead drop between big players in Liverpool and big players in Manchester.

The added genius was that it didn't sit on either of your patches. If the contents of the lock-up were found and outed, it wasn't on either Scouse or Manc turf. It was a Warrington problem.

But it all hinged on one thing. Buying off the storage centre employees—or at least a high-ranking member of its staff. Getting to the bottom of that was why Kharthik was here.

The place was busy with people dropping off belongings that would stay here for months, even years. There were a couple of drivers clearly using units here as delivery depots as part of their jobs at Amazon or Hermes. But one thing everyone had in common was the need for a door code. And beneath a multiple-security camera setup was a bank of windows with slatted blinds, half open.

The office.

You'd have to be stupid to try to smuggle something into here without staff knowledge. The scale of the items was critical to the investigation—multiple containers of class-A drugs. A person couldn't just drop all of that off for somebody else to pick up. Surely that would ring alarm bells? And now—a *body*.

No. Kharthik was convinced, even more so after watching this. At the very least, some Storage Plus staff had to be in on the plan. Shipment timings had to integrate with the staff scheduling. That meant someone with a managerial role. And that had prompted Kharthik to do his homework before leaving the office, inspecting a list of employees he'd arranged direct from Storage Plus' main office, going right over the head of this particular franchise satellite.

He knew who was on duty today—and crucially—who'd been in charge last night.

Now, armed with a staff printout and his warrant card, he tapped on the window to the office that looked over the loading bays.

It took a couple of seconds, before one of the openings between the slats parted to allow a couple of splayed fingers to poke through. A woman's face appeared. Turquoise eye shadow and thick specs.

Kharthik held up his warrant card, and smiled. The slats dropped, and he moved towards the main doors. He looked up. Camera coverage was tight. The tapes would surely be make or break.

The woman appeared on the other side of the entrance. She drew a small rectangle with her index fingers, and mouthed the letters *ID*.

He pressed his warrant card to the glass.

After a moment, she hit a panel out of sight, and the main door slid open.

'Hello, my name is Detective Constable Manit Kharthik, with Warrington Police. Could I come in for a moment?'

She gestured to the back with a flick of her head. They walked only a few yards before they were in the office overlooking the loading area. She immediately closed the window slats.

'Sorry. It's… it's not been a great morning. Gossip is already killing us. Half of these people are here moving stuff out, ending their tenancies, and we've been fielding calls from the media all day—not to mention calls from customers trying to get their rates lowered. There are always vultures.'

'It's Gayle, isn't it?' he asked. He remembered the name from his printout. Gayle Dean.

'Yes, Assistant Manager.' One of two.

'I believe the onsite staff spoke to police liaison last night. Gave his name as Mr Nigel Ferriby. Mr Ferriby said there'd be some CCTV coming our way, but as yet it hasn't arrived with us.'

'No,' said Gayle, sitting down. She didn't seem surprised.

Kharthik played the first card. *Softly, softly.* 'I'm here to see if we can speed that along.' He smiled properly this time.

'I don't know if we can,' she said, her glance hard. 'I went to look at them myself, and—well, there's nothing there.'

This wasn't a surprise. 'I wonder if you could elaborate, Gayle.'

'The CCTV system is housed over there.' She pointed to a set of monitors on a side desk. 'It's simple, but thorough. Regular cameras along each corridor. Obviously, when you store other people's belongings, you want to make sure it's safe, right? CCTV is the best way to do that.'

'And last night? When you say there's nothing there?'

Gayle looked like the weight of the world was descending on her shoulders. 'The system was turned off. It wasn't even on when your lot arrived. If that gets out, you might as well shut us down now.'

'Who turned it off, Gayle?'

'I don't know, but Nige was the only one on last night.' She walked over to one of the computers, which was turned on but idling with a screen saver of rolling clouds occupying the screen. She pointed underneath the monitor, at the black box. 'That drive collects the CCTV feeds. All you'd need to do is turn it off.'

'I assume it was off last night?'

'Yes.'

'But it's on now?'

She wiggled the mouse back and forth on the desk, and the screen jumped to life. 'This is where we keep watch, if we need to.'

The screen showed a grid of small rectangles, each offering a different view of the facility.

'So how much was missed last night?'

'I'll show you.' She sat down and navigated the cursor with practiced ease, arriving at what appeared to be a calendar. Every day of the month so far was filled in red, with the occasional small green slice at the end. 'Green is to show that there was a recording prompted by motion detection, which is only on the fire escape cameras. Red is when there's been a recording to the main system.'

She clicked on that day's screen. It showed a series of timelines, all unbroken red. 'These have all been running, right through today, and the recordings will all be there if I just click on them.'

She picked one and did just that, and a view of a corridor popped up. People were walking along it. 'This is the feed in real time. But if I go backwards…' She ran the cursor along the red slider under the image. 'We go back in time, and can pick any spot in the day.'

'Okay, I'm following so far.'

'But, look—when I go back and look at yesterday's entire day of recording.' On the screen with all the red timelines, they abruptly stopped, every last one of them, at 1.30 a.m. The camera started recording again at 2.30 a.m.

'The cameras had been turned off for an hour.' The phrase *inside job* glowed neon in Kharthik's mind.

'Yes. And that can only be done here.'

'With Nigel being the only employee in this room at that time. So there's nothing you can show me from last night in that time frame at all?'

'No. Only from two thirty onwards, when the place was crawling with your lot.'

Kharthik was buzzing. This was proof of conspiracy. 'And what about Nigel now? Have you heard from him today?'

'He's supposed to be in again tonight, but he's already called in sick.'

Kharthik's eyebrows raised.

'It doesn't look good, does it?' Gayle looked ashamed, but not guilty.

'I have to ask this, and I'm going to ask you directly. Did you have anything to do with what happened here last night, or the CCTV being switched off?'

Gayle's eyes started to swim with tears. 'No. I promise, no. But I hired Nigel, and I feel responsible for his mistakes. And this is going to result in me losing my job.'

'Okay,' he said. 'Let's try to get something definitive, something that will help, and that will look good for you and your employers. Can you help me?'

'Yes,' she said. 'I'll do anything.'

'Then let's start. If the CCTV was turned off to allow something dodgy to happen, then let's see if it's happened before.'

He sat next to Gayle for the next hour, cajoling her along, helping her methodically work back through the last month of recordings. They found no fewer than eight other occasions when the CCTV had mysteriously gone off—and always between one thirty and two thirty in the morning. They started in April, and ran bi-weekly until the previous night.

Kharthik leaned back. This was a serious enterprise. He consulted his printout from Storage Plus head office, tracing back the dates in question with his finger. There was no doubt.

Nigel had been on shift every one of them.

'He only began his job in April,' said Gayle, quietly watching him.

'Then I think we need to have a chat with him. Do you have an address?'

Gayle checked the neighbouring computer screen and scribbled on a hot pink Post-It.

'You've been really helpful, Gayle,' said Kharthik. He glanced at the ballpoint.

It was a local Warrington address. *Take this info back to the nick?*

No. Kharthik decided he was going to take the initiative. He was going to go to that address and catch this guy before he legged it.

'And Gayle,' he said. She looked up at him, anxiously. 'I'll make sure this doesn't blow back on you.'

CHAPTER 30

MONROE LISTENED, SWORE, then asked Madison to hold the line. When he eventually picked up again, he told Madison about a safehouse in a little village above Bolton, called Belmont. But before signing off, he offered one last message.

'I told him to step back! Does that man ever listen to instruction?'

Madison offered nothing; it would only make things worse. This wasn't a position she wanted to be in, calling in favours from her boss. She'd never been one who needed bailing out. She was happy in the deep end.

But this? This was black hole deep, and the Foley family needed all the help they could get.

Monroe blew out down the line. 'We don't have a handy branch of witness protection, just sitting on standby for fuck-up cops to disappear to when their decisions come back to bite them on the arse.'

'I understand, sir. I'm just trying to keep Foley and his family safe.'

'You could put him in the cells until this blows over, that's what you could do!'

'I don't trust anybody enough, not after last time.'

Madison guessed that even Monroe was realistic enough to know that, despite his assertions that the ship he ran at Warrington nick sailed honest and true, the spectre of DC Hoyt and his corrupt actions loomed large.

'Okay. This place in Belmont is normally used by Greater Manchester Police for training purposes—but in this instance it will suit us fine. Get Foley there, and get him out of sight. I'll look into this threat to life myself, get some boots on the ground. Am I correct in guessing that this threat will have come from that name again?'

Madison hadn't told Monroe about Brendan's altercation with Culpepper in the supermarket. In order to get him to agree to providing sanctuary to Foley, she'd needed to make him look as blameless as possible. 'I think it would be fair to say that— yes, sir.'

'Then we need proof of source. After that, we can bring Culpepper in. Finally get him off the streets. If it was for an unpaid parking fine, I'd take it at this point.'

Proof of source was tricky. Proving that there had been a threat made seemed obvious, given the amount of blood now pooling into the grids outside Leigh KFC. But it wasn't straightforward—there'd been no obvious threat to anyone, other than a few lives lost. Did they even know for sure that this had been down to Culpepper's gang?

But that snitch Leopold would know, surely? After all, he was the one who'd told Madison about the threat. Now, she resolved to make Leopold finally earn that title of confidential informant, and found out where this information had come from.

'I'll take Foley to Belmont,' she said.

Monroe nodded, and glanced at his watch. 'I'll have plainclothes officers meet you there to provide security. It's a bit of a trek—they'll be there in an hour from now.'

'Sir, given the circumstances, can I be in charge of the Foley's protection? Use my team?'

Monroe laughed. 'I hope that's a joke. You have two enquiries running and I'm afraid there's no way half of CID can bunk off on a Belmont jolly. A bit of faith in your colleagues wouldn't go amiss here, detective.'

Madison had to go with it, despite her misgivings. 'Done. But while I've got Foley, I'll take him there myself.'

They agreed to check in again when the Foley family was all safely in place. Ending the call, she flopped back onto the bed. Still fully dressed, uncomfortable in her jacket, she stared at the ceiling. The plain white lamp shade cradling the stark bulb. Everything here was function over form. Maybe, if they all got out of this, she'd actually decorate her home one day. Do something for herself. Not be so work obsessed. Live a little.

Fuck that!

She stood up from the bed, remembering her boxing matches. The bell ringing, the call to arms, proving that you're a winner. Why change now?

She exited the room, recharged with purpose.

'Brendan, we've got somewhere, it's a—'

She stopped in her tracks and glanced around the room— the empty room.

Foley was gone.

She ran to the front door, threw it open, and looked down at the car park from the balcony railings. No sign of him or her BMW.

The bastard.

CHAPTER 31

MIM WAS IN the PR firm's office kitchen, eating a yoghurt, idly wishing it was laced with Baileys. The empty shell of a sandwich packet sat at her elbow, a bottle of water half drunk in front of her, and a copy of *Cheshire Life* opened to a double-page spread of some rich wankers with rich wanker spaniels and their perfect rich wanker life.

It had been a terrible morning. Her late arrival had been very much noted and she felt under-prepared.

She thought about Brendan, and his new night-time activities. She couldn't picture him as a doorman. She couldn't imagine him managing drunk idiots, corralling them like pissed cattle, getting spat at, and asking people to behave. So why was he doing it?

Finishing the yoghurt, she tossed the spoon into the sink, which wasn't half a bad shot from where she was sat, and thumbed through the magazine. A door clunked from somewhere down the corridor.

She had long thought that Brendan would never leave certain things alone—certain things he should be nowhere near, for all manner of reasons. But she knew what he was like—dogged. In the early days, it had been an inspiring quality. Once Brendan Foley wanted something, he usually got it, and to be wanted by anyone with such fixed intention was intoxicating in itself.

His night-time occupation was a smokescreen of some kind—it had to be. A way of keeping tabs on certain players. Namely, the people who had killed his father.

She shook her head. Being a copper's wife was difficult enough without bringing bad choices into the mix. Too many bad decisions had been made of late.

Scooping everything into the waste bin, she paused.

Footsteps. Oh god, no. The last thing she needed was small talk.

She grabbed her blazer off the back of her chair.

'She in here?' a voice asked. Suddenly, a man appeared in the doorway. She wasn't sure if she recognised him, but there was something intimate in the way he looked at her. He was younger than her, with a shaven head, and eyes cool enough to be rocks in a whiskey tumbler.

'Mrs Foley?'

Dread pooled in Mim's stomach. *Oh, fuck…*

'Call me Mim.'

'I'm DS Tom Christopher. I used to work with your husband—'

'Is he alright?' She couldn't stop herself from immediately interrupting.

'Yes, he is. But I need you to come with me. Now.'

'My children, they're in nursery, and school…'

'We'll pick them up on the way.' He gestured for her to come with him.

'What is this about?' Mim asked, as she followed hurriedly. They were soon jogging down the corridor.

'I'll explain in the car, but there's been a threat made, and we want to take it as seriously as we can.'

Mim was only half-shocked. If her suspicions about Brendan's behaviour were right, then of course he'd been sticking his nose into affairs he shouldn't have been. She sighed. 'What's he done this time?'

Christopher took a second to answer. 'My job right now is to get you somewhere safe. We can save any questions for later. Maybe, you can ask him yourself.'

'Are the kids in danger?'

They dropped down the stairs and into the lobby. After determining the space was clear of danger, he ushered her outside.

'Blue Ford,' he said, pointing. 'Get in the passenger side. We'll pick your children up first.'

'Are they in danger, Tom?' she repeated, more urgently now.

He finally met her gaze. 'There's a threat against all four of you—yes.'

Mim hated Brendan then. 'You stupid, stupid man,' she whispered, as she slipped in the passenger side of DS Christopher's car.

The next few moments were frantic as Mim directed Christopher to the crèche. She ran in, flanked by the detective, unable to stop rising panic, and emerged moments later with a bemused but delighted Mick, his face covered in carrot purée.

Next stop was Dan's High School. Mim had a chance to call ahead so that Dan would be ready. When they got there, he was sat alone in the glass-walled lobby, full of questions. 'What's happened? What's going on? Where's Dad?'

'Dad's going to meet us soon,' she said, putting her arm around him.

'But what's happened? Why are we going home already?'

Mim didn't know what to say. Lying to her children was something she never wanted to do.

'I don't know, Dan,' she said, squeezing his hand, which—with him at seventeen—was already bigger than hers.

Christopher intervened. 'Your father would like you to come meet up with him. I used to work with him, mate, so I know—

just like you do—that when your father wants something, he tends to get it.' A pathetic attempt to get Dan on side but, unbelievably, it worked.

They hit Winwick Road, down to the M62. Just before the junction, Christopher unexpectedly pulled into a bus lane.

'What are we doing?' Mim asked, every sense alert now. 'What's going on?'

He turned to them in the back. 'I have to ask you all to do something for me, and it will sound weird. I need you to cover your eyes.'

'What?' said Mim, pulling her children around her. 'What the hell for?'

'We are trying to keep you as safe as possible, and one of the ways we do this is to make sure that you don't even know where you are. We just want to protect you the best way we can. Okay?'

'Mum?' said Dan, his voice quivering. 'What's going on? Where is Dad?' He was clearly beginning to panic now. He had been like this since his younger cousin Connor had died suddenly last year—easy to panic. Though, god knows, there was enough to panic about now.

She cursed Brendan again, silently. Damn him, and damn what he was doing to his children.

'It's okay, Dan,' she said. 'If your father thinks this is the right thing to do...' She looked at Christopher, for confirmation.

'We all do,' he said. Then he turned back around and slammed down on the accelerator.

CHAPTER 32

SALT BREEZE LICKED Harvey's forehead, as he listened to the surf. He'd worked hard for this view, this chance to sit on an expensive deck at the back of a seafront mansion. *His* seafront mansion. The glass of the balcony was streaked with that briny wind, but the decking was crisp and clean and drenched in sunshine. Whatever happened anywhere else, whatever he heard on the news—a bit like the news of a bloody shooting at a fast food restaurant over in Leigh, that just ripped through the Sky News morning programming—he could always sit here and let everything wash away.

It was half twelve, and he sipped from a glass tumbler, half-full of amber. He knew that putting the word out would create waves, just as he knew the price offered would add bait to the water. But wild bloodshed at a restaurant? At lunchtime, no less? That was as unexpected as it was ill-advised, and he didn't even know who was behind it.

He took narcissistic comfort from the fact that this had happened only because of the Culpepper name's power, reach and reputation. Of course, when Harvey Culpepper said jump, his underlings always wanted to outreach each other, impress him. They all knew that if Harvey Culpepper promised something—like a million quid, for example—he'd deliver it.

And that was why he was here now.

His phone rang in his pocket and he scrambled to pull it out. Dorian. He answered immediately. 'Is he dead?'

'No,' said his right-hand man. 'Two others are, though. Three more injured. One of them an innocent.'

Culpepper wasn't squeamish about collateral. But this was still bad for business.

'Who were they?'

'Still waiting to find out. But one of them was a hit squad from Preston.'

'Jesus.' His reward had obviously got out quick and was attracting serious underground attention.

'You said to put the word out, gaffer—'

Harvey hung up before anything else could be said.

Had his rage caused a spiral? People would say his ego had taken over, but he knew that a winner always backed their own horse—end of story. If that was ego, then so be it. People didn't get far because they wondered if they *could*—the top dogs just went and *did*.

'Dad?'

Harvey turned to find Mikey stood on the veranda. 'Yeah?' His only son was bang on twenty—shirtless, built like an athlete. An amateur boxer with aspirations of going pro, Harvey had done everything he could to make that dream become real. That had included giving him the means to devote his life to training. He'd never even had a job, much less anything that Harvey himself had had to do.

Lucky sod.

'Can I get a ride to the gym?'

Mikey was serving a twelve-month driving ban for motoring pissed up.

'Is your mum about?' he asked.

Mikey ran his hand through his hair. 'I'll have a look,' he said reluctantly.

'Mum *is* about,' said Charlotte, emerging onto the veranda in her gym clobber. Harvey noticed a fire in her eyes, and imagined it could only be because she'd heard about the reward too, and had an opinion on it.

'Can I have a ride to the gym? Dad won't take me.'

Harvey sighed, and swirled his drink. 'I'm busy.' He cursed himself for coddling this kid. Harvey's own dad had never coddled him, more was the pity. In turn, Harvey hadn't wanted his own kid to lack opportunity—but Christ on a bike, it made his lad a dosser.

'Yeah, you look well busy,' Mikey countered. *And,* Harvey mused, *it had made him a bit of a dickhead.*

'I'll take you in a minute, lad,' said Charlotte, her eyes still trained on Harvey. 'Go get your stuff. I want to catch up with your dad.'

Mikey sloped off, knowing from past experience not to argue. Harvey watched him go, shaking his head, as Charlotte strode up to him.

'You look upset, darling,' he said. 'Either that, or your yoga instructor gave you a proper going over.'

'We didn't discuss *this,*' she said. 'Rewards on ex-coppers' heads, gunfights cracking off, people caught in the crossfire. It's all over the fucking radio. Dorian told me—'

'Or was it Dorian who put the colour in your cheeks?' His bile was up now; he was on the defensive with his own wife, and that always made him aggressive.

'Don't you fucking dare,' she warned, in the age-old dance the two of them were so familiar with. The same routine they always went through when the shit hit the fan.

He tried to look past her towards the ocean, but she stepped to block his view.

'Foley has to be taken out,' he finally said. 'Now.'

'So he fucked up a deal. That means we have to get smarter, not go *cartel* on him. Yes, take him out, give him the worst fucking death you can think up—and God knows how good you are at that—but you do it on the quiet.' She was on a roll now. 'The national media, Harvey! You've thrown a spotlight on crime in the region, and we all know who the top name round here is. Jesus, you might as well take out a sign on the Cunard Building!'

'I have to run everything past you now?' They both knew what the truth was.

She didn't hesitate. 'If it could get us both banged up for life—yes.'

'Don't be ridiculous, Char. Everything we've done— together—could get us banged up for life.' He wasn't above pointing out that they'd both been in on his empire-building, right from the very start.

His tactics didn't work. 'If it all came out,' she reminded him, calmly. 'Which it never has, through playing smart. This stupid price on Foley's head could drag everything out from under us, and give the cops a Christmas.'

He smirked darkly, but it was a front. He knew she was right, but could never let her see it. 'Nobody on the blue line knows that order came from me.'

'Not now, but give them two minutes to rub sticks together. Only the biggest players can offer cash like that for a hit.'

'Mal and Ger were always good at sorting this out.'

'Yeah, but they fucked up, and now they're off in Europe, aren't they? Drinking sangria and tossing each other off on the beach. Happy days.'

Harvey still felt jilted by that—the fact that they'd never come home. He'd sorted it. He'd got Art Foley, Brendan's father, framed for the whole lot. It was tied neat, bow on top, media happy, police sated. They could have come back no problem—but there hadn't been a whisper. Not a single attempt at contact. After all he'd done for them.

Charlotte sighed and leant against the railings. 'Who was it? In Leigh?'

'A hit squad from Preston, or so Dorian tells me.'

'We have anything that can tie us directly to them?'

'There's nothing. No direct business between us. I don't even know who they represent. Could just be a bad lot for hire.'

'They got down the motorway quick enough.'

Preston was an hour's drive north from Liverpool. How they'd got onto Foley, found him so quickly—that was to be admired. If they hadn't then got shot to shit, they could even have been useful to know. Too late now.

'How were they shot up? Was Foley carrying?'

'If he had any sense, I think he would. But nah, a second party was having a crack at Foley too. Looks like there was a difference of opinion.'

Charlotte was quiet now. Harvey sat indignant. This would wash over. All these things always did.

A shout from inside the house. 'Mum, let's *go*!'

Charlotte rolled her eyes and trailed out after their son—but not before sending Harvey a parting shot.

'Sort it,' she said, spitting the words out.

Harvey sat, listening to the surf and beyond that his wife's retreating footsteps. A door slammed shut, finally leaving him alone with time to think. There was nothing else to do. He glanced at his phone, beside him on the arm rest. He'd sit here however long it took, until it rang again—and this time, it had better carry good news.

CHAPTER 33

SEABREEZE MARCHED INTO the nick, his head in an absolute melt. It felt like the world was spiralling, the careful codes of conduct they swore by all melting in the heat of a fraught early afternoon in July.

Entering the main swimming pool hall, the summer day outside pressing an infernal heat through the skylight. He walked around the edge of the pool; wires snaked everywhere.

The side of the hall was punctuated by dark wooden doors, each opening into a small cubicle. They'd never been dismantled; moreover, they'd become small, sweaty admin spaces. Most of them were six by four. The AV suite had been put in a family cubicle.

Seabreeze had access. Which, considering the situation with himself, Madison, Foley and Christopher, was a blessing.

He was known as a whizz and also as dedicated. Nobody would think twice about him coming in on a day off.

He booted up and leaned back in the chair. As the room around him began to hum, he tried not to think about what was at stake. Christ, everything was in the balance. Their careers, livelihoods, future prospects—it all hung there. Never mind what would happen if word of their actions got back to the Culpeppers.

He navigated to the CCTV databank, and found the time in question. It took him under a minute to find Madison, and the man, skulking between cars. He copied the time code, and brought up the four separate angles, arranging them together and enlarging them, to give him four views of the stranger's face. Despite the cap he was wearing, this was good enough to get a decent look at him. His smartphone up to the screen, he took a snap of each angle.

Then there was the question of what to do with all this. He could hack into various facial recognition tools from his setup back at home. But it would take time. Time they didn't have. He could use the various angles to come up with an approximation of this blackmailer's face. But it would never be perfect, and wading through those imperfections would again, take time. Feeding that guesswork mugshot into HOLMES or ViCAP would come up with options, but only if this person was in the system. But the system access, if done here, would be flagged, logged and recorded. A technological breadcrumb trail, and he didn't want that.

He could look at the clothes. That jacket looked unique, almost vintage-ey. He could source that, or maybe use that as a basis for search parameters on similar tools as the facial recognition databases. But again. This would take time. And logging.

He let out a sigh and looked at the face on the screen. The man who called himself Stig.

Stig. He'd never met a Stig before. It wasn't a name you got round here. He remembered Liverpool had a player back in the nineties called Stig. Stig Inge Bjørnebye. That was the only one he could think of.

What was the etymology of the name? Scandinavian? Bjørnebye was Norwegian. Had some crime players come across the North Sea?

He shut everything down, both his thoughts and the computer, resolving that he'd have to go home and spend time carefully trying to get a fix on this bloke.

Then it hit him. He didn't need all this tech stuff. The answer was a hark back from old school days. Stories at bedtime. Literature classics.

He suddenly remembered where else he'd heard the name.

Stig of the Dump.

Another word for dump? Tip.

The landfill. Where the bodies of Mal and Ger had been deposited.

On his phone, he quickly found the name of the waste management company which owned and operated the landfill in Birchwood. Navigating the menu, he found what he was looking for. *Meet the team.* He pressed it, and was taken to a series of headshots. He scanned through, right down through thirty names, to the bottom one.

There, in a hard hat and high-visibility vest, his face split with a half-smile, was a Winston Wilson.

Stig.

CHAPTER 34

GARLAND STOOD ON his porch, like an immovable statue. Jason's jacket still rested on the railing. He gazed at the sky, mulling things over. He'd refreshed his coffee cup getting on ten times now, from a jar of instant he kept under his chair, and boiling water from an old catering urn he had sat out here, powered by an extension cord. He filled it every morning from a five-litre watering can, kept the heat on all day. If it weren't for food, he'd never have to move.

That jacket, though.

He looked at his own, draped on an old dining chair. Every inch of the leather was covered with patches, and every patch a story. An achievement. An award.

His was full. Jason's was not.

It was a reminder of the life he'd led. And a cold nudge towards the problems it had caused, the traumas. Would Jason have chosen this life, had he known how he would end up? A dead jelly man, separated from his leathers, propped up in a storage unit surrounded by narcotics?

He swilled the coffee, his latest cup now cold. A lawnmower buzzed somewhere. It should have been a reminder of cold beers, warm skin and good times. But today, it just needled him with a headache.

He'd sat here for a long time, for reasons he couldn't quite fathom. He didn't know what to do. Not a clue.

They'd had a deal. It had been working fine. But something had made the Culpeppers kill one of Garland's—as a warning.

He didn't know why, and he wanted an explanation. Charlotte Culpepper, supposedly right up there at the top of the tree alongside her wretched husband, had said she didn't know either.

He should have grabbed her. Forced the information out of her.

But Garland wasn't like that. Call him old-fashioned, but he didn't believe in harming a woman. And Charlotte Culpepper, while a lot of things, was anything but dumb. Coming here was dangerous enough without coming to gloat about murdering one of theirs.

No. Garland thought she'd been telling the truth.

She didn't want Jason's death, that much was clear. She didn't want the huge potential fallout, so she'd tried to make a step to reparation by returning his jacket. By coming here so soon with a gesture, the fire had been swept out of the motorcycle monarch, leaving him with a conundrum.

But he had to save face, still had to do something to even this balance out. Something like this couldn't—and shouldn't—go unpunished.

It would send out entirely the wrong message—that message being that the Devil's Defects were bitches to Liverpool and Harvey fucking Culpepper. That simply couldn't stand. Manchester didn't bow to Liverpool.

But a huge other problem existed. One that he was keeping buried. The seismic issue of money.

He'd paid for a product that the cops now had. No cash with nothing to sell. It had all been seized. They were massively out of pocket—so much so that the mortgage payments on every house in Renshaw Circle would have to be missed. Not good.

The awful truth was that the Devil's Defects were cash-stripped.

He could plead with the Culpeppers to let him buy more, but the heat would be insane. The cops were wise to it now. He still didn't know how that bust had been made.

Another whine crested over the drone of the mower. A car, with a small engine.

Who now?

His boys started to emerge from the houses as a small kiddie car came down towards the cul-de-sac. A couple of lads at the end house gestured for the car to slow down, and a man full of nervous energy got out. He already had his hands pressed together in pleading. The lads listened to him speak, and after a moment walked the visitor down to Garland's house.

Garland sat back and eyed the man sternly as he approached. Did he recognise him? He didn't think so, but he clearly understood how to behave on Renshaw Circle. Unlike that Culpepper woman.

'Says he's got a message,' said Fin, part of the welcoming party who'd marched him up.

'It's the day for it,' replied Garland, giving the man a once over. He was slick with sweat, but they all were. His jeans were grubbed up and torn around the hems, where half-dead Asics trainers sat as worn out as could be. He wore a blue tracksuit top, a blotchy face and eyes that knew what shit he could be in.

'I had a visit from police, just now. Said they'd been trying to reach you—'

Garland held up a hand to stop his speech, ire rising in a hot flash. He waved away the Defects. When they were out of earshot, he finally spoke.

'You ignorant, braindead *prick*. You walk in here talking police, and you don't give a second's thought to decorum or discretion.'

'I'm sorry,' said the man, his hands dropping in front of his chest. 'I'm really sorry.'

'Tell me who you are, then tell me the rest.' The fury felt controlled now.

'I'm Alvin Leopold. My name is Leo.'

Garland rolled a hand, indicating that he wanted to hear more. Leo turned to check that the Defects were out of earshot. Some were keeping a wary eye.

He turned back. 'This woman copper came to see me when I was having a quiet pint. Told me to give this to you.' He held up a white business card.

'Did she mention me by name?'

A pause, which Garland didn't like. 'Yes.'

He liked the answer even less.

Garland stood out of his chair and walked over to the railing. Leo managed to deposit the card into Garland's outstretched hand, their eyes locked.

'You aren't fucking with me, are you, Leo?'

'No, I'm not.'

'You're aware of what might happen if you were fucking with me?'

'I'm not fucking with you Garland, I promise.'

'I don't know you, but you know my name. That doesn't sit all that right with me.'

'It's not difficult to know your name, I'm sorry. I didn't mean…' The man trailed off, and Garland looked at the card. It was plain, nothing. Cheap even. No fancy lettering or anything, just a white rectangle with some pen scrawl—two lines. Top line said 255. Bottom line gave a phone number. A mobile.

It took Garland a moment to work out why the number 255 was relevant. All leaders delegated—after all, it was the best way to lead—and sometimes finer details slipped. But all the fine print had to be taken into account. Garland knew that 255 was the number of that godforsaken storage unit in Warrington.

This could be viewed in any number of ways.

An olive branch. Seeking terms and a way forward.

It could be the opening play of a trap—coax the Defects out into the open, and drill them hard when their guard was down.

It could be a journalist, seeking a century-level scoop.

It could be another party, aware of what went on in 2272, wanting to start some blackmail scam.

'You sure this came from a cop?' Garland asked.

'Yes. Hundred per cent.'

This was all different. A cop. Reaching out on the quiet. The could mean *all sorts*.

'You're *sure* sure?'

'Yes. I've met her before.'

Garland looked up sharply. 'What the fuck you've met her before?'

Leo took a couple of steps back. 'I mean, she's a common fixture in Warrington. Everyone knows who the DIs are.'

'She's a DI, is she?' Garland's tone had turned sinful. 'You sound like old mates, getting together for little chit chats in the pub regularly?'

'It's nothing like that, Garland. She's just very hands on, is all.' He was panicking now, sweat beading his forehead.

Already, Garland was connecting the dots in his head. 'She knew she could come to you, didn't she? Knew how to find you? You're on their books aren't you.'

'No, Garland, no I promise…' The man was wilting fast. 'They wanted someone who knew the main players, and of course, you, you're one of the main players! They came to me because they knew I could get their message to the right person.'

Garland was at the top of the porch steps now. 'The right person? I thought she mentioned me by name, didn't she? Or was that a bit of an overstatement perhaps?'

'No, I—'

Garland flicked the business card off into the bushes.

'Please!' screamed Leo, as Garland grabbed him round the neck, and whistled down the street to the Defects. A couple of them suddenly ran to their respective houses.

'Come up here and have a chat with me on the porch,' said Garland, grabbing Leo by the ear and dragging him up the steps.

Down the street, two bikes started to rev their engines, which boomed high into the neighbourhood sky, drowning out any shouts for mercy.

'Please Garland, I'm just the messenger—'

Garland kicked Leo's legs out from under him with two violent swipes. The smaller man fell to his knees. 'Oh, yeah. What is it they say about that?'

'Don't shoot him!' Leo screamed. 'Don't shoot the messenger!'

Garland dragged him to the catering urn of boiling water. 'Who said anything about shooting?'

It all came to a head. The feeling of being pushed down, overlooked, belittled and subordinated. Those fucking Culpeppers. The money they'd lost. The money *he* had lost. The pressure, all around him, all of a damn sudden. He needed to remind everyone who he was. What the Defects were made of.

The pressure erupted.

He pulled the metal lid off the cylinder, steam escaping in a cloud, and shoved Leo's head in. The man screamed and thrashed as his head cooked. Garland gripped the back of his neck, as boiling water exploded over his hands. Those hands that had been shredded by asphalt so many times they barely had any nerve endings left. This sidewinder, playing any side he could, gargled noises that would give lesser men nightmares, until the thrashing became spasms, the bucking less committed—and Leo stood there, leant over, with his head in the giant tin, like a guy who'd got carried away bobbing for apples.

Finally, Garland stepped back, went to his chair, and slugged cold coffee. He'd have refreshed the cup if it weren't for the minor detail of a dead informant stuck in the water. He wasn't bothered—fresh boiling water would clean the urn right out. He looked down the street, and nodded. The engines were cut, and Renshaw Circle was quiet again. A couple of the bikers came down after a couple of minutes, guys who knew their place in the hierarchy. They could offer some assistance here.

Garland moved to the top of the porch steps. 'Fin, photograph him. Harris, there's a business card in those bushes. Fetch it for me.'

The two men busied themselves. Pictures duly taken, the card retrieved and handed over, the two men waited for instruction.

'Get rid of him,' said Garland, casting a dismissive glance at the slumped body. 'That development out near Runcorn Bridge should be about right. You know the drill.'

Both men nodded. They did know the drill. COMUDEV were a housing and development company. They had a couple of sympathetic ears in their project management department, greased by paper emblazoned with the Queen's mush. One who told them when foundations would be poured, and another when concrete would be on site.

Honestly. A person could be amazed at how many new builds had bodies hidden in their foundations.

CHAPTER 35

THEY STAYED OFF the motorways and stuck to the A and B roads, flirting with Northern textile towns. Leigh, Atherton, Bolton, then out towards Winter Hill, its mast visible for miles around.

The roads were hot and heavy, and progress was slow. He checked on his passengers regularly. Firstly, to make sure they were all right. Secondly, to make sure they still wore their makeshift blindfolds.

Mim Foley was chewing her lip to pieces, worry so evident despite the blindfold. All Christopher felt he could tell her was that he'd seen Brendan and he was fine, and that he would be joining them. She hadn't asked anything further after they'd picked up the older boy, Dan, who sat stoically next to her in back. He was the spit of his dad, right down to the hand-wringing. The baby, Mick, was restless in the back seat. Poor little lad.

Little lad.

Don't think about it.

Don't think about the little nugget floating about in Emma's belly.

Don't think about the expedited tests, possibly going on right this minute.

Don't think about possibly having to say goodbye to the little guy, and all the hopes and happiness with it.

Don't think about not having a little lad just like that one in the rear-view mirror.

He returned his focus to the road, the car climbing with it. He pushed the revs, just hard enough not to slow down. Nevertheless, some boy racer in a hatchback overtook him on the climb, obviously unaware that he was dangerously jetting past a copper. He didn't rise to it, just focused on the task at hand and his cargo. A few more turns, and Belmont reared up ahead.

A single street, lined by cottages. As emergency safehouse locations went, this wasn't bad at all. He managed to travel the entire length of the village without seeing a living soul, save for a white cat in a window, balanced on a chair back, watching its limited world drift by.

It took less than a minute to get right through and out the other side of the village, before a high turn took them onto Longworth Road, and along a reservoir. Even though it was baking, the barren openness of the terrain—the hardy yellow grasses, the bracken, and the uninterrupted water—lent an air of bleakness. Winter here would be bollock-hard and lemon-bitter.

A white cottage loomed on the crest of a grassy knoll, over a short stone ford.

Their destination.

The road forked immediately before the house. Christopher took the right, then immediately turned off onto the cottage driveway. A sign read Schofield House, words chiselled onto weather-beaten slate. The back of the house had a short turning circle. The place was like a tomb.

Behind the house, Christopher turned the car a tight one eighty so the bonnet was facing the exit, and killed the engine. Silence closed in immediately.

'You can look now, gang,' he said, turning.

They took off their blindfolds, and Dan was the first to take in the surroundings. 'Where's Dad?'

Mim stared out at the house. 'How long will we be here?'

'I couldn't say, Mrs Foley, but I know it's the best place to be at the moment. Let's get you inside.'

They exited the car, and stepped into the sunlight. Mim handed Mick to Dan, who placed the kid on the ground to toddle in the gravel. Christopher found it hard to peel his eyes off him—the simple innocence.

The back door stood open.

'Just wait here a moment, please Mrs Foley,' he said, before he stepped inside.

The rear porch was a damp conservatory, transparent corrugated roof discoloured to a murky pink. The conservatory had another door, locked. He knocked twice.

Within a few seconds, the door was opened a few inches, and a woman's face looked out. 'DS Christopher?'

'DC Golds?'

She opened the door wider.

'GMP,' she said.

'Warrington Police.' They shook hands. 'Thanks for your help today.'

'It's a pleasure. Road trips are always better than paperwork.'

'Amen to that. Is he here?'

'I was to expect him with a DI Madison. Neither have appeared, I'm afraid. Firearms team en route, or so I'm told.'

Not here yet? That wasn't good. Not good at all.

Christopher turned. Mim was watching him with a dark, worried expression.

Christ. What was he going to tell her? And where in the blue hell was Brendan Foley?

CHAPTER 36

THE SKY OVER the North Pennines was as grey as the tarmac. Brendan weaved Madison's Beemer around a sheep's carcass. The moors either side of the road were never-ending waves of dull yellows and oranges, pocked by the small white shapes of sheep more vital.

He knew he should have told Madison what he was doing, where he was going, but he hadn't been able to find the words. Couldn't face the inevitable accusation: 'Are you out of your mind?'

But he trusted Christopher. His family were safe. There was comfort to be had there, at least.

Keeping a close eye on the onboard satnav, he saw that the journey was coming to an end.

The road snaked right to left along the abandoned slate face of a disused quarry. A crossing emerged, stepping stones over white, shallow water, the grey skies giving the water an angry depth. The mere sight set Brendan's guts into a tumult.

He hadn't spoken to his brother since their faces had been cast in the pulse of strobing purple neon, in a strip club deep in Manchester's Chinatown. Both men drunk, fresh from the death of a son and nephew—off the back of which, everything had gone to hell. Brendan had reluctantly visited the club in order to warn his younger brother that their father was about to be arrested, and that he should get his affairs in order. He'd tried to coax Ross into going home, but his brother had torn away from him—overwhelmed with drugs, adrenalin and the old fatigue of a family falling apart yet again.

He hadn't seen Ross since. The following day had been the motorbike drive-by attack, with Ross as one of the targets. Brendan had no idea how he'd survived.

A bridge rolled him over the River Wear, whilst his mind wandered back towards the past. After that meeting, he'd lain awake for hours night after night, wondering about that attempt on Ross's life. Who'd perpetrated it, what had happened, where the murder weapons were now.

He'd read the reports, passed to him in yet another favour from Madison. Forty-four bullets ripped through a car on the East Lancs road, whilst Brendan was sat next to the man who'd arranged it. Brendan had never felt so impotent. It was probably one of the key moments that had punched a hole in his desire to be a policeman. No matter what you did and how you did it, you were always held accountable to the same standards and codes of practice—even in the face of moving goalposts. Anyone could play dirty. Could a person ever see justice as a cop?

He caught himself now, and reined in the bitter thoughts.

His car crawled through the village of Stanhope. A nice place to settle, he thought. The perfect place to escape. Lie low. That is, until your estranged brother shows up.

Was he right to barge in on Ross, even if Seabreeze's information was correct? What was the brotherly thing to do here?

People had tried to kill Ross, and failed. Would rooting him out now drag him back into harm's way?

Even worse, the same people who had tried to kill Ross were now trying to kill Brendan. The Foley name, the dynasty connected to this damn lineage, was nothing more than death and blood. He'd tried to step away from it all, only to fail.

Was he risking everything by coming here?

In short, yes.

Couldn't stop driving, though.

The final turn appeared ahead of him. Heather View. He followed the bend round and over that damn river again, on a one-way bridge. The river here churned even more violently. It did nothing to calm Brendan's nerves.

He started to see the rectangular windowed boxes on a rising hillside, row after row of them, and he turned right under a rising barrier. Suddenly, there were kids everywhere, playing, chasing, laughing. Bikes darted, pedal carts scooted, even some hoverboard things with seat attachments jetted by.

He weaved between the children, slowing to let them pass, and weaved his way to the back corner of the park. Up another hill, where the trees got taller, past a sign reading Evergreen Way.

He knew the one he was looking for. Seabreeze had been thorough. He owed him big.

There were fewer kids up here.

There. The tired-looking one.

The other surrounding caravans were clean, sparkling.

He left Madison's car on a grass verge and started walking. He didn't want to announce his arrival. Not yet.

Why was he here again? He tried to order his thoughts to come up with something, but his brain emptied.

It all boiled down to one word. *Recruitment.*

He'd come here to try to bring his brother home. Together, they could bring down the Culpepper empire. He was sure of it.

The fact that Harvey Culpepper was trying to kill Brendan was just a side issue with admittedly compelling timing.

As he drew closer, he couldn't see beyond the net curtains. The caravan didn't look bright or welcoming. Nor even lived in.

He took a deep breath. All the villains and all their dens he'd walked into without a moment's hesitation—but his own brother? Different gravy. He just about forced himself to knock on the door.

A moment passed. A shift of weight beyond the door. The creak of footsteps. Then the door swung open.

CHAPTER 37

KHARTHIK HAD KNOCKED twice. Contemplated for a second whether to break in.

The house was dead. A newbuild that didn't look so new anymore.

Aware of prying eyes, he knocked again.

When there was still no answer, he walked around the side of the house, past the spilling wheelie bins. No cars in the drive, either. He didn't like this—not at all. If all the evidence was accurately pointing where it seemed to be, then the people this Nigel guy was dealing with were redtop levels of bad news. Mean and gratuitous.

Should he be here at all?

The back of the house was as unloved as the front. Dog shit everywhere; the smell in the baking heat was nauseating. He crossed round to the glass patio doors and looked inside. It didn't take long to work out that the place had been abandoned in a hurry. Utensils littered the kitchen countertops. An empty plastic pedal bin. Kharthik felt a strange respect for Nigel for having the presence of mind to take the bins out before fleeing, but then that baked crap smell entered his nose again, causing him to wince.

He started walking back around the house again when he heard a car door slam. Unsure of his position—*Should he really have been round the back of the house?*—he took it slowly down the side passage, and peered around the corner.

A man was walking up the driveway to the front door.

He wore a blue short-sleeved shirt and a thick black goatee beard. He banged hard on the door, twice. Kharthik stilled and pulled tight into the red brick.

Who was this guy? Who did he represent?

When the man seethed *'Fuck this shite!'* in the thickest Scouse tones imaginable, everything was answered in one go.

He suddenly felt a swell of righteousness, and he stepped out from the passage.

'Can I help you, sir?'

The look the man gave him was chock full of dismissal. 'Yeah, you can fuck off all the way back to your own country. How about that?'

Kharthik grimaced. He'd heard far worse, but still, the depths that people's standards could plummet to always surprised him. 'Bless you, I haven't heard that one in a while. Did you really just say that to a police officer?'

The man's nostrils flared.

'Racial epithets aside, can I ask what you're doing here?'

'Visiting a mate, but he's not in, is he?'

'No, it does look a little empty, I'll give you that. In fact, I'd go one further and say he's done a runner.'

The man immediately glanced off to the side, betraying the whir of internal cogs.

'That's right,' Kharthik said. 'Give it some thought. Your inside man has done a runner, hasn't he?'

That snapped the man's focus back.

'Warrington Police fancied a word with him. And usually when things go a bit pear-shaped, all sorts of creatures come out of the woodwork. I fancy a word with you.'

The man immediately bolted. Didn't bother with the road, or his car, just sprinted full pelt at the hedges at the far end of the street, and a footpath opening that parted the tall green overgrown bushes.

Kharthik ran after him.

There was a handful of yards in it to begin with, but his quarry didn't really have much in the speed department. Nevertheless, he got to the hedge first and hurled himself through, turning left along a shaded ginnel that carved a dusty dirt path between the other hedges and the fence panels of back gardens.

Kharthik was nearly on him, when his vision was blurred by a barrage of swirling white dots, which he ran through. Midges. He felt them pepper his cheeks as he tore through them—only realising too late what the distraction had cost. The man had stopped to face Kharthik, bringing his hand up, holding a black gun.

The pistol's noise boomed along the passageway. Immediately, the man corrected his aim, and fired again.

Kharthik felt a pain he'd neither expected nor imagined, but he still smashed hard into his opponent with the heaviest shoulder barge he could.

He sailed into the hedge. Kharthik didn't stop, and dragged him to the ground viciously, rolling the man onto his front to sit on his back. He took hold of a wrist, applied pressure at the top of a shoulder blade, and forced a forearm up the man's back. He didn't know where the gun had got to, but he felt in control— even more so when, as the man bucked, he pushed his face down and pinned it into the dirt.

Then he remembered—he didn't have his cuffs on him.

They were in the car.

Controlling the man with one hand, he whisked his belt off, and bound hands together.

'Let's hope I don't have an accident as we walk out of here. Last thing you'd want is to be spotted emerging from a back alley with a supposed foreigner. Especially one with his pants round his ankles. I mean, people would talk. Oh, and I'm all the way from the exotic shores of Runcorn, just to be clear.'

Kharthik read him his rights, even though his left arm was singing. Blood was drenching the tan of his suit. He twisted round and spotted the wound at the top of his shoulder. Actually, on inspection, even higher. He'd taken a shot in the muscle tapering up to the neck.

He'd been lucky.

This guy, not so much.

He went through his pockets and found a wallet. Driving licence with a Liverpool address. And a name.

Dorian Torrance.

'Well, Dorian, I think it's time we got going, don't you? Places to go, people to see, drug deals to talk about. And I hope you're in the mood for singing, because we've got a sellout audience all set, and they're fed up of waiting.'

CHAPTER 38

MADISON HAD TO get, of all things, an Uber—she was damned if she was heading off into Manchester in a panda car. Thankfully, when she arrived at Pendleton Mission, the doors were open, as promised.

It wasn't as she'd expected it at all. Just another forgotten building, in a forgotten part of Greater Manchester. The building was still adorned with exhausted weather-battered signs from previous inhabitants, but Madison knew that now this place was run by... the Devil's Defects.

As she took the front step, her phone buzzed in her pocket. She glanced at it, hoping it was Brendan with an apology, an update, handing himself in... Any of the above would have done.

But no. It was DS Kharthik.

Instantly, the smell of burgers hit her nostrils. She realised that she hadn't eaten in far too many hours. No, she'd catch Kharthik later. He could definitely wait.

She entered to the smell of grilled beef, accompanied by an audible sizzle, and her mouth drenched. The place was interesting, almost church-like. Tall windows reached up to a vaulted ceiling, and sunlight streamed in shafts of orange. Long rows of tables occupied the centre, and people sat on benches. At one end was a bar, optics empty, fridges bare. The floor was swept, yet betrayed all sorts of recent life. She didn't think this place would pass too many health and hygiene checks. A row of people shuffled, plates outstretched, towards a glass-panelled kitchen section at the far wall.

No sign of Garland Roarke, however.

Word from Broom had been that she wouldn't be able to miss him. *Look for the biggest, gnarliest bastard in the room.* Biker tropes. A few were about, but they all struck her as too young. *Grizzled.*

Her search was interrupted by a raised voice. 'Fancy a cheeseburger?'

The voice came from the rear of the kitchen area. Everyone looked over to Madison in a Wild West pastiche. *Smart move*, she thought. Designed to put her on the spot, ruffle her feathers.

But it would take a lot more than watchful eyes to put the pressure on Iona Madison.

She walked over to the kitchen, and came round the side of the grill. As she looked into the kitchen's interior, she saw a bearish figure dressed in an apron, jeans and a chef's hat.

The creature turned, flipped a burger into a bun with a deft roll, and held it out to her. 'Ketchup?'

This was him. This was Garland Roarke.

'Anything hotter?' she replied.

Her next fight was three weeks off, so an injection of protein wouldn't be the worst thing in the world. And, given how good the burger smelled, she didn't think she could turn down the offer if she'd tried.

'Tabasco's on the counter,' Roarke replied, passing the spatula over to another biker. 'Handle this for me, Fin,' she heard him say, as he gave her the burger.

Up close, he was six and a half feet of sinewed body. The look on his face made it clear that he'd been there, done that and bought the T-shirt, just so he could wipe his arse with it. The bona fide *gnarliest bastard in the room.*

'Thanks,' she said, taking the burger and moving to the counter for the hot stuff.

'I do love a girl who likes her hot sauce,' he said, walking to one of the tables beneath a window.

'Piss off with that bollocks, or this conversation will go a lot differently,' she said, sitting opposite him, burger dripping.

'Hey, you came to me,' he said, holding his hands up.

'With a possible lifeline, but any more of that shite and redemption is off the table.'

He chuckled. 'You think a man who runs a group called the Devil's Defects has any plans to court redemption?'

'If you don't play ball, you are fucked. We've a Devil's Defect in custody, we've got one on a slab, both of them involved in a high-profile drug deal that went *very* wrong. And you just told me you were in charge. So yeah, I think words like *lifeline* and *redemption* would be quite useful to you at the minute.'

He didn't miss a beat. 'What those boys get up to in their spare time has nothing to do with me. Devil's Defects is about finding a place. And here is where we found it.' He spread his hands out, gesturing to the mission.

Madison stood. 'Thanks for the burger, but you've wasted my time. I'll pass everything we have—which is a *lot*—on to the Crown Prosecution Services.'

'Sit down. Don't make me look bad in front of my boys.'

'You are making it harder and harder to want to offer you anything.'

They stared at each other. Madison was smart enough to know they both needed something from the other, and despite the polar opposite start points, deep down, their best bet at getting those things was each other.

'You want the Scouser, don't you?' Garland said. Madison nodded. 'Then sit back down.'

She hesitated for a moment, then sat.

'What do you want for him?'

'Long stretch. Inside. Little to no chance of ever getting out.'

'I could go along with that, but I don't want it ever coming back that it was me who helped put him there. Understood? It never, ever comes back to me or the Defects.'

'That can work.'

'What do you have in mind?'

'There's two ways. You could be a registered CI—'

Garland put down his coffee. 'You say that again, and it's me who'll be walking from the table. I'm no snitch. No Defect will ever be a snitch.'

Madison stared at him, thinking of the Defect she had in custody right that moment, and how they might have to add the prefix 'protective' to the word if Garland Roarke ever found out what had been discussed in the interview room that very morning. 'Option two, we put together a sting operation.'

Garland's body relaxed. 'I'm listening.'

'You both need to agree to meet. It needs to look as though a deal is about to go down between you—big weights of narcotic to get the high arrest tariff. Whilst he's waiting for you to show up, one of your guys goes in and says you're not coming, but tries to conclude the deal on your behalf. If Culpepper accepts, police arrive, take them both in. Your boy gets thrown back in the pond.'

'This is snitching.'

It was time to show Garland who really held the killer hand. 'I think you need a reality check. We've a man at the nick right now who's gone full songbird. *Your* man. He says so, and so does his ink. We have enough circumstantial evidence to tie you to the dead drop delivery and for clarity I'm talking about the sheer weight of Class-A we found there. You are fucked… unless you play ball.'

'Nobody walks into my place and threatens me. *Nobody.*'

'Bless you. You know, I really feel for you macho types who obviously got your life lessons, your stupid jacked-up code, from old action movies and a prehistoric sense of what it means to be a man. But the world doesn't give a shit, Garland. About your misplaced honour or your sense of right. I definitely don't. At this point in time, I've got you. Bang to rights, in the nick till you're dead. But it's not you that's killing people and putting hits out on ex-coppers and their families. The offer is this. You man-up—that's the expression you like to use isn't it?—and help me bring down Culpepper. The slate is wiped. You choose to carry on with the naughty stuff, then we can dance all over again. But that's on you.'

Garland didn't move, but his gaze held fast. Eventually, his jaw unlocked. 'What is it with women today?'

'We got sick of crap men.'

As far as Madison was concerned, negotiations were underway.

CHAPTER 39

THE HOUSE SMELLED weird.

That was the overarching sensation Seabreeze had as he walked up the driveway of the address he'd got via a quick call to the landfill site office. He wondered if it was because of the number of wheelie bins parked under the front window. He counted eight. Did eight people live here? Eight different apartments? Surely not.

No, something about this place was way off. And that *smell*.

It wasn't that generic bin smell, more a deep, baked-in grime that had been years in the making. It made his stomach roil. There were four cars on the drive, which gave initial credibility to the idea that a number of people lived here, but on closer inspection, the cars' windows were rimed with mildew and the tyres were uniformly flat. This place was a dumping ground, and no amount of four-bedroom, mock-tutor desirability could mask it. Stig of the Dump was just about right.

The building loomed over him. Every curtain was dragged shut, discoloured linings facing the street. He spotted two cameras in the eaves, one high on the right, one midway up on the left. Oddly, they were different models, one a little domed orb, the other a small white protruding cylinder, angled at the drive. He didn't know if they were on, and there was no way of telling—but it didn't bother him all that much. This guy was threatening cops. He'd decided to play dirty. It just happened to be that he lived that way, too.

Seabreeze needed to get inside. Get a handle on this guy and find some leverage to turn the tables back in their favour. He was sure the place was empty, having cased it for an hour. As he watched, he'd checked the DVLA database from his phone. Wilson owned a Toyota MR2, a car Seabreeze hadn't seen in years. In any other circumstances, he would have liked a look at it, but its absence emboldened him.

Walking round the back of the house, he began to hear a pulsing hum. The once-white rendering of the walls was cracked and peeling off in great sheets. Seabreeze felt a wave of sympathy for the building; it would once have been a beauty.

Finally round the back, he couldn't believe his eyes. Forty wheelie bins at least, covered the entire back garden. High hedges and huge conifers reached desperately to the sun. The whole area stank, fetid and sweet, and the heat from the day was not helping at all.

He shuffled up tight to the phalanx of bins, to get a look at the back of the house. Immediately, he could see that the back door was covered in black rot and mould, with dark foot-long shards of wood peeling away from the frame.

He could get there if he climbed over the bins.

Holding his nose, and cursing the fact he'd chosen to come out in spotless Nike 77 Blazer hi-tops, he hoisted himself onto the nearest bin. It was sturdy. Full. Of what, he had no idea.

Think Jordan, think. Eyes on that door.

He hopped from one bin lid to the next, making his way across, praising his luck that he was naturally slight and athletic. You couldn't be a big lad doing this.

One of the bins shook when he stood on it, and wobbled. He looked down to catch his balance, and saw a platoon of rats burst from a hole in the side of the bin. His stomach flipped, and he let out a scream he'd later hope nobody heard. He ran the rest of the way across the bins, dropped down off the last one to try the door, which swung open in its frame. He slipped into the house, and closed the door behind him.

A wall of stench hit him like a knee in the gut. He wretched, mouth filling with saliva, bile creeping up his throat.

He found himself in a kitchen, full of waste and junk. The sink was a stacked Jenga of abandoned crockery. There were two tables, each surface covered. Every square foot of the floor was stacked with newspapers, magazines, letters, serials, takeaway menus. The scale of mess was overwhelming. Bin bags sat on the countertops. There was the sweet garbage smell of rot.

The kitchen units were all closed shut, aside from the nearest one. That was half full of small, neatly stacked parcels, wrapped in newspaper. He managed to drag the door next to it open. That unit contained more parcels, stacked neatly one on top of the other, row on row. It didn't take him long to discover that all available cupboard space was filled with these parcels. He went back to the first cupboard, and took the nearest package. The paper was carefully folded, a solitary sheet of tabloid print. The odour in the room rose in sharpness, as he unpacked a perfectly presented human shit. Reflexively, he gagged and threw the whole thing at the sink.

Seabreeze couldn't stop his mind doing fast maths. These kitchen cupboards were full of years of neatly organised and meticulously catalogued human bowel movements. He backed out of the kitchen, and into a hallway that was full of junk. Wall-to-wall garbage, save for a narrow path through the middle.

God, this place is a nightmare come to life.

The smell here took a different note. As he made his way down the narrow path between items—a toaster, a clothes rail, a huge, winding pile of electrical flex, cardboard boxes, plastic boxes, a stuffed fox, a giraffe-print lampshade—he realised he didn't know what he was looking for. Not really. Just something incriminating.

Was hoarding illegal? He didn't think it was. Surely Wilson wouldn't want the state of his home life broadcast… but maybe he didn't care. Maybe he thought this was normal. There was likely nothing here that could be used as leverage against Wilson. So, as bile rose again, he realised that he'd have to get his hands dirty.

But where on earth to start? There could be something here that Wilson shouldn't have. Something illegal maybe. But where? It would take a full forensics team weeks to go through everything here.

How could a person live like this? He felt a pang of pity for Wilson, and the difficulties his mental state must pose.

He made it all the way along the hall to the front door, peering through the grease-smeared glass. Nothing amiss. His car was still parked up on the pavement opposite the house. He had to make a start; time was running out. People kept their valuables near their beds sometimes, didn't they? Or at least in their bedroom.

He went upstairs, but that was treacherous going, as the steps were home to towers of shoeboxes which he couldn't bring himself to open. Despite the congestion, he struggled to imagine the man he'd seen on the station CCTV being nimble enough to navigate through this mess. He was stout and doughy, but he clearly must be possessed of a hidden agility to get through this daily Krypton Factor of collected shit.

The landing was more of the same. It made him desperate to get home, hit the shower, scrub himself with anything and everything short of bleach. The stench was sweeter again up here, and he dreaded to think what was causing it. He could hear the scuttle of insects, but couldn't see them, and it made him cover his mouth and nose.

Of the five rooms upstairs that branched off the landing, only three were accessible. The others were all full of junk, and it began dawning on Seabreeze that maybe this guy was using his job at the tip to scour for more treasure. It must kill him, he thought, this man who's so obsessed with possession he can't even flush away his own waste, to see all that stuff get discarded every day. Maybe he was a second chance kind of guy.

That meant that, of the remaining rooms, one was a bathroom. He'd be damned if he was going in there; God knew what horrors it would hold. Steeling himself, he turned to the first bedroom.

The door was held open by stacks of curled football programmes and pro-wrestling magazines, and he glanced inside.

Lying on the bed, top and tailing like caterpillars on a teenage sleepover, were two shapes wrapped in plastic. Seabreeze recognized them immediately. After all, he'd been one of the people who'd tossed them into the landfill on that night he wished had never happened.

All their conversations, all their wondering… what could Wilson have? What evidence could he possibly possess that tied the four of them to the deaths of those two gangsters last summer?

Now and here, their questions were answered.

Winston Wilson had fished out the bodies of Malcolm Jevons and Gerry Toyne, keeping them for a rainy day.

Seabreeze stared. These items—these corpses—plucked from his nightmares and brought back into the present. Nothing about this could get any worse.

Except it could—because as he backed out of the room, he heard the greasy front door below clunk open.

CHAPTER 40

BRENDAN'S BROTHER HAD the look of a man whose beatings were worn like medals.

Losing your wife. That would be the bags under your eyes.

The weight gain, the shoulder sag that suggested a devolution. Chalk that up to losing your dad.

The haunted glaze to the stare. That would be the murder of your son.

The whole package spoke of defeat.

Brendan sympathised. If he didn't get his own act together, he'd be in the same boat soon. Still, he found it hard not to stare. His brother had survived a drive-by shooting that had taken all his friends, crawled out and ran. Didn't stop running until he ended up here. Told nobody what he'd survived, and had somehow eked out a way to carry on.

'You're not so much into the black stuff anymore?' Ross said now. His eyes didn't waiver from the head on his Guinness.

'Still partial, but I'll have to drive back in a bit, so I'm pacing it,' Brendan replied.

They were sat at a table against the wall in the Riverside Bar and Grill, which was the on-site bar for residents at the caravan park Ross had chosen to call home. Children milled about, racing each other to the arcade machines, then back again to their parents, nagging them for coins in exchange for a quiet pint. More than once, Brendan had thought it was wrong of him to be here at all, what with the price on his head, but he was reasonably confident, thanks to the distance he had travelled from his corner of the country, that here was safe.

Ross drank, and signalled with a small nod to a bar person beyond Brendan's shoulder that he was after another.

'So, this is what you've been up to?' said Brendan, taking his first sip of the stout.

'Don't look so snooty about it, it's worked out fine so far.'

This was so typical of the brothers. Polar opposites, bonded by nothing more than shared blood and a damning lineage. They'd never been on the same page ever since their teens, when Ross had eyed their father's criminal exploits more favourably than Brendan. Their interests had forked with a stubbornness few could have predicted or understood. Nevertheless, Brendan wanted to do what he could to bring their separate journeys closer together. Life, he reasoned, was too short.

Plus, he wanted his brother's help.

'We aren't that dissimilar now, you and me,' he told his younger sibling.

'And how'd you fathom that?'

'I couldn't hack being a copper anymore, not after all that. So, I'm just a regular bloke now. Not on the force anymore.'

If anything was going to shock Ross, Brendan had found it. His brother finally looked up from his pint. 'You jacked it in?'

'I couldn't carry on. Not after what happened to Dad, and… the rest.'

'You can say his name. I won't have a breakdown.'

'And Connor.' Sixteen years old, one bad mistake. Listened to the wrong voice, and was killed for it. Life was full of the harshest penalties. 'Didn't have the appetite anymore.'

'So what are you doing now?'

'Working the doors in St Helens.'

Ross's eyes widened theatrically, and a glint of his old character shone for the briefest second. 'You're having me on. You?'

'I'm not.' He felt his mouth twitch with a smile.

Ross shook his head in disbelief. 'Bobby to bouncer.'

'Believe me, I've heard them all.'

'Where in particular?'

'Nexus and Flexion, mostly.'

'Oh, you've properly fallen from grace.'

'Why do you think I picked them? All sorts of interesting clientele in there.'

Ross suddenly caught on. 'You're... you picked them because of who they're connected to?'

'And all the intel that comes with it.'

Ross's face lit up with understanding. 'You've not given up, have you?'

'Not one bit. I'm still going to bring those bastards to justice. At least, I'm trying.'

Those eyes of his brother's darkened. 'Do I detect an ulterior motive? You've not arrived here simply to check on your little bro, have you?'

Brendan didn't often feel sheepish, least of all in front of his brother, but he did now. 'I could do with some help.'

Ross went still. Unsettlingly so. He was known to be a hothead. 'You...' he said, with a pointed finger that could have seemed playful to any bystander. '... you are quiet for months. I was this close to Swiss cheese and you couldn't have given a shit. When I went, I bet you were fucking glad. I bet you were delighted.'

'I can't tell you how wrong you are.'

'The troublesome younger brother, vanished. How convenient. You were thrilled. But now—now? You need help, you've been banged up, because you've stepped into a world you don't understand. And you're in over your head. So you think, *What scumbag do I know who has an idea how the bad people do business?* Enter baby brother.'

'You're wrong.'

'Fuck you, Brendan. You've no idea.'

'I do. Turns out, yeah, I've poked my head where it doesn't belong. There's a price on me now, too. And on my family.'

Ross went quiet again, but this bout of silence burnt far less. 'The cut on your head.'

'Two teams tried to kill me in Leigh.'

'Sent by?'

Brendan only had to nod. *Culpepper.* 'He's put word out, with a price that gives you instant retirement. Mim and the kids are under police protection.'

Ross rose to boiling point in a hot second, but managed to simmer just as quick. 'And why aren't you? Don't they look after their own anymore?'

'I'm supposed to be with them. But I came to you. Brother to brother. I need your help.'

'Knock off the *brother to brother* crap, Brendan.'

'All right, are you happy that Harvey Culpepper is still putting out hits on the Foley name? Are you going to settle for that? Because I'm not. I can't.'

'I'm out of it. I'm not coming back. Nothing would bring me back to the North West.'

'This man took everything from you. Everything. Now he's threatening your brother and his family. Doesn't that mean anything to you?'

Ross held his arms out, a king sharing his kingdom. 'When you spend a bit of time in the sunshine drinking the good stuff, it's surprising how quickly you forget.' He lowered his hands, the darkness returning. 'Especially when there's nothing left to go back for. Friends, wife, father, son… all gone.'

'What about Mum?'

'Mum doesn't know what day it is.' Moira Foley was in an assisted living facility as dementia robbed her of any sense of her final years. Art Foley, dead and buried, had been her carer, showing that even the most self-involved had slivers of selflessness.

'She does. She does. She knows your face when she sees it.'

Guilt brought the colour to Ross's cheeks. 'How is she?'

'She's in a home, Ross. Twenty-four-seven care, because she needs that now. And yeah, she's losing it, but she's still there enough to know her son when he walks in.'

'Does she… ever ask after me?'

'Of course.' Brendan didn't want to tell the full truth—that with every passing day her memory of him blurred. One day, she would likely forget him altogether.

'What do you even want me to come back for?'

'I want you to help me take Culpepper down.'

'What does that even mean now? You're not a cop, what can you do?'

'He's doing business with a biker gang in Manchester, big business. Shifting huge weights of cocaine once a month. They were using a lock-up in Warrington as a dead drop. Culpepper drops it off, a biker collects the drugs later. Warrington's just a convenient destination.'

'It's still our turf.'

Brendan shook his head. 'There's no such thing as Foley turf.'

'If you'd gone into the family business there would be.'

'I'd never have done that, and you know it.'

'So now what are we? Those guys who sit in the corner at the swingers' party while everyone has a turn with his wife? Cos that's what this feels like.'

Brendan glanced around, his voice dropping to a harsh whisper. 'I thought you didn't care. I thought you had a new life on permanent holiday.'

They were at an impasse again, bickering brothers doing exactly what they'd always done. They truly didn't know any other way, but in the past it had usually been characterised by sly words, and quarrels left unspoken, never mind resolved. This was much more. But what should Brendan have expected?

Ross picked up his pint and glugged it theatrically before wiping the back of his hand across his mouth. 'Just the way I like it.'

Brendan stood up. 'I need to get back, then, if you're not coming. But I promise you, whatever you think about me, I am really happy to see that you're all right.'

Ross nodded once and looked away. 'Get your family safe.'

It had been a stupid idea coming here. But still, he felt compelled to have one last try. 'This would get revenge for dad. For Connor.'

'I've changed my mind. Don't you say his name.' Ross's eyes suddenly sparked with grief and anger.

'Connor would be ashamed of us both,' Brendan said, after a moment. Then he walked out of the bar, past the snotty children and the half-drunk parents, and away from his brother.

CHAPTER 41

THE KIDS WERE inside and settled, but the atmosphere was far from calm. Tension was heavy as a boozer's breath. Madison still hadn't shown up, Christ himself didn't know where Foley had got to, and the GMP copper Golds was in the kitchen on self-appointed tea duty, with nothing to do.

Christopher walked around the cottage perimeter again, constantly on the lookout in case anyone was looking to cash in on Culpepper's reward. Foley's family was in his hands, and at the mercy of the region's police forces. He would not let them down.

The house was on high land, and gave enviable views over the Black Walk Water reservoir. The Black Walk was a footpath that ran around the perimeter on the northern side, and off into the hills behind the cottage.

By now, he knew where all the exits were, what the best roads were to get out and quickly onto a main traffic artery, understood the lay of the land and the best vantage points to use for defence. But the harsh reality was that he had no real tools of protection here. If killers came with firepower, just like they had done at that KFC earlier, he'd be stood here with less than a knife at a gunfight. He felt exposed and blunted.

The sun, dipping to the west, painted the reservoir in burnished molten. But the beauty of the scene wasn't much comfort. *If word of this place gets out to the wrong people,* he thought, *we are fucked without a firearms team.*

He glanced in the front window and saw Foley's two boys. The little one on the floor cavorting about. The older boy, face puckered with worry.

Why on earth wasn't Brendan here for them? If they could just keep the boy growing in Emma, he'd never leave their side at a time like this.

He rounded back to the rear of the house. They still hadn't been joined by any other cars. Backup was supposed to be coming. Where was it? This was properly out in the sticks, but surely this family needed more protection than just the two detectives. He'd texted Madison, asking her to give him a call. On the hands-free in her car, she'd updated him that Foley had gone walkies. Where was *she* going? She'd said she was following up on something and would explain later.

As he reached the back door, he was met by Golds, going the other way. 'I'd bought tea stuff,' she said, 'but they don't have bin bags. Be a darling and chuck them, would you?' She pointed at the wheelie bin stood neatly by the garage and gestured with a mug. He took it and saw it contained a handful of used tea bags. 'There's a full one waiting for you inside.'

Christopher took the cup. Everything about this place was odd. It was as though it was occupied by ghosts, everything too clean and too tidy for a family. And why didn't they have bin bags?

He opened the lid of the wheelie bin. Even this seemed barely used, with only the faintest whiff.

His hand froze, about to tip out the tea bags as a hammer bolt struck.

The body at the morgue—the one that was all battered on the inside. The garbage smell that had accompanied the corpse—the one that the mortician hadn't fully been able to explain. The stench had been nothing more than residual. Just like this bin right here. His mind went to the rust. Some dumpsters were made of metal, huge lumbering things.

It fit. All of it—suddenly it fit.

The man, Jason, must have been in a large dumpster before he'd died.

Now he had to ring Madison again, even if she was off following some lead. He tipped the tea bags out, wincing at the cold tea that dripped over his fingers. He slammed the bin lid shut, scrambled for his phone, and tried her number. No answer, so he sent a text with the bare details, nothing more.

As he pocketed his phone, there was the spit of tyres on gravel. And not just one vehicle, he could tell instantly. Someone had arrived—but as he turned to clock them, he knew straight away—this wasn't the cavalry.

CHAPTER 42

'DOES THAT MAKE sense?' Madison asked, her attention stretched all over the place. Christopher's message had sent her straight on the phone to the mortician.

'Yes, a hundred percent,' answered Mackie now. 'Not just a pretty face, our Christopher. Such an explanation would make perfect sense, and account for all the chemical compounds present on the body. In fact, the more I think about it, the more I think it could only be that.'

Madison stood by her desk, having raced back to the nick. No time to sit down. All the spinning plates were on the cusp of crashing to the ground. Christopher's hunch could be a major break, and she couldn't let it slip by. 'So what are we thinking? He drowned in a big metal garbage dumpster full of water?'

'No, there's not enough water on the lungs for that. He coughed quite a lot up. It was organ trauma and eventual failure that saw him off—so not a drowning.'

'Alright. We know what he died in, that it had to be something to do with the Culpeppers, and that it was recent.'

'All correct, but that middle part is assumption on your part, nothing to do with me.'

'Granted.' Madison breathed out. 'Where would you get a lead on large metal dumpster bins?'

'Far from me to tell you how to do your job, but most bins I see around and about—not that I know much about the world of bins, you understand—are plastic. Steel seems more reserved for the commercial and—'

'Industry.'

'I think you've got yourself a start point.'

'Thanks, Mackie,' she said, sincerely. She sank onto the edge of her desk. Just to take the weight off her calves for a moment was bliss. 'I'm really learning on the job here, aren't I?'

Mackie's voice softened in a way that Madison had previously thought impossible. 'I always thought your predecessor, Foley, was an incredibly young appointment, no matter how good he was. And you're somewhat younger than him again, aren't you?'

Madison didn't answer.

'You're doing brilliant, DI Madison. And you're shaping up to be the best I've ever worked with.'

Madison hated it, but tears swam abruptly in her vision. 'Thank you.'

'Follow your instincts. You'll get there, I've no doubt.'

As she wiped her eyes on her sleeve, she noticed that another Post-It had been added to the desk. She craned her neck to read it: DORIAN TORRANCE IN CUSTODY. PRESUMED CULPEPPER ACCOMPLICE. KHARTHIK.

When one door closed, another opened.

'I'll be in touch. Bye, Mackie.'

She hung up. It had been the most insane day yet, but there was still so much more to do. There was the matter with Dorian—whoever the hell that was—but she also had to get to the safe house.

She checked her watch. Weighed all of her commitments against the promise she'd made to Brendan.

Decision made, she walked straight into the unit hub. Kharthik wasn't there, but Broom was, a picture of diligence, eyes glued to her computer screen, a hand navigating with near psychic precision between a packet of breadsticks, a small tub of dip and then up to her mouth. She never once broke gaze from the screen—quite the feat.

'We've someone in, I believe?'

'Yes, boss. Dorian Torrance is the name we have for him.' She ran through the circumstances of the arrest, as told to her by her colleague. 'I've Kharthik's report. I think he's down near the custody suite now, keeping an eye on him.'

'He fired on an officer?'

'Yeah. A couple of times. Report's got it all.'

'And Kharthik is all right?'

'If anything, he's high as a kite.'

'Cool. Time is of the essence here, and as much as I'd like to stay, I can't. So, after your heroics this morning, if you're up for it…'

Broom's breadstick paused halfway to her mouth as her eyes widened. 'I am.'

'Okay. You lead the interview, Kharthik in support. Obviously, we've got him on firearms offences and firing at a police officer, so he's fucked regardless. Maybe he'll talk like your birdie this morning.'

Broom grinned at the opportunity she'd just been given. 'If he's even half in the mood, I'll have him crooning.'

Madison nodded. 'I know you will. I'll be back to check in later.'

She turned to leave when Broom stopped her.

'Boss? Can I ask? What's going on? You're off out, Christopher is nowhere to be seen, I can't get in touch with him. What's happening?'

'I'll tell you when I can, Broom. But you need to focus. If this bloke in custody is even half as slick as his employer, you're in for a runaround.'

'Yes, boss,' she said, returning to her computer. Madison caught her throw a small fist pump as she left and couldn't help but smile. The world still had good, dedicated people in it, you just had to know where to look. Then, when you've got them, you get them on your side.

She left the main pool hall, up the steps and out through the old wooden doors, then jogged down the corridor to the front desk. She'd have to arrange a pool car to get up to the safe house, as it was a bit of a trip away—but then she saw Monroe bustling from the adjacent corridor, leaving in a hurry.

'Sir!' she called, jogging to catch up with him.

'Yes, DS Madison?' He paused at the front door, already grasping the handle, his mind clearly elsewhere.

She checked around her. Patel was staring hard in the opposite direction, a little too obviously pretending not to be listening.

'Thank you for arranging their safety. Are they all okay?'

He smoothed his tie, but the tension was evident. 'Word from Christopher is they're fine. And don't worry, it's the least we could do for Brendan after everything. But he's not checked in there yet.'

Madison was enthused to see him take his old employee's well-being so close to heart, but she didn't have the headspace to dwell on it. 'He's not? I was going up there now.'

'Me, too. I feel I need to take a direct hand in this. One of our own is under attack; I can't leave his protection to chance.'

'I understand, Sir.' Madison flushed with admiration for her boss. He didn't have to do this, but by taking a personal hand in protecting the Foley family, he was showing just what kind of man he was. The kind of man that you'd want to work for.

'As it happens, I have a car waiting. Do you want to hop in?'

'That would be wonderful, sir.'

She followed him out into the shadows cast by the dipping sun. She felt her muscles relax for the first time all day. Finally, something was going her way.

CHAPTER 43

HARVEY CULPEPPER HAD spent the afternoon in siege mode, keeping his head down, and letting the hell he'd unleashed rain down far away from his sanctuary.

He had moved to his study with a cafetière of freshly ground beans and a pot of hot water, an espresso cup and a sausage roll. He'd sat there with the test match cricket on in the background—England versus India—three phones laid out on his desk, answering whenever one called for his attention. The rest of the time, he brooded.

He was frustrated, and there was a new feeling he was becoming acquainted with, one that the unpredictable rhythms of the cricket never quite managed to distract him from.

Isolation. He felt cut off and alone.

Charlotte was out and about, and worse, she was disagreeing with him. That had never happened before.

He knew she'd taken the jacket back, and in a sense, he could see why—although he'd never admit it. If he couldn't get things back up and going again with the Devil's Defects, who was going to pop up and take that amount of merchandise off his hands? He still had kilos of the stuff. He could perhaps shop it about, see if someone down Birmingham way, or possibly further south, would want to take it.

But players of that scale didn't just emerge.

Harvey was forced to admit—he needed the Defects.

They needed each other.

So maybe Charlotte was right. Maybe it had been a bad idea to kill that lad, despite what he'd done. The kid had gone off Terry Ten Men and tried to change the arrangement, and whether that was coming from Garland Roarke or not, you didn't renegotiate terms, and you didn't do it in the underhand way he had.

It just wasn't cricket.

And now, fresh off the upset of last night's outrage and affront, he'd put out a big money hit on an ex-copper and his family.

Another four. England were performing, god bless them.

It wasn't the killing of Brendan Foley and his family that bothered him, far from it. It was the fact that when you announce a reward for something like that, it goes neon and viral. It travels like wild weeds, attracting all comers, and, while part of Harvey loved the chaos it sparked, that sort of thing was bad for business—not to mention costly and in danger of drawing attention.

Harvey had never done anything like that before. He'd always had his head screwed on tight and let business run the day. What was good for business, after all, was good for him. Emotions taken right out of it.

One of the phones burred softly on the desk's leather inlay—the middle one. That was interesting. Each of his phones had a different purpose, but for the middle one to ring? This usually meant something good.

'Hello,' he answered, before listening. After a moment, he spoke with that pure confidence he knew so well, practised and smooth. 'I'm sure we could work something out.'

He listened again and smiled. 'I've an idea. Would you let me make a connection?'

The caller's reply made Harvey Culpepper smile.

'Very good,' he said. 'All right, leave it with me. Nice one.'

He hung up. Buzzed with the adrenaline of a possible resolution, he picked up the phone on the far left, and placed a call. As it rang out, England hit a clean sparkling six over midwicket.

BRENDAN DROVE OUT of Stanhope as fast as the car would carry him and jetted between the rolling swathes of yellow, the dried grass covering the moors of Weardale mirroring his own worn-out, barren feelings. There was music to face. Ignoring road traffic laws, reasoning that nobody would see him out here on the moors, he called Madison on the hands-free.

'Where the hell have you been?' she said by way of hello. From the sound of an engine and her tinny voice, Brendan could tell she was in a car too.

'Don't ask,' he said. 'I'm sorry I had to go, I'm sorry about your car, but... I had to go do something. It doesn't matter now.'

'You're too right it doesn't matter. You've got GMP and Warrington police pulling out all the stops for you, least you can do is as we ask.'

'I'm sorry, Iona,' he said again. 'Are my family safe?'

'Oh, now you ask! Yeah, they're fine. They're at a safe house location, I'll ping you the details. Get there as quick as you can.'

'Thanks. And Iona, I'm so sorry about all of this. But thank you for helping me and my family.'

She was quiet for a moment, and he was sure she was talking to someone else—*who was that?*—when she sighed. 'It's all right. But they need you. I'm on my way there myself, so I'll see you shortly.'

'I'm going straight there.'

'Thank god for that.' He could hear the sarcasm in her voice, and it made him smile.

Perhaps things would be okay after all.

CHAPTER 44

MIM POURED HER third cup of coffee into the sink after realising, midway through the dregs of the second cup, that the caffeine buzz was doing nothing for her nerves. Fidgeting, her hands empty and useless, she stood by the back door.

In the short time they'd been at the safe house, and with every passing moment that her husband had failed to appear, she'd felt a growing finality creep over her. Not about their plight, nor about their immediate survival.

But about her relationship.

Brendan had jeopardised them. With hard-headed moves and ill-advised schemes, he had set them on a crash course with tragedy.

Yes, he was stubborn. Yes, he was driven.

But there came a point when both of those characteristics stopped being praiseworthy and morphed into selfishness.

He was sullen. Morose. The family had survived other tragedies, but this time he was lost. The family needed him and needed him not simply to do the right thing by them—but to put them first, regardless. And Mim couldn't shake the feeling that he'd failed in this most important part of being a father.

That wasn't what good husbands did.

As she listened to the birds from the rolling moorland behind the house, she felt safe in the knowledge that the two detectives were patrolling the front.

At least they were protecting them.

Her mind was made up.

If they got out of this, and when the dust was settled, she'd have to leave Brendan for the sake of her boys. Good parents prioritised their children, and no priorities were ever felt more keenly than a mother's.

She felt tears gather in her eyes, but they didn't spill—because she knew that leaving Brendan would be the right thing to do. He was on a crusade of self-harm. A downward spiral of self-destruction. And now that meant that bad things were coming for them all.

It took her a moment to register a movement from behind the garage. Three men dressed head to toe in black, including balaclavas. She had to tell the police. Christopher. Golds. The men moved silent as a dream, but one detail was all too real—they were holding guns.

Fortunately, they hadn't spotted her.

Moving on instinct, she retreated back into the house—to her children, their safety uppermost in her mind. It was what any good parent would do, and it bolstered her decision to leave Brendan once this was over.

Assuming any of them lived that long.

CHAPTER 45

WHEN HE HEARD Mim shout from the back of the house, Christopher knew that they were on their own. No firearms team could make it here in time.

He ran from the front windows, where he had been keeping watch, straight back into the hall, and he nearly crashed into Mim coming the other way. Her eyes had gone pin sharp, her jaw set. 'They're here,' she said. 'Three of them.' He didn't have to ask what side *they* were on—but he did find it alarming that they'd found the Foleys so fast.

'Get upstairs,' he instructed, and she took the stairwell. He went for the back door and got there in time to see a man in black fill the porch door. Christopher threw it shut, twisted the back door key, and slid the top deadbolt. It was an old door, of the *Keep Trespassers Out* variety, and would offer some resistance. But if these guys had brought guns, that would be a different story.

'We won't hurt anybody if you let us in now,' came the shout from the kitchen.

'Golds!' shouted Christopher back down into the belly of the house. She appeared from the front sitting room.

'I've called it in; GMP is coming.' She joined him.

'Did they give a time?'

'ASAP.' She undid her jacket, to show a holster on her hip, from which she withdrew a sleek pistol.

'Are you firearms?' It was rare to find a copper, not least a detective, who had firearms training. It was like a Christmas present in Christopher's eyes.

'I don't advertise it.'

'Count of five,' came the shout from the other side of the door again. 'Five, four—'

'We have a firearms-trained officer in here with a gun pointed at this door,' Christopher shouted through. 'Go back to where you came from, so we can avoid any injuries.'

That cut the count off and left a short-lived silence before bullets started firing through the door, splintering the wood, chips exploding all over the kitchen.

'Go through to the dining room, see if you can drive them back via the rear windows,' Christopher shouted over the hail of cracking wood. Golds crouched and scrambled through. Seconds later, gunshots rang out from the dining room, which paused the assault on the back door.

Golds was singlehandedly giving them a fighting chance.

Before the attack on the door resumed, he grabbed the wooden kitchen table, upended it, and pushed it against the door, followed immediately by every chair he could find.

But then there was the sound of glass breaking from the front. He left the kitchen and ran through to find a man in black breaking the last shards of pane away from the front windows in the sitting room, and it was clear now that this group were circling the house. As he ran across the faded carpet, Christopher wondered again how on earth they'd managed to find them so fast. Just how connected were this group? Who even were they?

He grabbed the coffee table, sturdy despite being decades old, and swung it as hard as he could at the man climbing through the broken window. The man saw it coming, and twisted, catching the tabletop flush on the shoulder, which must have hurt like hell. It did, however, slow down the man's progress just enough for Christopher to shoulder charge him back out of the window—but Christopher caught his arm on the last jagged teeth stuck in the window frame, shredding his jacket sleeve right through to his forearm. He bit his lip at the cut, blood seeping from two distinct wounds. He heard Mim shout from the upstairs landing. It sounded like: 'Get out!'

They were inside.

The man on the other side of the window brought a gun up—but Christopher was right there, and grabbed his wrist with two hands. The gun kicked twice, bullets flying around the sitting room, but Christopher held firm. It scared the life out of him, feeling the gun spit like that, knowing those bullets were meant for him—but he remembered that he had a new son he was waiting to meet, and he wasn't going to miss that.

It gave him a burst of righteous strength, and, like stripping a wire, he managed to pull the gun clean out of the attacker's hands. It was heavy and steady and gave confidence. As soon as it was in his hands, he turned and pointed it back at the man, who dropped out of sight beyond the window.

Turning back round, Christopher followed the sounds of a struggle, and ran back into this unsafest of safe houses.

THE MAN EMERGED from the dining room. He had a gun in his right hand. Mim also saw that he hadn't spotted her, crouching on the upper stairs. As he came around the corner, he poked his head into the kitchen, gun first, and she saw she had a choice.

Sit on the stairs and wait to be spotted, then be shot like a dog.

Or dive down, make a go of it, and try to get that gun.

It was only when she was mid-air, sailing towards the man, that she knew she'd gone for the latter.

Her hip made first contact with the intruder, right between the shoulder blades, and it crushed him into the door frame, his body collapsing, forcing all the air from his lungs. But as they landed in a heap of limbs on the kitchen threshold, she felt him kick and roll away, and that gun started to swing up towards her.

It terrified her, watching that black shark eye of the barrel point spin to look at her. Then she heard her youngest child crying, muffled behind one of the upstairs doors. It gave her a jolt of unfathomable resolve. She dived forward, pinning the man's head to the floor, which stopped his arm from rising, and she found herself screaming 'Get out!', punching and kicking any part of him she could get to, fighting for her life and her children's.

A crash from inside the kitchen made her look up, but only for a second, to see a boot kicking through an open hole in the door. A hand reached in the gap and shoved the table back, as chairs toppled. The boot started kicking again, allowing sunlight to flood in alongside the size tens.

She fought and scratched, and ripped the man's balaclava off. Dark hair sprang out in all directions and the stink of sweat filled the air. The gun went off in his hand, but the bullet only managed to fly above Mim's head and into the ceiling. It was followed by another, which popped the lightbulb in the hallway and rained glass down on them like malevolent raindrops. The tide was turning, when fresh gunfire suddenly rained over their heads, causing them both to duck. Mim didn't know where it was coming from, until she saw Christopher jump over them both, shooting at the kitchen door, forcing whoever was trying to get in to retreat.

She felt liquid in her eyes, staining her vision red, as the man rolled out from under her. She didn't have the strength to stop him. He ran towards the front of the house away from Christopher, firing behind him as he went. Mim scrambled back up the stairs and resolved to stay there as a barrier between the shooting and her children. Mick was crying, but tears were better than anything else. Then, she could hear a car horn blaring, and she hoped and prayed that sanctuary was imminent.

CHAPTER 46

MADISON AND MONROE heard the gunshots before they even laid eyes on Schofield Farm.

They shared a horrified glance, then Monroe booted the accelerator. The car kicked forward, around the reservoir on the left, and there was the house.

Two black shapes were at the front windows, one of which was smashed. Flashes from the other windows betrayed the fact that more shots were being fired.

Monroe flew the car up the side road. Black-clad figures darted around to the rear of the building. 'Sounds like it's all happening at the back.' He shoved the door open, but Madison stopped him.

'Wait! Turn the car around, so that we can be ready for a quick escape,' she said. 'I'll go in the front, get the Foleys out. Be ready.'

Monroe looked at the house, uncertain—but an extra sound of gunfire seemed to make his mind up for him. 'Don't play hero, grab the Foleys and pull them out.' Then he nodded and said: '*Go.*'

Madison leapt out of the car and climbed up the inclined rockery that led to the front garden. Gunshots still rang out from the rear, but she felt no fear, just drive and purpose. *Find Foley's family. Get them out.*

She checked first, then hopped in through the broken front window, landing in an empty sitting room that was strewn with debris. The rest of the house sounded like it was playing host to a riot. She moved quickly to the door and peered around the frame into the hallway.

A man ran straight into her, darkly clothed, trying to tug a balaclava back on. His eyes landed in the cut-out holes, just in time for him to see her. He pulled his hands up, one with a gun, but Madison was quicker, spinning into a highlight reel left hook. The man's jaw crunched under Madison's knuckles, which themselves cracked with the perfection of the impact. He crumpled into the doorframe and slumped there, dazed. She reached for her cuffs, wondering what she could attach him to, but her eyes were drawn to the far end of the corridor.

DS Christopher was at the door to what appeared to be an overturned kitchen, fighting off a would-be attacker. And clambering up the stairs was a woman Madison assumed to be Brendan's wife. She was drenched in blood. Using Christopher's cover fire, she left the downed assailant, reached the stairs, and grasped Mim Foley's shoulder.

'Miriam,' she said. Mrs Foley turned round, eyes wide with fear, her hand raised, ready to fight back. 'I'm police! DI Madison, I'm here to get you out.'

The panic faded from Mim's eyes, but only partly.

'Where is everyone?' Madison asked.

'The boys are locked in the upstairs bathroom,' Mim replied breathlessly.

'And Brendan?'

A shadow passed over Mim's face. 'He isn't here.'

Jesus.

'Let me check upstairs, then let's go.' She left Mim crouched on the stairs and ran upstairs. She counted three bedrooms and the single remaining door, the only one shut, had to be the bathroom. She went to it, as the gunfire slowed on the floor below. 'Boys?' she said, knocking quietly. 'Police. Open up, let's get going.'

'Is Mum okay?' asked a fraught voice.

'She's absolutely fine. There's a car outside.'

There was the sound of a bolt sliding, then the door swung open to reveal a teenager who looked like a rough approximation of his father, albeit twenty years younger.

'Hello, you two,' said Madison, feeling a flush of protection, as she ruffled the toddler's curls, trying to remember if Brendan had ever told her his name. Tears streaked the youngster's red cheeks. 'Hello, young man, how are you?' She gave a wide smile, which the little one tried his best to return.

'Stay low,' she told the older boy. Dan, she thought he was called. 'When we get downstairs, turn right and head straight for the front door.'

'Okay,' he said.

'It'll all be over soon.'

They went carefully down the stairs, the commotion now appearing to be located outside the house at the back, and she silently prayed that her colleagues were all right. Mim met them on the stairs and took Mick, who gurgled at the sight of his mother. Madison checked the kitchen—Christopher was pointing a gun through the ragged gaps in the broken back door. He saw her.

'Go, go,' he shouted. 'Get them out the front. But be careful.'

Madison nodded and turned to the three Foleys behind her. 'Follow me, heads down, move quickly,' she said. They moved along the hall to the front of the house. Madison grimaced when she saw that the man she'd left dazed was gone. No time to sweat that now. There were answering gunshots coming from a back room behind them, but they kept heading determinedly to the thick front door with its diamond wedge of glass window.

Madison peered through. She could see the roof of the chief's car on the road below. He'd left it in the perfect spot. She turned to the Foleys.

'Straight down the garden. Don't wait for me. There's a car at the bottom. Get in it.'

She threw the door open and emerged into the sunlight, the grand reservoir looking so big and close they could all just step straight into it. The gunfire at the back of the house sounded distant, and unrelated, like there was some industrial work going on nearby.

They ran down the garden and leapt off the small drystone wall onto the roof of the car, before sliding off and getting in, all the while playing pass the parcel with Mick. Monroe jumped out.

'Take them,' he said. 'Back to the station, make them safe.'

Madison almost shouted in reply. 'No, I need to help Christopher!'

Monroe's jaw was set. 'Our goal was to protect the Foleys, that is the best way of doing so.'

'Sir—'

'That is an order, DI Madison. Your predecessor wasn't great at following those and look where it's got us all.' He pointed at the house. Gunfire rang from inside.

Madison relented and ran around to the driver's side. 'What about you?' she asked.

'I'm going to take charge.'

She felt clarity and protocol kick in. 'Three attackers at least. Mostly at the back of the house. Christopher is in the kitchen. One attacker unaccounted for near the front.'

'Thank you.' Monroe stalked purposefully around the house, up the side.

Madison got in the front of the car. He'd left the engine running, and the Foleys were in the rear seats, buckling up. She pressed the accelerator, the engine roared back at her, goading her on, and they gunned it out of there with a squeal of rubber which echoed clear across the water. It was only as they were moving that Madison realised she had been in and out of the car in under two minutes at Schofield Farm. Two minutes that had saved three lives.

CHAPTER 47

THE BLACK-CLAD group, this kill party, had been forced back to the garage, Christopher's gunfire twinning with Golds' from the dining-room windows to push them back. So far, he'd been careful not to hit anyone—the paperwork would be complicated enough when he had to explain that he was firing a gun as a detective—but he was damned if he was going to let these people get at the Foleys, no matter the trouble it might land him in.

And they were winning.

Nobody had been shot, but the kill party had lost guns, plus the tactical advantage. The police and the Foleys… so far, they were surviving this siege.

Golds appeared. 'I can't see them anymore. I think we've pushed them back behind the garage. She swapped an empty magazine for a fresh one from her hip.

'God, I'm glad you're here,' Christopher said.

'That got hairy in a heartbeat,' she replied.

'Any idea who they are?'

'No.' The two of them scanned the back garden. 'But they weren't the best of the best. Average. I'm assuming a little group that wanted to make themselves famous by cashing in on this reward—the big worry is how they knew we were here.'

It could be that one of their forces had a leak—size unclear. Whether it was merely letting slip that GMP had a safe house out here, or far worse—someone in GMP or Warrington Police was dropping big hints, most likely with a cash blowback in mind. Either way, it was corruption, and corruption was bad news for everybody.

He started moving the chairs to open the destroyed back door, tiredness pulling at him. When he emerged, and saw the rear driveway was empty, the relief was febrile, almost liquid. He checked the rest of the house. Empty. They were alone. They'd survived it.

They'd got away—Mim and those kids. Escaped with Madison.

He walked round to the front of the house, stood on the front stoop like it was his homestead, looked at the reservoir and smiled broadly. *We're going to manage this,* he thought.

His mood was boosted further when Monroe appeared walking up the drive. He was red in the face, somehow even more livid in the light of the golden hour and beaded with perspiration.

'They've gone. Off over the moors,' he panted. 'I watched them go, tail between their legs. Got a few descriptions we can work with as well. I'm just sorry we didn't get here sooner to join in the fight.'

Christopher smiled. 'No worries. And thank you, sir.'

'I think there's a commendation in here for you somewhere. Or at least a yearly Christmas bottle of scotch from the Foley family.'

They stood together and overlooked the water as adrenaline receded.

'I think you better take this for your report,' said Christopher, handing Monroe the pistol. 'I know, at least, I definitely shouldn't have it.'

Monroe took it like it was a dead animal. 'I'll handle it.' He pocketed the gun and took in the view for the first time.

'What now?' Christopher asked, as the first cool breeze of evening hit his skin.

'Now, we have to take down Culpepper. That's the only way forward. As long as the threat remains active against Foley's life, then this game of soldiers just keeps repeating until we are done and dusted—and people die.'

'I think Madison has a plan there.'

'Only question is, where's Foley?'

With all the timing of a poorly scripted movie, Madison's car came around the bend below the house—with none other than Brendan Foley behind the wheel. The car stopped sharply.

Christopher felt a strange sense of anger when he saw him, while all Monroe could do was laugh bitterly. 'Come on,' said the Super. 'Let's get a ride back to the station.'

By the time they'd got around to the driveway circle, Brendan had parked and was getting out.

'Don't bother,' shouted Monroe. 'They're with Madison, on their way back to the station.'

'Where the hell have you been?' asked Christopher.

'Is everyone alright? My family okay?' Brendan asked breathlessly.

'All fine, all fine,' said Monroe. 'You need to get us back to the station. Your family's on the way there now. And you have some explaining to do.'

'I suppose I do,' Foley said quietly, while looking at the back wall of the house, adorned with bullet holes and strewn with masonry chunks. 'This place looks like a warzone.' He turned to the other men. 'Thank you. For everything you've done here to make them safe.'

Christopher hesitated, then nodded in acknowledgement. Foley should have been alongside them.

'Give me a moment,' Monroe said, walking to the house.

Foley and Christopher got in, the former closing his door and hitting the ignition without a moment's pause.

'Where were you?' Christopher asked. He couldn't stop the note of accusation in his voice.

'I had something to take care of. I needed to… I knew they'd be safe with you, mate.'

'They needed *you*, Brendan. Those boys needed their dad.'

Brendan fell silent.

After liaising with Golds at the back porch door, Monroe jumped in the back.

'Golds has got the scene, officers imminent,' said Monroe. 'It's their safehouse, after all. I'll just have a bit of explaining to do. But, given the circumstances, I think I can do that by phone. We've a family to protect, after all.'

At that, Christopher looked pointedly at Brendan, but he was already reversing.

They set off, leaving the battered safe house up on the hill. GMP would probably have to sell it—there was nothing safe about that place anymore.

'You know where you're going?' he asked Brendan.

'Yup.' He looked bruised—not just on the outside, but the inside too. Whilst they'd been saving his family, Brendan had clearly been up to something that wasn't much fun as well.

Christopher's phone burred in his pocket, and he saw Emma Morgan's name come up on the screen. He answered, but before he could even say hello a rush of words spilled into his ear.

'They rushed through the results! They've just rung me. We can keep him!'

With the impact of a hammer strike, Christopher felt his heart fracture wide—but in the best way possible. It was opening, making room to allow the warmth and love of a new life to take root. He hadn't been able to allow himself this before. But now, with these results, he could.

'Did you hear that, Tom? We can keep him—we can keep our boy! You're going to be a daddy! For real, you can say it now, you're going to be a daddy!'

His eyes started to burn, and a new feeling came with it. A happiness so acute, he'd never experienced it before. He felt like he might burst. 'I love you,' was all he could whisper.

'I love you, too. So much. We can talk about names, buy a pram now, can't we?' He could hear the hope in Emma's voice.

'Yes, we can,' he whispered, realising that he'd been clinging on to the same hope all this time. His throat closed, tears swelling, as a new future opened up before him—a place in his heart that he'd refused to acknowledge until now for an unborn son.

'I'll see you later.' He couldn't say more, acutely aware of the men pressed in around him.

'I love you t—.'

CHAPTER 48

'I DON'T KNOW what he was so excited about, but at least those were nice last words,' said Monroe, a smoking gun in a shaking hand, while pieces of DS Tom Christopher's brains sat de-skulled all over the dashboard.

In sudden horror, Foley nearly barrelled straight off the road. In the rear-view mirror, Monroe at least had the manners to look shaken and appalled with himself.

'When he gave me the gun… I couldn't help it. And I take no pleasure in what I just had to do, Brendan. None at all. But if it was going to happen, it had to happen out here where there's nobody about.'

Brendan was numb—at the sudden obscene violence, and at the abrupt loss of his friend.

DS Tom Christopher was a *good* man. And he was slumped next to him with a hole in his head, the remnants of his phone on the floor, and stuff that should have been inside him was *everywhere*. The emotional conversation that Brendan had overheard, the final thing the man had felt and experienced…

'I'm sorry you had to see it,' said Monroe again, and it was only then that Foley saw that the pistol was now trained on the back of *his* head.

'You… you *bastard*,' was all he could say.

'I know,' said the chief superintendent, with a sigh. 'I know.'

'Why?' Brendan was openly crying now. He punched the wheel and screamed. 'You bastard, *why*?'

'Stay calm, Brendan, please. I know it's not easy given…' Monroe peered over the back of the passenger seat to see the mess. 'Jesus Christ, we'll never get anywhere like that. Pull in somewhere quiet when you can.' It was like he'd defaulted to practicality in the face of abject horror. He started to rummage in his suit jacket pockets, alternating the pistol from hand to hand, never moving it from the back of Brendan's head. They were still in the middle of nowhere, so it was easy to pull up a single-track farm lane, and over by a hedge.

Monroe got out quickly, retraining the gun on Brendan as he now stood by the car. He pulled a white handkerchief out of his trouser pocket.

'Put Christopher in the boot, and clear up,' he said, handing Brendan the handkerchief through the open window. 'You don't have to do that great a job with it; we just need to get there without attracting any unwanted attention.'

Brendan got out, sniffing softly. 'You fuckin' traitor. You're taking me to Culpepper, aren't you?'

'Yes. I've three wives, remember… and a million quid is a million quid. The price is the same whether you're alive or dead by the way, so unless you want to end up in the bed with the dearly departed, I suggest you get a move on. Really doesn't matter to me, either way. I'll keep a lookout, so chop chop.'

'I hope you burn in hell.' Brendan walked round the side and opened the door. He had to catch Christopher before he slumped out onto the grass verge, and in doing so, it showed the man's fatal injuries in all their destructive glory. His shaven head had a small hole at the back, a black-red dot as big a twenty pence piece, with a cavernous opening forged in split bone on the front, above his right eye—which was still, somehow, intact and open. 'I've got you, mate,' he found himself whispering to his dead friend. 'I've got you.'

PART 3

BAPTISMS FOR GHOSTS

CHAPTER 49

HORROR BOLTED THROUGH Seabreeze with electric potency. Here, in a hoarder's bedroom, with a couple of corpses that took their last breath the best part of a year ago. And someone had arrived.

He stared at the bodies on the bed before glancing around the room—nowhere to hide. Except...

God, he was going to have to get beneath the bed. The one with two shrouded stiffs on it, like some sort of macabre morgue slab. Could he bring himself to do it? But what choice did he have? Seabreeze looked at the two bodies and rolled under the bed frame. Or, at least, he tried to. He couldn't fit into the gap, so he ended up lying at the foot of the bed, and shuffling himself in beneath the very centre line of the mattress, like an earthworm burrowing into filth.

Being found in a civilian's home—even *this* home—was trespassing. And Seabreeze wasn't a police officer. He was support, at best. He had no right to be here.

But careers and livelihoods were on the line. Getting caught would inevitably lead to the discovery of the bodies. Further career suicide.

So he burrowed as if his life depended on it.

Steps on the stairs. A voice getting louder.

He covered his mouth and nose to ward off the stench of mould and dust, and froze.

'She didn't take us serious, boys. Not one bit.'

215

It had to be Wilson—and he wasn't alone. Fear added a nice extra layer to Seabreeze's horror. The more sets of eyes there were, the lower his chances of a clean getaway became.

'We'll have to show her. Show the other three, too. You fuck with us, you get yourself *fucked*.'

He was ranting, and his accomplices were obviously happy to let him vent. Did that suggest Wilson was the leader? 'We're going to show them all,' he said. 'Treasure is treasure at the end of the day, isn't it, boys?'

The voice turned loud and near. Seabreeze guessed that Wilson was looking into the room to check on the bodies. 'Fucking jokers,' he seethed, before moving off down the hall.

'You won't believe it, Mum,' he called ahead. 'World's gone mad.'

Mum.

Holy shit, thought Seabreeze. Had he broken into someone's house while an old woman was inside? She was dead, wasn't she? He'd been so sure the place was empty. So much for that. This situation had gone from one layer of hell to the next.

He couldn't hear any other footsteps on the stairs, so his accomplices must be cooling their heels downstairs somewhere, although Seabreeze couldn't picture a single place anyone could relax in the downstairs of this garbage-themed fun house.

He just didn't know how to get around this. How to make a clean getaway. People upstairs, people downstairs, and he was stuck under a bed on which lay a couple of year-old corpses.

'The disrespect is huge, Mum,' Wilson was shouting, marching back down the hall. 'The disconnect between law and the public has never been greater. She didn't take me seriously. At *all*.'

There was an impact, two in quick succession. Wilson was hitting something, taking out his impotent rage on a wall maybe.

Seabreeze didn't think any part of this man was stable. None of him. He was a cracked little despot, living in a kingdom of filth, somehow with minions.

'I will show her. I will show all four of them. That's the last time I get disrespected like that. Even if I have to drive you both to the old baths myself.' The voice grew louder on the last couple of words, and the air in the room shifted. Footsteps creaked across the floorboards towards the bed; the vibrations travelled up through Seabreeze's fingertips.

Then the bed groaned and dipped. Seabreeze quickly turned his head to one side—just in time—as the mattress springs sank closer all the way down the frame.

My god.

Wilson had laid down on the bed. Right between the two cadavers.

'We'll show them, won't we, lads?'

And it all became clear to Seabreeze. Nobody was here. Not a soul. This man, this fractured, tortured man, was talking to ghosts.

Then, with the suddenness of a spell, Wilson began to snore, and Seabreeze, his nose full of mould and dusty fibres, and his mouth pressed tightly shut unless he wanted to suck the grime clean out of the carpet, started to panic.

CHAPTER 50

'YOU FIRED TWICE on an unarmed officer,' said DC Isabelle Broom in the interview cubby at Warrington Police station. 'Do you dispute that?'

Dorian Torrance sat opposite with his solicitor, a crap-suited slickster who looked like he'd dipped his hair in chip fat. She knew he was the lawyer used by the Culpepper family and associates; he'd been to this station before. Looking at him now, with his confident air, Broom realised that she relished it whenever her opposition lived up to their full cliché. Corrupt solicitor in the pay of a gang leader? Bring it on. She'd loved their interview, the spectacular to and fro before landing the killer strike, which unravelled the perp's story in a withering instant. She had known *exactly* what she was doing.

Dorian looked at the solicitor, who nodded once. 'No comment,' parroted Harvey Culpepper's right-hand man.

'And the gun?'

Again, predictably. 'No comment.'

Broom had an answer prepped and in the chamber. '"No comment" is a phrase that you see people instructed to use all the time, but it hardly assuages assumptions of guilt. "No comment" on repeat sounds like you don't want to talk. Which sounds like guilt. So, if you're innocent, which, from the front the pair of you are putting on, I'd suggest is highly unlikely— you might like to try something else.' She paused for dramatic effect. 'Especially when the man who says you shot at him is sat opposite you.'

She gave Kharthik the scantest of nods. '"No comment" really isn't going to fly too well in these circumstances. You're going to need more than that.'

Dorian leaned right into the mic, locked eyes with Kharthik and then Broom, and spoke the words again in a drawn-out taunt. 'No... comment.'

Broom looked at the solicitor. 'This is the course of action you have advised your client to take?'

The slickster solicitor leaned into the table mic. 'You heard my client. If you missed it, I suggest you rewind the tape.'

Broom leaned back. 'So, what are you suggesting happened? How do we all happen to be sat here today? Did we all just end up in this room by happenstance?'

Nobody answered; Broom had known they wouldn't. But this was the first of many knife twists she had planned.

'In your own words, Dorian, can you tell me how you came to be here today?'

'It's a misunderstanding?'

'How would you define firing an unlicensed firearm at a police detective a misunderstanding?'

'I didn't say anything about that. I am saying, you've got the wrong guy.'

Broom turned to Kharthik, who shook his head. The set of his jaw took her back. She'd never seen him like this.

Kharthik suddenly leaned into the mic and with a prickle of unease, Broom felt control of the situation loosen.

But before he could even open his mouth to speak, an ear-piercing noise filled the room—no, the whole building. An alarm. The fire alarm? She wasn't sure. This interview was over. For now.

CHAPTER 51

THE MISSION BAR was busy, as it always was when dusk crept in to curl good intentions at the edges, and lure nice guys out to play. Shots were poured amongst a sea of leather, patches that had once divided were worn now in communion, as toast after toast was raised to Jason—a casualty of playing hardball with businessmen who had no class.

With every deferential nod, every pat on the shoulder, every commiserating half-smile, Garland could see how serious his quandary was.

Some things just weren't done.

If it got out that he was fraternising with cops, that he was thinking of selling his lifestyle out, he'd become a pariah. Relationships would shatter. Everything would fall.

But only—*only*—if it got out.

He could see by the empty bottles already amassing, that sooner rather than later the evening would morph from respectful wake to a raising of hell. He couldn't afford to get tuned. Certain decisions couldn't wait. But if he ducked out early, people would talk. Could he claim that he was leaving for business? That might work. At least to his boys. His Defects.

In a sudden leap, he nimbly climbed onto the bar, and stood in a wide stance. The barman handed him up a bottle of vodka with a pouring spout attached to the bottle neck.

'Oi, oi, oi!' he shouted, and a volley of repeating cries repeated his call back at him, word spreading through the crowd that Garland was getting ready to address them. He wasn't entirely sure how to say what he needed to, but this was what leaders did. They shaped a story, moulded the truth, to make things happen. The reality behind the myth-making was often far different, but that wasn't what mattered. Uniting the crew—that's what was really important.

In this case, he had to pay respects to a man who'd cost him hundreds of thousands, who'd brought the police directly to his door, and had clearly acted behind his back. To make matters worse, Garland still didn't know what he'd done to make that Scouse bastard kill him.

'What a scene,' he said, casting his glance across a sea of faces. 'I see patches from all over the country. I can't tell you how proud that makes me feel. We are grateful. *I* am grateful. It's amazing how easy it can be to see sense, it's just sad that it has to take something like *this* to make it happen.'

In that moment, he knew his decision was made.

Garland was out of pocket. Desperately so. He was tied to mortgages that, without a change in circumstance, he couldn't hope to pay. The Defects had done well in puffing themselves up to plug the hole in the Mancunian drug supply chain, but without cash and manpower, that would disappear very quickly.

But... all of that would disappear if the Culpeppers were gone. Garland and the Devil's Defects could take their spot, take their contacts, and expand to cover both territories, and every one of the thirty miles in between.

Beyond, if necessary.

He realised with a start that he'd stopped addressing the crowd, so he styled it out with a deep, shuddering sigh.

Leaders had hard decisions to make, with their charges' welfare hanging in the mix. And while his followers wouldn't approve of snitching, it would certainly keep their pockets filled. It was just a question of how to make it work, and how to make sure he came out of it clean and shining. A plan was forming as he stood there, saying words that were nothing more than placeholders, while the real mental machinations took place.

That copper, Madison, had offered him a way out—and as much as he hated accepting anything from a copper, it was a genuine chance at not just clearing the slate, but if he played smart as hell, it would give him and the Defects a shot at something much bigger. If he played this crowd right, he would have an army at his disposal for those much bigger plans.

Decision made. Now to spout some bullshit that would tick all the right boxes.

'Too long, we've been outsiders. For too long, we've been looked down upon, and dismissed. Marginalised, laughed at. We've let that happen. We all have…' He glanced around the room again, pointedly making eye contact with face after face. 'Not one of us is free from blame. Petty squabbles have distracted us from what our way of life is all about. Brotherhood. What good is brotherhood if we turn away from the man stood next to us? What does it mean to extol a code, but not live by it? It leads to the events that bring us here. The Devil's Defects is just one name, one patch, under a huge tribal banner. This affects every one of us, and colours us all with that same shame. Togetherness has been forgotten. Togetherness is what we must reclaim.'

The room was silent, the audience mesmerised.

'But we put that aside for now. Because tonight is about a brother lost. And so… to Jason.' He held up the bottle like an Olympic flame. 'The lad was loyal, willing and dedicated. He'd put brotherhood before anything else. Tonight is not the occasion for anger or blame. Tonight is for celebrating the life of a young man who, like so many brothers before, has gone too soon. We drink, we laugh and we remember—together. To those who've gone…'

Every glass in the venue was lifted heavenward, as Garland finished his customary toast line.

'We say goodbye, our son.'

A sombre chorus resonated to the rafters.

'Now, let's get pissed up and smile. Bar's free. Fill your boots to the toecaps.'

Cheering erupted, but another voice cut through, from beneath Garland's feet. 'To Garland Roarke!'

Garland glanced down. It was Fin, looking up at him with an almost familial love. Garland hated him for it, just for a second, but when the crowd repeated the toast, and drank to him, he forgave him.

Poor Fin. If only he knew.

He climbed down from the bar, taking Fin's proffered hand to protect his knees, and dropped to the floor. With the vodka bottle, he filled every outstretched glass, and made his way through the crowd. Bikers got tainted with all sorts of stereotypes, and a lot of them were accurate—hell, Garland himself even played up to a number of them to protect the Defects' image. But no outsider would ever give credit for, nor understand, the level of love in the room. The mood was buoyant, all beefs quashed.

If he pulled this off…

He opened the chipboard door to the back office, and slipped inside, allowing the door to swing shut behind him. He stood alone in the dark for a moment, then dropped onto the sofa, not bothering with the light switch. He dragged out his mobile phone and the screen cast a half-light, as he began to place the call. If this was ever going to happen, it had to be while the iron was hot.

CHAPTER 52

MADISON'S NERVES WERE abuzz. They'd been lucky at Schofield House. Damn lucky.

When they'd been stuffed into Monroe's car, and Madison had jumped behind the wheel, it had seemed like the safest place in the world to be. Bulletproof glass and a reinforced chassis, Monroe's job ride was their best option. But where to go?

There was only one option. The cop shop.

As she cruised across the top roads, then down from Rivington Pike, Mim Foley bravely held it together while her sons cried into her shoulders, their age differences entirely forgotten. Madison found thoughts of Hoyt following her all the way down the road—the copper who had secretly been on the Culpepper payroll. Surely, that particular mole had been weeded out and dealt with. Surely the force was clean. But still… they'd been discovered in their safe house. They'd been ratted out.

'Can I ask you something?' Mim said, out of the blue. In the rear-view mirror, Madison could see that her sons were finally hushed and sleeping against her.

'Anything, Mim.'

'You understand my husband better than I do. I want to know something.'

Madison felt acute discomfort. 'I hope you don't mean—'

'I'm not talking about that. I just want to know why… Why didn't he come with us today? Why didn't he come to protect us like he should have? Like any husband would do?' Finally, despite all her strength, Mim started to cry, silently, to not disturb her boys.

'I know. It doesn't look good. But Brendan is the most committed man I've ever met, and he was a brilliant policeman. If he wasn't there today, it was for a reason.'

Mim turned her face to hide the pain etched there. 'He always told me how much he tried to keep work and home separate. This was one of those days when we really could have done with the two of them meeting.'

It was hard to respond to that. But Madison still found herself reasoning away his behaviour. 'I think he realised the target was firmly on him—that no one would go after you and the boys if he wasn't there. It was a gamble to keep you safe, and unfortunately it didn't work.'

'I don't know him anymore. Since everything that happened last year, with his dad and everything, he's just not the same man.'

Madison wondered how much she knew. What did Mim Foley know about the events that led to her husband leaving the service? And how incriminating was that information where Madison was concerned?

'These are conversations for husband and wife,' she said. 'What I do know is that your family has been through an awful lot, and we need to get you all safe and together as quickly as we can. I won't rest until we've done that, okay, Mim? I promise you.'

In the back, Mim smiled at last. 'Thank you. Brendan always spoke very highly of you.'

'Brendan was the best cop I ever worked with. But things change. I don't know what makes him tick anymore, but I can promise you his sense of duty is still there, strong as ever.'

'What did he do to bring this on us all?'

Madison didn't know how to answer. Cop code was funny, and pointed and irreversible. Brendan wasn't a cop anymore, but you didn't dob your colleagues in to other coppers or family. You looked after each other.

But that woman in the back, so strong, so resolute—so used up by this situation—clearly deserved better than what Brendan was giving her.

'He did something, didn't he?' Mim pressed. 'Something hot-headed, and stupid, and now he's got lunatics shooting at our kids.' The sobs started again, harder this time, and her eldest child woke.

'It's alright, Mum,' said Dan. 'It's okay. Dad will come.'

Madison's heart broke looking at the boy, who for all the world believed in his dad and the choices he made on their behalf. But there was no denying it, and no way to doll it up into something more palatable. Brendan Foley had sentenced his family to death when he started meddling in criminal affairs as a civilian.

Conversation dried up again for the remainder of the journey, and eventually, they pulled into the nick car park. The day had been a blur, the weight of events pressing on everyone in the car. As Madison parked up, she threw a glance around the parking space for two things. That creep Winston Wilson, and her own car, on the off chance that Brendan had come back here.

Neither were in sight.

'Wait here a minute, and keep your heads down low,' she instructed, before hopping out. She was loathe to leave them there, but she didn't want them out in the open without knowing exactly where she was taking them. She glanced up at the security cameras. It was funny how she wished they were gone the last time she was stood here, but so thankful for them now. Then she leaned back in through an open window to look at Mim. 'I'll be no more than two minutes. I'm just going to sort out a room. Keep an eye on that door, okay? That's where I'll be coming from.'

Mim nodded and whispered, 'Thank you.'

She ran around front, entered the station, and saw Patel on the desk.

'Sergeant,' she said as she reached her. There was nobody else around, a lull caused by a recent shift change, Madison guessed. The station recalibrating, and settling in for the evening's events. Patel was drinking from a mug, and as she neared, Madison smelled peppermint. 'I need a room, but quiet. Off the books. What have we got?'

'I…' Patel looked dubious.

'I can't put these people in an interview room, and I can't let anyone else in the nick see them. This must be completely secret. But the Super knows.'

'I'm not sure what I can do. I could call custody—'

'No. Nobody is to know. Please, Patel. What can we do?' She looked imploringly at the desk sergeant.

'Who are they?'

'If I tell you, will you help me?'

'Yes.'

'You know the firefight over in Leigh today? It was a hit squad trying to kill one of our ex-coppers. They missed, but people have been trying to kill his family all day. Their safe house and protection was compromised. I have them outside now. Copper's wife and his two sons, teenager and a toddler.'

Patel needed no more encouragement. 'This isn't a usual station, as you well know, and it's not like any space is unaccounted for, but… I suppose, if the Super knows, you could use his office? Considering the emergency and everything, and there's a sofa in there for the little one.'

'I think that would be amazing… I'm sorry, what's your first name?'

'Sanaya.'

'Iona. That would be amazing, Sanaya. Thank you. If you unlock it, can I bring them in through the fire exit?'

'I can't deactivate the alarm.'

They looked at each other, understanding stretching between them. 'The alarm would be a great distraction to get them inside,' Madison said.

'I didn't hear that. I'll meet you at Monroe's office.'

'I can't thank you enough.'

'It'll be the most excitement I've ever seen, Iona. You can have this one for free.'

Patel came from around the desk and they both jogged down the corridor, echoes following them. This wasn't the main corridor, and Madison was relieved. Two officers running in a police station would always fuel the gossip circles. Lives were still at stake. Madison branched off, following her nose to the fire escape. It was a large building, but its guts ran simple, and it didn't take her long to find the fire door in question. It was dark, as all the corridors here were, and cool. A tiny, oft-ignored part of Madison felt like lying on the floor and curling up, away from the heat, the noise, the stresses. Instead, she pushed the handle, and the station alarm immediately started to blast overhead.

She threw the door open and the evening crashed in—purples and pinks bullying their way into the dark corners. She saw the car, Mim, Dan and Mick, and indicated to them, waving a hand furiously through the air. They immediately jumped out. Madison held the door open, scanning the car park. The alarm was still blaring. She imagined the staff all filing out of the front, whilst she and the Foleys slipped in the back.

'Come on, come on,' she hissed. As soon as they were inside, she pulled the door shut, and re-engaged the handle lever. The darkness fought back admirably. 'Okay, this way.'

Madison set off at a rate, keen to get them to the safety of the Super's office. A couple more turns—and there ahead of her, as promised—was Patel, holding open the door to Monroe's office.

'Thank you,' said Mim, as she passed the sergeant.

The three of them stood in the middle of the room, taking in their new surroundings with numb bewilderment. The alarm abruptly stopped, and the sudden quiet was deafening and burdensome.

'Stay here, until I come and get you. Only me, Brendan or the Super, who's that bloke on the wall over there.' Madison pointed at a selection of framed photographs on the wall behind the desk, showing Monroe at various stages of his career, and at various stages of moustache growth.

'Okay,' said Mim. 'Bring Brendan back, please.'

'I will.'

Madison left, and thanked Sanaya Patel profusely as she started back down the corridor. Her phone began to ring in her pocket, and she pulled it out.

A private number.

Thinking of all those spinning plates, she answered.

'Yes, who is this?'

A voice answered. It sounded steeped in gravel and gargled with oil. 'Is that any way to answer your phone to a member of the public?'

Garland Roarke. She grimaced. The man made her skin want to leap right off her frame. 'I assume this means you have something to say?'

'Here's how it will go. Midnight tonight, Culpepper's Dockyard. Culpepper will be there, and so will a lot of that white powder you're so keen on. The main building as you go in. Take the big metal lift to the roof. He'll be there with a few of his cronies. You'll have him bang to rights.'

'Tonight?' she hissed. 'I can't put together a sting by tonight!'

'The call's already been made. Those are the terms. If you want him, that's how you can have him.'

'We don't want to get him for possession, we need him with intent to supply. If it's possession he could be out in a few years.'

'Not the quantities we're talking about.'

Madison couldn't think straight, no matter how she tried to frame it in her head. This would be a major operation. One of the biggest stings going. And she had—what?—three hours to put it together? With everything else that was happening?

Garland interrupted her racing thoughts. 'You asked me to help you get him. I'm giving him to you.'

'You have to be there,' Madison blurted out, knowing with those words she'd somehow accepted that this meeting, this attempted arrest of Culpepper, was the only way.

'No fucking chance.'

'You do—and I remind you, it's either you or him I'm bringing in. Either way, for me, it's a high-profile collar and I get a pat on the back, probably a medal, definitely a mention in the station newsletter. I can come to your door right now...'

He growled, 'I'd like to see you try.'

'Grow up, you troglodyte. Or we can both go to Culpepper, you as a confidential informant, and I take him in.'

'I'm not going there. End of story.'

'Then I'll be seeing you soon. Now, if you'll excuse me, I've a raid to organise on Renshaw Circle.'

She hung up.

She waited in the cool corridor, her heart pounding, imagining what was happening where Garland was right now. Ring back. Come on...

The phone rang. She waited a full ten rings before answering. She didn't say a word.

'Midnight,' said Garland Roarke, before hanging up.

Madison breathed out hard. She was tingling with the undiluted adrenaline at the prospect of a major arrest. But she was also nauseous.

How the hell was she going to pull this off? She needed to call Monroe. This had to go through him.

CHAPTER 53

SEABREEZE COULDN'T BREATHE. He'd been under that bed so long, listening to the rhythmical snoring from above, with the mattress pressed down on him, that he was sure almost all the oxygen in the room had been used up. The stink was beyond reproach or explanation, and he didn't want to even open his mouth. What he had done, however, was concoct a plan.

He shimmied his hand beneath him and manoeuvred his phone out of his pocket. The screen splashed blue light over his face as he clicked it on, and immediately scrolled through his phone contacts. Fiona. His soap star squeeze.

HELLO LOVELY. TESTING OUT A NEW TIP LINE AT WORK. COULD YOU CALL AND TELL THEM THERE'S BEEN A MURDER AT THIS ADDRESS? THANKS DARLING. YOU'RE A STAR. AND SAME AGAIN TOMORROW NIGHT?

He added the confidential tip line number for Warrington nick, and the address he was stuck at. He almost laughed at the uneven tone of the message but needs must. He double checked his phone was still on silent, but a response came through while it was still in his hand.

YEAH, SURE. SAME PLACE OR COME TO MINE?

Internet was patchy at hers, and the broadband kept messing up the 4K stream. SHALL WE DO SAME PLACE? I'LL COOK.

The repartee was actually helping distract from the enormity of what he was trying to pull off, and the tiny window of opportunity he had.

PERFECT, Fiona replied.

Twenty minutes passed, during which time Seabreeze tried to think of anything but his current predicament. He felt like an athlete, a sprinter, with the big race about to start any minute. Only it wasn't a starter pistol he was listening for—it was a siren.

When he first heard the soft wail, his body flooded with adrenaline, and as it grew louder, he jiggled his legs slightly to get the blood flowing through them.

The car pulled up, the siren was killed, and the doorbell rang. The snoring above him stopped with an abrupt snag of breath and phlegm. The bed began to shift.

'What the bloody hell is that?' said Wilson. The mattress roiled as he climbed off. As soon as Seabreeze heard the feet on the stairs, he was moving, pulling himself out from under the bedframe, gasping for air. As he managed to see things properly for the first time in hours, he saw the blue lights swooping around the darkened bedroom from outside. The sun had dipped fully since he'd gone into hiding.

The bodies were still on the bed, but he didn't stay, as he heard the front door open, and voices begin to bounce back and forth.

He'd been imagining the house, its shape, its layout and blueprint. His instinct for detail often kicked in unbidden. He remembered, from when he'd been casing the place earlier, that there was an en suite to the master bedroom. That it looked over the rear garden, and that it wouldn't be too big a drop to land on those bins.

The entire house was dark as he stepped onto the landing. Watching his step, he went as fast as he could down the hall to the master bedroom. The door was already open, filth and garbage predictably piled up, but his eyes saw the bed. In the darkness, on a pink, floral bedspread, replete with valance, tucked in up to the chin like a wee one on Christmas Eve, was a body. Springy white hair sat up from a dark shape, which Seabreeze thanked the heavens he couldn't fully make out, awful images in his head of Wilson washing his rotting mum's hair.

All it meant was that Winston Wilson was a full-on looney-tunes psycho.

Chased by abject horror, as if the cadaver could loom up at any moment, he went into the bathroom—it smelled like an abandoned aquarium that had been left to rot. The smell was so pungent, he couldn't breathe, and he saw what looked like dark water filling the bath.

Resolving that he just didn't want to know, he leapt for the window, to swing it open.

Feet in the house. Thumping. Raised voices. Someone was coming up the stairs. Fast.

He peered out and down at the landing pad of wheelie bins. His career and those of his friends all rested on his ability to get down there, get away, and stay on the ball.

These bodies were going to be taken. And he needed to follow them, needed to remove any evidence of their involvement. He didn't quite know how he was going to do that yet, but that was the plan, and the train had left the station. He was on this ride and would have to see it out.

Looking down, he prayed he wouldn't land on one with any rats, and just as the first shout of 'Oh my god!' rang from within the house, Seabreeze squeezed through the window in a jumble of limbs and leapt through the air.

CHAPTER 54

GARLAND HAD ONLY just returned from Jason's wake, when he mused that the night was dark and full of terrors—or fast women in faster sports cars. He sighed—*What now?*—as he heard an engine approach Renshaw Circle. The same one that had come earlier in the day. The same one that had brought Charlotte Culpepper. His dogs looked to Garland for instruction. He waved them back, called them off.

The car looked sleeker in darkness. Meant business. He wasn't worried though. He could handle this woman. He could handle any Culpepper. Their future was in the palm of his hand.

She parked in the same place as earlier in the day, which felt like long weeks and months ago now, and wasted no time in stepping out. She looked like steam would sizzle from her if she was dipped in water. Made up for a night out, eyes big and bright. Belted waist pulled in tight, making her a full figure eight, in a dress that clung on for dear life. He almost shook his head.

She looked at the street behind him, at its emptiness. 'You trust me this time?'

'I feel no threat from you, lady.'

She smiled. 'And you don't scare me either, old man.'

Garland was careful. By now, she'd know about the midnight meeting, and his supposed attempt to get back on side with her husband, pull business back into the right place, and get things moving again. But he had to move cautiously. He was helping to put this woman's husband away tonight, and he couldn't deny it gave him a thrill, knowing the truth that was coming for her in the not-too-distant future. 'So what are you here for, then?'

'It's more personal,' she said. 'Something has clearly gone wrong in the communication between our two sides, and I'm pleased that the proper moves are being made to put things right. I can't speak for my husband, but… I'm happy things are being sorted. I wanted to thank you for reaching out in the way that you did. And I think a personal touch is all the more important. So, thank you.' Unexpectedly, she inclined her head in deference.

Garland wasn't so easily charmed. 'Is this your role now? Emissary? The grease between the main gears?'

'I wouldn't say just that.' She stepped up onto Garland's porch. Uninvited. He stiffened.

'Ease back,' he said. 'I'm glad you're happy and everything, but ease back.'

She ignored him. 'Going forward, you should bear me in mind when it comes to keeping business prosperous. I know how things work. Harvey knows I know.'

'I'm glad. Now get the fuck of my porch.'

Her eyes rested on a bottle that sat on the deck next to the armchair. 'Is that whiskey? Can I have a nip, in the name of business?'

'Your ears bunged up? Get off my property.' Garland sat tight, hissing now.

Instead, and outrageously, Charlotte took another step closer. 'You need to understand something,' she said, as she held her palms up in an offering of peace.

The old Garland would have punted this woman off the deck, straight into the bushes, and have her car burnt out by a couple of lads whilst the rest drove her back across to Liverpool with a bag over her head. But this Garland, for some reason, was different. He sat in his chair, his insides coiled, and watched her.

'I'm an asset,' she said. Another step. 'And I take my role seriously. And when it looks like things might fail, I go the hard yards to fix things up and press through.'

Another step. She was almost at the chair now. Garland held his hand up. 'That's as far as you go, girlie.'

'And my husband won't always be the top dog. He won't always be the one who calls the shots.'

Before Garland could register the meaning in her words, Charlotte had climbed into his lap, straddling him. She hitched her dress up just a touch, pushed her hips in close, and sat there, on the grizzled biker's lap. His rage was huge and tidal at the affront, and as he moved to throw her off, she pushed back on his chest with gentle force. He felt paralysed.

'The mistakes were made on his watch,' she said, softly, playfully, looking into Garland's eyes. She unfastened the top button of his denim shirt. 'And I won't be that sort of leader.'

Garland couldn't help himself, and moved a hand onto her thigh. A bomb set off in his stomach. 'What are you saying?'

'I'm saying, there are better horses to back, long term. Better relationships to work on.'

Once she'd finished with his buttons, she slipped a strap from her shoulder, then the other and allowed the top half of the dress to fall to her waist. Garland was transfixed. She took his hand and placed it on her bare chest. His hand, Garland Roarke's hand, shook with anticipation. She moved to his waist, and with nothing more than a tinkle of belt and a shimmy, Garland felt the world turn impossibly perfect and ecstatic. She moved against him—this woman, who was the wife of a criminal he was about to snitch to the police, and he felt all at sea.

Confused, but in spasms of rolling pleasure, he finally let his hands grasp at her.

The words slipped out, almost helplessly. 'Then if I were you, I wouldn't be at the meeting tonight,' he whispered.

'Thank you,' she whispered back—then the pleasure he felt consumed by suddenly carried a different quality. Hot—too hot and too wet. And then... detachment.

He looked down—and saw a knife handle in his gut, buried to the hilt.

'That was all I needed to hear,' said Charlotte, in that same seductive whisper.

Garland tried to move, but he couldn't. Instead, she used both her hands to drag the knife, still embedded, up his stomach, to his chest. Garland could only watch with a curious detachment, as his body blossomed open.

He tried to say something but couldn't. There was no pain. The only sensation he felt—the last emotion he'd ever feel— was shame.

CHAPTER 55

'YOU PATHETIC FUCKING pig,' Charlotte whispered into Garland's face. She didn't move, left the blade where it was, still stuck in his torso, and waited for his vitality to shrivel away. She didn't even turn as the first shouts of terror rang out.

She pulled her dress up to cover her modesty. One of the straps twisted, so she took a second to untangle it, laying it flat against her clavicle. All the while, Garland stared at her lifelessly and she never broke his gaze, the knife still buried good and deep in his guts.

She finally moved away from the body, rearranging her dress, annoyed to spot a blood spatter marking it. 'Fucking typical.'

She left the porch and called ahead. 'I'm clear.'

And the hit squad from Preston—who'd fucked up so badly at the KFC in Leigh—started taking their chance at redemption.

First, they entered the houses. Double tapping everyone in sight, two shots, in the head, of every person they saw—which wasn't that many, because so many were still getting pissed up at the Mission. Timing, indeed, was everything. Once the houses were cleared, Molotovs were tossed on the roof. A smash of glass, and the hot breath of a blaze igniting with sudden scale. And it was none of that shite you see in movies; no, this squad, despite initial impressions, knew what they were doing, and made them with a precise mixture of ethanol, tar and gasoline. Guaranteed to do the job, and the buildings went up eagerly, the rooftops eaten by flames in seconds.

Charlotte walked back to the passenger side of her car, while inferno bloomed on the buildings all around her. She opened the glove compartment to get at the baby wipes and watched her team as she wiped herself down of any trace of Garland's blood.

She was pleased with how they'd done.

When you break away and do something new, you need to know that you've got the right people around you.

There was a shout, a loud smash of glass.

Whilst still wiping Garland's blood from her décolletage, she saw a man on the front lawn of the house at the far end, scrambling to the ground, trying to right himself, desperate to get away. Clearly, a straggler, who'd missed the initial cull. She recognised him as the younger one, Fin. He must have come back with Garland like a loyal lapdog, never leaving his master's side. Maybe he was set to go to the meeting in Liverpool too. Either way, none of that mattered, nor would it change his outcome.

The Preston hit squad swarmed him, kicked him all over, until one of them shot him in the head. Good-looking kid he was too. They promptly took a limb each to stuff the body back through the broken window, into the house he'd run from, which was now positively ablaze.

Yeah, Charlotte thought, as she ran the baby wipe over her bare arms, the first prickles of heat from the various blazes warming her skin. *The right people.*

The squad waited until all the houses were burning adequately, then moved to join Charlotte. Around them, Renshaw Circle burned, and with it the Devil's Defects were overthrown, disbanded and very literally disintegrated.

She nodded to them, smiled, replaced the wipes, then moved around to the driver's side.

'Do the same with the Mission on Sankey Street, then get to the rendezvous point. It's happening tonight in Liverpool, so all we do is lay low and wait.'

She took one last look at the house at the end. Garland Roarke's. The man was still there in his chair, the knife still stood proud, as fire licked and eagerly ate. It wouldn't be long before the house—and body—would all be gone.

'Let's be off,' she said, before getting into the car, and swooping out of the cul-de-sac, the heat licking at their wheels.

As soon as she had driven the Beemer away onto the entry road, an old articulated lorry, borrowed just an hour previous from a haulage firm depot in exchange for a hefty insurance payout to yield a nice shiny new one, reversed across the junction, and blocked the entire space. Tyres were shot and burst, locking the lorry in place until something even bigger came to haul it away. The hit squad were cleaning up before they hit the road too. The lorry wasn't moving for a while, which would give the buildings time to smoulder to little more than dust, and for all parties of this new branch of organised crime to escape.

Charlotte smiled into her rear-view mirror, enjoying seeing the final pieces of the perfect plan slot into place, as she shot off into the Mancunian night.

One of the North West's criminal kings had just been thoroughly dethroned, and by morning, the East Lancs—its thirty miles and the cities on either end—wouldn't be a man's world anymore.

It would be a new era entirely.

The era of the Queen. Of Charlotte Culpepper.

CHAPTER 56

AT FIVE TO midnight, Harvey left his office, signalling to his boys that it was time to go.

The six men shouldered the canvas bags that had been at their feet.

'The stairs,' he ordered.

He was nervous. Usually, Dorian and Charlotte were with him on matters such as these—his right-hand man and his queen. They were not only worthy advisors, but good luck charms. And he felt exposed to the core without them. But he needed this deal now more than ever. He needed cash flow to resume, and he needed things with these bikers to get back on an even keel.

A deal. That's what he needed.

As he walked up the steps to the roof, the iron stairwell clanking in the dark, he thought, for the first time that day, that killing Jason had perhaps been a bad idea. He had tried to pull the price down, in an effort to please his boss, but offing him had set off a wild and uncontrollable chain of events that had brought nothing but attention to his enterprise.

Where the hell was Charlotte? She'd always been loyal and stubborn as a mule. Had she been picked up too, like Dorian? But on what charges? Her hands were completely clean. Perhaps she was off with that young upstart from yoga? No, surely not. Playing with puppies was one thing, but at the end of the day, you always needed the big dog.

He exited onto the roof via an old service door, and the entire Liverpool city spread before him, twinkling like diamonds, with a haze reaching into an endless navy sky.

His city.

His fucking city.

All these people would do well to remember that.

He walked out to the far side. It was a large space, and he didn't need all of it—but he always made sure he was facing the door when anybody came up.

Something caught his eye.

On the horizon, off towards Manchester.

It looked like a thumb smear on the distance, but no. A thick, fat column of black smoke was rising from the ground. And slightly to the right—a touch further back—the crane-dotted skyline of Manchester city centre stood, its buildings watching with quiet stoicism.

Doubtlessly, there had been a major fire near Manchester tonight.

He admired the sight. Chaos could be a beautiful thing.

He checked his watch, turned to face the door, and the service lift door which stood next to it.

Midnight.

Let's get this over with.

THESE OLD ROOFTOPS were another world—especially when you'd watched night lower onto a city, while watching an inferno swell to life in another.

Whatever was going on over there, under the other end of the vast purple blanket, was going to be life-changing. Police officers were able to enjoy calculated detachment. But what would it mean to the people involved? Survival possibilities. And that one was not good.

'It's a big one, that,' said Kharthik in a low voice, as the creak of a door made Madison spin round.

They'd been up here for ninety minutes or so, as soon as Garland had put the pieces in place. She couldn't get a hold of Monroe, so had pressed on with faith that somehow, this was the right thing.

She hadn't been able to raise any help except for Kharthik, his interview with Dorian rendered useless and terminated. She'd been prepared to come alone if he hadn't been so insistent. But they'd been under fire before, so she knew he could handle it.

Yet this was so unknown.

She wanted this to be on her, all her, so that whatever the fallout was, nobody was joining her on the sinking ship of Madison's career—or life.

She had to face it. Trying to arrest a major criminal, on his turf, surrounded by his people, with another career criminal as part of the sting, and his people, who weren't...

But, if she pulled it off? If...

She edged around the corner of the fat vent that she and Kharthik were crouching behind, and hoped her knees didn't crack so violently that they'd give her away in a demeaning instant.

He was here. The man she'd come to arrest.

She'd only laid eyes on Harvey Culpepper once before, and in that moment, she'd been under attack from a volley of punches in one of the hardest fights of her career, as she watched him reduce Brendan Foley to tears at ringside on the front row. Then, he'd been a picture of calm. Now? She'd been around enough crims to know the odd tell, and while he was still putting on the act and preening to the six men that were with him, she could tell unmistakably that he was off-balance.

The playing field had never been more even.

She watched him walk out onto the roof. He glanced at the fire, then turned back to the service lift doors. His men did the same, stacking the neat black bags in a small, squat pyramid.

If all that was narcotics, then this was a *big* bust.

Big enough to define a career.

Also, big enough to have Madison and Kharthik thrown right off this roof.

The men didn't talk; they watched the doors. Madison checked her watch. Two minutes to midnight. She blew out, the sound lost in the whistling breeze that crested the rooftop. Culpepper stood motionless, staring at the far end of the rooftop, at the doors and the black beyond. Whether he knew he was on a precipice or not, she daren't speculate.

One minute to go. Until the meeting was scheduled to start.

A calm sense of cool descended. Take away the hype and bluster, the fear and anticipation, the stakes and the odds—Madison *lived* for moments like these. Wasn't this what it had all been about? To get to this moment?

Whilst Harvey's men stood motionless, her opponent started to pace. He began to look untethered, his body betraying him. He was rattled.

Madison didn't know how this played out; the intricacies of the little power moves. Was this unpunctuality a gentle middle finger from Garland? She imagined that was more likely than a spot of traffic, especially at this time of night.

One minute became five, and Madison's own calm began to shrivel. Kharthik looked at her, but all she could do was shrug and shake her head.

Had Garland reneged on the deal?

Surely not. A man like Harvey Culpepper wouldn't take kindly to being stood up at the altar.

But she needed Garland here. She didn't want to arrest Culpepper without him. A charge of possession was a grand scheme of nothing without a corresponding intent to supply. And for that matter, Culpepper hadn't even touched those bags. That lawyer of his back at the nick would have the CPS in fits, turning Madison and Kharthik's words inside out:

I didn't know what was in those bags, your honour. My friends just brought them up to that roof in the middle of the night.

Excruciating minutes crawled by. Even the heavies began glancing at each other when, at 12.09 a.m., the lift started to clunk and screech.

Deep below them, in the belly of the building, someone had called it. The elevator was rising.

Madison's calm returned. Kharthik's body stilled.

Harvey Culpepper appeared and moved dead centre, flanked by his boys.

The doors at the other end of the roof peeled open.

In a square of dim light, the calm seemed to judder like an old movie reel.

And, from inside the lift, a man stepped out onto the roof. He looked terrible. Exhausted, bruised.

It was Brendan Foley, staring daggers at Culpepper, as he walked out onto the roof.

Then a gun appeared behind him, pushing him on.

Madison's heart leapt at the danger, but managed to stay in her throat. Brendan had been captured and brought to Culpepper personally. The man entering behind him emerged into the light.

Recognition hit; she felt faint.

Nudging Brendan Foley out onto the roof, into the arms of the man who had tried everything to kill him, was Madison's own boss.

Superintendent Monroe.

CHAPTER 57

WHEN HARVEY CULPEPPER glimpsed the person walking out of the lift, all he could do was applaud.

'Oh, this is perfect,' he said, dry palms clapping together. 'Just *perfect*. You only went and did it.'

'I've come to collect,' said the man behind Brendan Foley.

'You can collect all right. I might want a photo though, just so I can remind myself it really happened.'

The other man's face froze. 'You can stick your photo up your arse. I just want my cash.'

'Oh, you've definitely earned it. Monroe, isn't it?' He glimpsed a flash of guilt over the superintendent's face and relished it. 'My fucking word. He cashes in.'

Monroe spoke in a dark, flat voice that carried the trace of a tremor. 'The money. Where is it?'

'I'm good for it, don't worry. And I might stick a little bonus in, if we can have a phone number. Maybe an open line of communication?'

'Other services are not for sale.'

'Oh, I think you are. I really think you are. Just shows, boys, doesn't it?' Culpepper turned to his men and nodded to Monroe theatrically. 'Everyone has a price.'

'This is a one-time thing. The money.'

Harvey thought on his feet. Getting a sympathetic ear with Warrington Police's own superintendent—well, that would be worth all the hassle of this night alone—almost to the point that it didn't matter if Garland Roarke showed up. Warrington would become a real prime territory that was all his. That's what happens when you have the police. Immunity in that territory.

'Do you really think we'd keep quiet about you bringing the hero copper to us? You must be mad. I already want to sell the rights of the last thirty seconds to Netflix.'

Monroe spoke loud, looking for any kind of authority. 'Anyone finds out about this, I go full bore at you and your organisation. Both officially and unofficially.'

Harvey laughed, an uncharitable bark. 'You've no legs to stand on. What did you think? You could walk up here like dropping a kid off at nursery, and walk away with a million quid and go back to being the Super? It doesn't work like that. Why do you think I insisted you delivered him yourself? Yeah, it sounds good, keeping it in-house, but witnesses to this subterfuge are gold. These boys know who you are, I know who you are of course, and you've been here. I ever need to leverage anything against you, I can find a thousand traffic cameras that put you and him in a car together, on your way to Liverpool—the night dear Brendan here went *poof.*'

Monroe didn't say anything.

'Speaking of our mate, Mr Foley... Well, then. Go on, lads. Get the tank.'

THE TANK WAS a phrase that didn't sound good no matter how you said it. And it sounded even worse when it resulted in four of Culpepper's men running past Brendan and that snake Monroe. Back to the lift and access doors. Brendan felt the touch of Monroe's gun, but still risked a look when the rumbling started.

Monroe obviously felt the same way. The two of them watched, dumbfounded, as a giant dumpster appeared—

lumbering around the corner, out into the middle of the roof. It took three of the burly men to push, and one to steer. When they got clear of the wall, they stopped and took a breather.

It was only then that Brendan recognised one of the men pushing.

Declan. His boss on the doors at Flexion.

He knew he shouldn't have been surprised. He'd picked that job to be close to the people Culpepper used from the world of the doors.

'Declan,' Brendan said. 'Mate…'

Declan breathed hard a few times. Brendan could only stare.

Culpepper walked up to the tank, and looked in. 'Ah, good. It's still full. Honestly, it's a bitch to fill when you're waiting. Go on, hop in.'

Brendan didn't follow.

'You want me to get in there?'

Like it was the most obvious answer in the world, Harvey answered, 'Yes.'

Brendan was not going to get in there willingly. He'd do anything at this point to get at Harvey, even if it cost him his life. At the end of the day, that was all he wanted. To pay Harvey back for what he'd done to his family. The fear he'd created. No matter what Brendan's feelings were towards his father, his death had been orchestrated by this man, right here. But that was the word, wasn't it? *Orchestrated.*

'You've never been man enough to do any of this yourself, Harvey. I'm right here. Come and do it.'

Harvey laughed again. 'If that's what you think—boy, I have a surprise for you.'

A bat appeared. Metal, black with red lettering down the side, its edges shining like a fat circular blade. Lethal. The game changed.

Brendan tried again.

'A bat. Ooooh, big scary hard man, isn't he… Come on, you wanted to take me out—so come on, let's be having you. Come on, do it yourself. You've never once lifted a finger. Make me feel special, do me personally.'

Brendan wanted to get him close but had no idea what he'd do once he got him there. He had no weapons, and worse, the only weapon he could see was pointed at his own head. But every minute breathing was another minute alive. Another minute he could use to find a way to get to his family and save them.

'I want my money, and I want to be off,' said Monroe.

'Coward,' said Brendan.

'Yeah, stick around,' said Harvey. 'You'll like this, I promise. See what you made happen.'

'You hear that, Monroe? What *you* made happen. All *you*.'

'Shut up!' burst Monroe. 'The deal was to bring him in. Alive, if possible. I've given you that, haven't I? A million cash was the reward, and I want that now. I've done my part, where's yours?'

Brendan reached his own boiling point. 'You make me sick, you know that? Just fucking sick.' He felt dizzy with betrayal.

Culpepper smiled, and this time, Brendan saw a glint of canine. 'Pipe down, the pair of you. Foley, get in. Get in, or I'll off you now and spend the rest of my days hell-bent on putting every Foley head on a spike. Get in now, and I'll call it there. Come on, now. Think about it. Your little mum, that wife who's clearly way too good for you, those two beautiful boys…'

'Shut up, I'm on my way.'

Brendan walked to the dumpster and peered inside.

Moonlight winked back at him, rolling softly, and it took a moment for his eyes to adjust, his nose catching the sickly sweet smell of rot.

He was looking at a liquid surface.

The dumpster was full, almost to the top, with water.

'Get in,' said Culpepper. 'Now.'

CHAPTER 58

MADISON COULDN'T BELIEVE what she was witnessing.

Superintendent Monroe had taken an ex-copper to a crime boss in order to be killed—all in exchange for a cash payout.

Christ. How much did he need the money?

No wonder she hadn't been able to get in touch with Monroe about the proposed sting—he was keeping his head down, on his way here.

But that meant he didn't know Madison and Kharthik were here.

And that gave her hope.

She watched Brendan drag himself over—God, he looked terrible—to peer into that massive bin.

She was stunned when that dumpster came out. Christopher was right—and where was he for that matter? Never mind a pint, he deserved a big pat on the back for cracking detective work, and a commendation from the Super... but the Super was standing over there, having betrayed them all.

Christ, what a mess.

And now Brendan was jumping into the dumpster.

What do we do?

She was answered by a click next to her. It sounded familiar to her in a way she couldn't pinpoint.

As she turned her head, she saw that she was right.

It was the click of the hammer on a revolver.

A revolver, which was in the hands of DS Kharthik, who looked ready to roll.

She stared at him, eyes wide with confusion.

He answered simply: 'Let's just say I forgot to catalogue it earlier.'

Dorian Torrance's gun.

Kharthik would be in a world of trouble if it came out that he hadn't followed the proper chain of evidence procedures, especially when it came to a firearm that was used to try to kill a policeman—but it paled into insignificance next to all the real trouble that was around all of them at that very moment. It gave them a fighting chance.

'You know how to use it?' She hadn't undergone any firearms training.

'Fair idea,' he answered.

'Do you think they're armed?' She nodded to the six men loitering by the bags.

'I do.'

THE WATER WAS tepid, but Brendan thought that made sense, given that he was essentially climbing into a huge pot of liquid that had been in the sun all day. He hoped it was going to be quick.

The water smelled off, but it was not unpleasant. He thought about his family, his mistakes, his choices. Stupid male pride was the reason for all of this.

Male pride, the Foley curse.

Horror and revulsion, with *himself* and nobody else, hit harder than ever, pulled tears from his eyes.

He just hoped his sons would turn out better.

He breathed out, thinking of them.

And Mim. How he'd let her down. How he'd let them all down. Not just today. But ever since.

They all deserved so much better, though they'd all been doomed from the start. From the second his father had decided to play crime, he'd condemned his family line to a life fraught with risk, danger and the constant shadow of impending tragedy.

Brendan had been unable to step out of it.

He hadn't been strong enough.

He was a failure.

Please, just make it quick.

Culpepper approached and waved the bat.

'Lads, keep an eye on the door. We've guests to welcome.'

The men didn't move. The bags remained well-guarded, ready for pickup.

'You've got me so wrong, Foley. You haven't a clue. You see, I *love* getting my hands dirty. Fucking love it. But you'll notice something about me, and that's the distinct lack of bars. Never been in prison. Never been arrested. Never done a minute. And that's because of constant invention. So let me talk you through how you're going to die.

'It's going to be awful. Toe-curlingly awful. You're going to be begging for it to finish, but it won't, because you deserve every last second of it. And I've been waiting for this so long, I'm going to savour each and every one of the seconds I drag this out.' He tapped the dumpster with the bat. 'And I'm not going to lay a finger on you.'

Brendan felt panic begin to swell, burn, overwhelm him.

'The most impressive advancements truly come from the strangest places. And in this instance, the third world. You see, those fellas worked out that you can use the conductive, sonic capabilities of water to do some terrible things in the right conditions. Like this.'

Culpepper swung the bat like he was trying to launch a home run, and smashed it into the side of the bin. The clang was painfully loud, and he felt his body assaulted deep inside by an excruciating blow that resonated long after the noise had disappeared into the night. Every single cell in his body seemed to howl, burn and throb with electric abandon, as if pulsing acid was poured through every nerve, every vein, every capillary.

'Hurts, doesn't it!' Culpepper shouted.

Brendan felt his world spinning, his heart pumping. He wretched. His core felt hammered into a new shape that didn't work.

'*That* was a shockwave in a confined space. And it's like being punched in every last one of your organs, all at the same time. Grim, isn't it?'

Brendan had to close his eyes to stop from blacking out. By beating the bat on the metal wall of the dumpster, it was sending sonic waves through the water into his body, battering him, without touching him. He felt a little like his bowels were going to drop if Culpepper did that again.

'Look where my hands are,' Culpepper said, waving the bat around. 'Nowhere bloody near you. All that precious DNA evidence, all those lovely fingerprints—right where they should be. Nowhere near you.' He glowered into Brendan's face. 'But believe it, sunshine, every ounce of pain is coming from me.'

'Fuck off and get on with it then,' Brendan spat. Considering the impact of the first strike, he didn't think he could handle much more before consciousness went, and he'd drown.

'Are you watching, Chief?' Culpepper said, pointing the end of the bat at Brendan's bobbing head. 'Foley's caused you more than a few headaches hasn't he—I bet this is bloody lovely to watch.'

Brendan couldn't have held Monroe's glance if he'd tried. His eyes were dipping and drifting down, his mouth in the water, when he saw something move on the other side of the roof.

CHAPTER 59

'HOWEVER YOU SPIN this,' Madison called, 'it looks bad, bad, *bad*.' All the men on the rooftop turned to find her pacing out into the open, camera phone in two hands, filming the whole thing. 'Don't let me stop you. Just want to make sure I get all your good sides.'

Everyone froze, the only sound being Brendan's coughing as he tried to keep his head above water.

'Hang in there, Brendan,' Madison said. She looked down at the screen. Her phone *was* running, and they were all in shot—including Monroe, who had turned a shade of grey. 'Especially you, Chief Superintendent Terry Monroe. Especially you—you sneaky, two-faced piece of shit.'

That provoked Monroe into life, and he swung the gun up immediately to face her.

'Throw the phone over the side. Now. Throw it off the rooftop this second.'

She ignored his instructions. She'd never follow one of them again.

'Why don't you just shoot me? Is killing *two* of your employees a bit much, even for you?' She didn't move the lens. 'You know, here we've even got a good look at you, Mr Culpepper—and your heavies, too. Lots of piccies for the papers.'

That sent Monroe pale as a cataract.

'You'll never get the video off this rooftop,' said Culpepper with venom—but there was a hint of glee on his face. He loved this. Loved the chaos. 'Boys, go and relieve detective Madison of her phone, will you? And watch out for her left hook as you go—there's dynamite in those hands.'

Madison watched the men approach, panning the phone around to catch all their faces. As the first one neared her, she finally spoke. 'I wouldn't. You touch me, your boss's head goes missing.'

A sharp *crunch click* split the night air in two, sharp enough to draw everyone's attention—to DS Kharthik, who was suddenly stood behind Culpepper, revolver pointed at the back of the crime lord's head.

'Fun,' Culpepper said. 'I can't see you mate, but you've light feet. That's Dorian's piece. I'd know that hammer action anywhere.'

'Foley, climb out of the tank,' said Kharthik.

Monroe turned away. 'Shit.'

'It's a bit late for hiding your face now, *Sir*,' said Madison.

Without wavering the gun barrel, Kharthik swivelled to assess Brendan's situation. 'Can you get out?'

'I'm not sure,' Brendan answered, as water gurgled from his jittering lips.

'You've a gun too, Superintendent. I suggest if you want that reward, you start using it,' Culpepper snapped.

Monroe stared uselessly at his own gun.

The men crowding Madison started to get agitated. They wanted out; this had all got too hot.

On the other side of the roof, she could see Kharthik was hoisting Brendan out of the dumpster, his other arm diligently holding aim on Culpepper.

And in the wall behind Monroe, the lift doors slid shut, and the lift began to clunk its way back down the building.

'Ah, business. At last,' said Culpepper. 'The balance will probably swing back my way here, just so you know.'

Madison could see the relief on his face, obvious even in the darkness.

CULPEPPER KNEW THAT if he was going to get the deal done and get off this roof the way he wanted to—alive—he'd have to kill all the cops.

He was glad those bikers had finally shown up, but he couldn't allow testimony of a major drug deal to leave the rooftop. His hands were tied, and these clowns didn't know what was coming.

He risked a smile. Those bikers hated the law more than they hated him. And this copper behind him, quick as he was, didn't have the balls to murder Culpepper in cold blood. This was Liverpool, not LA.

Culpepper just stood, twirled his bat and listened to the lift.

'You know, the more I think about it,' Culpepper said to Madison, a sly grin locked in tight, 'the more you're doing me a favour.'

He pointed the tip of the bat to the floor and leaned on it as if it were a cane. 'This video shows me doing nothing. Not, really. Maybe a little banging about, but that's all. It's not like I'm a recognisable member of a regional police force waving a gun about on a rooftop.' He offered a side nod in Monroe's direction. 'In fact, it's only you lot that appear to be armed.'

Madison countered with steel. 'Should we open the bags, then? They are yours, aren't they?'

'Are they? I haven't touched them, I don't recall.'

Brendan finally sloshed out onto the floor, coughing, holding his stomach, as the lift grew louder.

'Christ, are my friends in for a surprise,' Culpepper said.

The door opened, a square of harsh blue cut into the purple brick of the lift shaft.

A man stepped out. Holding a shotgun. Culpepper didn't recognise him at first, but after a couple of seconds a flashback to this man emerged from the fog in his mind—and with the memory, came horror.

CHAPTER 60

BRENDAN HAD JUST got his breath back when the lift doors opened, and his brother Ross walked out onto the roof, shotgun raised.

'Thank fuck,' he whispered, as consciousness began to feel something of an opaque concept. He didn't know how this had happened, but thank God it had.

Ross stepped out. Brendan could see immediately that he was on a hair trigger, which—when holding a gun—was not ideal.

'Drop that gun, Monroe,' he called over.

Monroe dropped the weapon to the ground with a clatter. 'Over there,' Ross said, walking Monroe over to Brendan and the dumpster. He looked over to Madison as he went. 'You lot, away from her.'

The men approaching Madison stepped back.

'Ross,' said Brendan, but it came out barely a whisper. 'How did you—'

'We've known about this place for years. When you said you were coming back to take him on, with or without me, there's only one place I'd know to look. When I couldn't get hold of you, I thought I'd have a little look. Quite a few cars about for a quiet night at the docks.'

'Thank you,' Brendan coughed.

'You were in that?' Ross nodded to the bin.

'Yeah, turns out if you hit the sides when you're in there with water, it hurts a lot.'

Ross turned with malevolence to Monroe—whose level of shame was clearly swallowing him. He couldn't meet anyone's eye. 'And that's your boss, isn't it? I mean when you were still a copper. He betrayed you, did he?'

'Yeah.'

'Then hop in, chief.'

Monroe looked at him dumbly.

'In the bin. Now.'

Monroe glanced around, beseechingly, looking for help. Nothing.

He breathed out fast.

'Please,' Monroe said.

'Get the fuck in,' Ross said.

Monroe climbed into the dumpster, gasping as the water reached his shoulders.

Ross walked over and grabbed Monroe's gun from the floor. He handed it to his older brother. 'Don't let the chief go anywhere.'

Brendan almost reached for it, but paused. If Madison's video caught him holding a gun, he'd go from victim in this scenario to a convictable villain. But taking the gun was their best and possibly only chance of getting off the rooftop alive. 'Madison, turn the video off.'

'Brendan, don't you join in on this,' she protested.

'If we all want to get out of here, Madison, *please* turn the video off.' His eyes pleaded with her, begging his old colleague to do as he so needed her to. She shook her head softly, sadly, and lowered the phone. Brendan took the gun and pointed it at Monroe. It felt foreign and heavy in his hand; he'd never held one before. First time for everything.

Ross looked at Kharthik now. 'You, keep an eye on Mr Culpepper, please, mate. Can't have him doing anything daft now.'

Brendan had to turn and swap the gun between hands in order to follow his brother, as he walked with purpose across to the bags, the shotgun barrel pointing at the men near Madison. 'Let's have a look here.'

The metallic swish of a zip's teeth parting, and it only took Ross a second to let out a whistle. 'Oh, yes. This will work nicely.'

Brendan didn't know what his brother was doing. 'Ross, we can go.'

'It won't stop, though—will it, Harvey?' Ross said to Culpepper, whose confidence finally looked punctured, doubt and fear now etched on the face and in his wrought body. 'You'll never stop killing Foleys, will you?'

'Ross, we can go,' Brendan pleaded, as sick realisation was dawning. *Ross isn't just here to save me.*

'No. Not yet.' Ross approached the men, but called over to Madison. 'My brother trusts you. You can go if you want.'

'No,' she said. 'I'm taking Culpepper in.'

'Like fuck you are.'

Madison sent a desperate look to her ex-colleague. 'Brendan, tell him. We are taking in Cuplepper and Monroe!'

Brendan was gripped by confusion, fringed with hate. Hate for Culpepper. Hate for his father, and the fact that his sons still couldn't step out of the lives he'd put them in. But Ross was right. As long as Culpepper was alive, he'd be a threat to his family. But Brendan couldn't allow this, surely?

He wasn't a cop anymore because he'd believed he could find justice another way, but the justice he sought was always supposed to be in tandem with the law. That was the whole idea.

Yet there was nothing lawful about where things were going here.

ROSS FELT A pure spurt of fury, nothing more, as he walked to the group of Culpepper's goonies by the bags—but in amongst all that rage was an emerging pillar of opportunity.

He'd been robbed of everything. The world he and his father had quietly built. His father—the man he had been devoted to. His wife, who'd realised there was little to their marriage beyond the ties of family and convenience. And worst of all, the hammer strike he'd never recovered from—the death of his beautiful son, Connor.

It didn't matter to him that it was his father who'd inadvertently sent Connor on a job that had got him killed. It wasn't Art Foley's intention, and families, by nature and practice, were messy, convoluted and unpredictable.

But for whatever it was he'd lost, he could get revenge—and then some.

By seizing *opportunity*.

And Brendan had given him that, whether he liked it or not.

'Now, who here has any real allegiance to that man over there, Harvey Culpepper?'

They all nodded, and glanced at Culpepper, like dogs looking to their master for approval.

'So if I wasn't holding this gun, you'd be all over me, doing his bidding.'

'If you weren't holding that gun,' answered one on the end with a grey flat-top. 'I'd be ripping out your guts and making balloon animals with them.'

Ross felt the old impotence loosen its grip on his rage—finally—and raised the shotgun, and blasted a hole as big as a Mitre size 5 football in the man's chest.

Nobody moved, shock descending.

'I take no pleasure in that at all.' Ross was lying—he really did. 'But I need to show you I'm serious about your options. And I'm really fuckin' serious.'

Suddenly, the men looked straight ahead, locked to the spot, desperate to show a collective backbone, even though it had just been jellied. Ross walked the line, shotgun alternating chests as he did.

'Does he look after you? Does he treat you fairly? Does he pay you right for the risks you take?'

Metres away, under the cycloptic eye of Kharthik's pistol barrel, Culpepper looked electric with spite.

The nods were less convincing this time.

'So you'll forgive me for asking—would you take a bullet for him?'

That didn't bring so many nods at all.

'And in return, would he take a bullet for you?' Ross turned slightly to address Culpepper. 'Well, tell them, Harvey. Would you?'

This was the point at which a leader could show whether he was an inspirational beacon of fellowship or a tyrant despot. Harvey Culpepper answered by sending out a gob of phlegm in Ross Foley's direction.

Ross laughed. Male pride, the nail in so many coffins.

'I think you have your answer.' He lowered the shotgun barrel.

'There's six bags there. You each pick one up, and I'll take the last.'

His brother spoke from behind him. 'Ross, please. Don't do this.'

'Reclaiming our birthright, this,' Ross replied. 'How many times do you get a chance to do that?'

'Ross, this isn't right,' Brendan pleaded. 'I didn't bring you back for *this*.'

'Come and stand next to me. We can do this together, like it was always meant to be.'

'No. No. You must be mad.'

Ross turned back to the men. 'You have contacts. I have contacts. Each bag, you sell it, put fifty per cent back into the enterprise. My enterprise. But that other fifty is all yours, you keep it. You five and me, all equal shares and between this six, it's equal shares the way forward. Do you want to be doormen forever?'

The men said nothing, but Ross knew the cogs were whirring.

He turned back to his brother. 'Brendan, now is the time. Come in on this with me, and we bring the Foley name back in an instant.'

Brendan didn't answer for a moment, didn't know what to say, until: 'This is madness,' and he walked to Ross.

Ross brought the shotgun up, held it loosely towards Brendan. 'Don't make me. I'm begging you, don't, but there are some things you will never understand.

Brendan stopped. 'This was about protecting us. Protecting my family. They're still in danger Ross!'

The brothers stared at each other, until Ross shook his head, and turned back to the men. 'Lads, if you're with me, take a bag each. Let's go and get rich.'

One at a time, the men stepped forward and picked up a holdall.

'You wretched bastards!' said Culpepper.

Ross strode over to him, confidence high now. 'You've lost everything. Your boys are my boys. You don't even know where that wife of yours is. You're done, Harvey. Now, get in the bin with the chief. Let's see what all the fuss is about.'

CHAPTER 61

BRENDAN HAD GONE from one hell to another in the space of a couple of minutes—and where his words were failing him, Kharthik's suddenly weren't.

The young detective stepped forward, the barrel of his gun switching from Culpepper to Ross. 'I'm afraid I can't let you do that.'

The sight of a gun trained on his brother tugged sharply on some lost fossil of fraternal bond. 'Put it down, Kharthik!'

'Foley, you can't seriously let this go ahead?' Kharthik didn't even glance away from Ross.

Madison filled in the blanks. 'He's right Brendan. Think about this,' she cried.

Brendan's gun lowered from where Monroe was still treading water in the bin. He let go and the gun dropped.

'Ross, they're right,' he said. 'You can't do this. You can't shut down one thing to start another.'

'You're with me or against me, bro,' replied Ross.

The word *bro* cut deep.

'Put the shotgun down!' shouted Kharthik.

'Or what? You're not going to shoot me,' Ross responded. 'That's not what coppers on these shores do.'

'I will if it stops those drugs from hitting the street.' God knew, with everything he'd been through, he'd feel this more than most.

Brendan couldn't bear it. Couldn't handle the threat to his family anymore. His father last year, those moments believing his baby son had been murdered before the sheer relief when he found out he was fine, the fear all day today when he knew Mim and his boys were on the run everywhere. 'Just stop! Stop! Guns down, everyone, please!' He shouted.

The night around them fell silent, just for a moment.

Kharthik was the first to lower his gun. 'I'll do everything I can,' he told Ross, 'to pull you in for what you're doing here tonight.'

'I don't doubt that.' In turn, Ross walked over to Culpepper. He got up close to the older man, who seemed like he was shrivelling visibly, like a little chastised pecker out in the cold. 'You killed my dad. And my fuckin' son. Get in that bin, *now*.'

Culpepper shuffled forwards, and approached the great steel dumpster. He started pleading in a shaky voice. 'The chief here was going to get a million quid for bringing Foley to me. If you help me, it's yours.'

The words echoed without reply.

'You're on your own,' said Ross, before dropping the shotgun and ripping the bat from Culpepper's grip. He swung it ferociously. Once, twice, on Culpepper's arms. Two loud cracks rang out, two breaks. Culpepper didn't even have time to scream when Ross swung the weapon again, once, twice, on each knee. Snapping patellas sounding like abrupt applause. He began to topple, but Ross hoisted him into the bin.

'No!' shouted Kharthik, racing forwards. Brendan found himself jumping in between Ross and Kharthik.

'Bags in the lift, lads—then come and help me,' shouted Ross, who began immediately smashing the side of the bin.

The men trapped inside screamed gutturally for their lives. Brendan knew the pain. Couldn't work out whether either of the men in there really deserved it. Decided they just might. They roiled against each other, panting and bellowing, sounding like injured animals left to die, their mortality stretched out and stripped from them. Monroe vomited, and couldn't stop heaving once he'd started.

'Jesus, that's a bit much,' said Ross, as he rounded the dumpster, and threw the lid over.

The last thing Brendan saw of Chief Superintendent Terry Monroe and the bastard Harvey Culpepper was the two of them locked in an agonised embrace as their organs were liquified. The lid closed, and Ross locked them both in, muffling out their screams for mercy.

EVERYTHING ABOUT THIS was wrong.

Madison had had enough. She sprinted across the rooftop, as the men were loading the bags into the lift, probably thinking about what colour Range Rover they were going to buy.

The screaming from inside the bin grew deafening, like animals in a tin abattoir. She was on Ross Foley in a flash, and had him by the shoulders.

'Ross, stop this,' she said, pinning his arms up his back—but she hadn't even locked in the hold when she was dragged off the man by two pairs of arms. She fought, bucked and kicked. Got free and started swinging like it was the last round of a title fight, and she was down on the cards. It took two more men to hold her, and all four of them eventually had her pinned.

Ross held the shotgun to her head, which was about the only part of her he could see. 'Stop now, please. Mate, you too, over here, play nice or all the king's horses and all that.'

Kharthik dropped his own revolver and was shoved on the floor next to Madison. They were held face down on the deck.

Madison realised there was no chance of escape. 'Brendan,' she said, breathing heavily. 'Please, you have to stop this.'

Brendan looked at her, but there was a far-off detachment in his eyes.

'This isn't the justice you want,' said Madison.

'What other justice is there for what they've done?' Brendan asked softly.

Ross finished banging on the side of the bin; the howls inside were reduced to gurgles now. He cracked the lid. Brendan didn't want to look. Ross blew out hard. 'Jesus Christ,' he said. 'Serves you right, you filthy fuckers. Fancy a look?' He looked at his brother.

Brendan shook his head. 'This isn't right,' he said again.

Ross turned on him. 'These fuckers betrayed you and killed our dad, your nephew—my son. If anything, it's not enough. Lads? Let's give this the heave-ho.'

Madison felt sick. 'Brendan, Ross, you can't do this... This is against everything you stand for, Brendan.'

Brendan stepped forward again, and again, his brother raised the shotgun in his direction.

'I mean it,' Ross said. 'Don't.'

Two of the men went to the bin, and Madison realised that there were now three men holding her and Kharthik down, as opposed to four. But face down, arms pulled back to breaking point, nose pinned to brick, there was nothing they could do to intervene.

'Over the side,' said Ross. 'One, two, three.'

'No!' shouted Brendan, but he still didn't move.

Kharthik started to buck and writhe, earning him a couple of kidney shots for his trouble.

All the while, Ross Foley and the two doormen rolled the dumpster to the edge of the roof.

'Sleep tight,' shouted Ross, as the back two wheels dropped off the lip of the roof. The weight shifted backwards, and with a scrape and scream of metal, it fell and dropped out of sight.

Silence. For a couple of seconds.

Then a distant crash followed by the hiss of settling water.

Nobody said anything. Ross looked over the edge.

'And the king is dead,' he said. 'He's not getting up from that.'

Brendan dropped to his knees.

The fight left Madison in one purging sigh.

Even Kharthik finally gave up.

Ross walked back and picked up the shotgun. 'Brendan, it's time to go.'

Brendan didn't say a word. Just shook his head, eyes red.

'The doors always open for you,' his brother said. He led his new colleagues towards the lift.

Madison rolled over, suddenly free, and saw Ross Foley pointing a shotgun at her, keeping her in place. He only lowered it as the lift doors closed.

They listened to the lift judder down, away from the roof, towards a new era. The era of Ross Foley.

EPILOGUE

MADISON AND KHARTHIK had walked Brendan down from the roof. The pain across his torso was excruciating, every step was painful—but his brain was numb. They took a quick stop-off at the bottom of the building. The dumpster had split on impact, spraying the contents across the forecourt. Monroe and Culpepper were nothing more than soaked bundles, so broken they were barely recognisable as ever having been human.

Worse came when Brendan, with faltering breaths, opened the boot of Madison's car to show them what Monroe had done to DS Christopher. Kharthik couldn't believe it, went silent and pale, then walked back to the building. Madison blanched equally, before the tears came—then sobbed, hunched over the body in the boot.

All Brendan could do was lean against the car, spent, and listen to Madison's snotty breaths.

It wasn't long before she railed against Brendan with anger. 'How?' she spat. 'How am I supposed to square all this away? How am I supposed to make this right?'

'I don't know,' Brendan said. 'The truth is the only way.'

'The truth...' Madison's sobs rolled uneasily into wracking, hopeless laughs.

Brendan couldn't answer.

After a few moments, Madison upped and spoke with Kharthik, who, after a minute, nodded his head. Brendan walked over, but Madison held up a hand: 'Back off. This is for the police to sort out. You can listen to that, just this time, won't you?'

Brendan put his hands up in apology and paced backwards.

The two officers spoke, and Kharthik took out his phone. Nodded again—then gave Madison the gun. She put a hand on his shoulder, said something else, then came back to the car.

'Get in,' she said to Brendan.

He did as he was told, not before shouting a weak thanks to Kharthik.

Madison handed him the gun. 'You're going to get rid of that. Properly. No one finds it. You've got that?'

'I don't—'

'Do not fuck with me on this, alright?'

Brendan pocketed the gun.

They rode in silence for a while, the enormity of what had happened settling on them like a blanket of snow.

Brendan eventually asked. 'What's going to happen now?'

'I'm taking you to your family. Kharthik has called it in. Then I'm taking Tom to the mortuary.'

'And me?'

'Me and Kharthik got there in time to see Superintendent Monroe and Harvey Culpepper fight over you, then by accident they both fell off the roof. I got you to your family, Kharthik stuck around to secure the scene. You were unconscious the whole time. Got it?'

'Thank y—'

'Don't you dare say it! Don't you dare say thank you. I'm done being your fall-back, getting you out of whatever shitty decision you've made next.'

They rode in silence the rest of the way.

THE STATION WAS ghostly. Patel was on the desk, her lips parted and her eyes red-rimmed.

'I heard,' she said.

Madison shook her head, and walked Brendan through the building. Heads began to pop out of doorways, the grapevine buzzed and the place was busier than it ever normally would have been at nearly one o'clock on a weeknight.

Madison shooed them back, as they reached the Super's door.

The Super. Madison still couldn't believe it.

She knocked three times. 'Mrs Foley, it's DI Madison.'

The door was unlocked and opened, and inside, Mim Foley stood there, exhausted, fraught, but safe, next to Dan, who rushed at his father.

'Dad! You're okay?'

Father and son embraced. 'I'm sorry, son,' Brendan said. 'I'm so sorry. Are you okay?'

'Yeah, Dad. It got bad, but I think we're all right.'

Madison stepped to one side to allow their embrace, and caught sight of young Mick, asleep, swaddled in a jumper on the sofa. Not a care in the world.

Brendan took a step towards Mim and tried to embrace her, but her body stayed rigid. She looked at Madison, as he kissed her cheek.

'Are we safe now?' she asked Madison, her gaze nothing short of livid.

'Yes. Everything is over,' Madison replied.

'Thank you.' Mim walked over to Mick without a word, and picked him up. He didn't stir. She carried him to the door. 'Dan, come on. Let's go home.'

'Thank God for that,' said the boy, buoyant for the first time since Madison had met him.

When Brendan turned to join them, Mim stopped him with two words.

'Not you.'

Her words offered no compromise. Brendan stood and watched as his family walked away from him. Madison didn't know what to say. But both knew; Mim Foley was right.

Footsteps grew closer. It was Sergeant Patel, and she started speaking before she even got through the door.

'DI Madison, you can't take DC Christopher to the mortuary. You'll have to take him to the hospital. A & E.'

'Why? He... he can't be saved, Sanaya.'

Patel paused to catch her breath. 'I know... but there's a fire at the mortuary.' She stared into Madison's face. 'It's all going up.'

ON THE OTHER side of Warrington, at the top of a multistorey car park with a view over town, Jordan 'Seabreeze' Seabaruth watched the pyre throw out its flames, right by the hospital. He wondered what on earth he had done, and if there could ever be any forgiveness.

ACKNOWLEDGEMENTS

I have been so lucky to work on this book, and on this series as a whole. To bring a story set in Warrington to a wider audience has absolutely delighted me, and I'm thankful to everyone who has helped make it happen.

To Sean Coleman, Trina and the team at Red Dog, my gratitude is eternal. I adore working with you, and am so grateful for the support and opportunities you grant me.

Huge thanks to Imogen Papworth, Harry Scoble, Alys Hewer and Sembene Manji whose work on the Audible side of things has always been incredible.

Warren Brown—man, I will always be grateful for you saying yes to this. You elevated this material so high, the platform changed and so did my career. You've done more for me than you know! Thank you, mate.

Massive thank you to the best in the business, Karen Ball, whose work makes my books better than they ever have any right to be. A complete genius.

To my agent Maddalena, I can't thank you enough for guiding me, keeping me on the right path, inspiring me and getting the best out of me. Your notes and suggestions are out of this world, and I'm so much a better writer because of it. Always grateful.

To Lisa Howells, thank you for supporting me and my work above and beyond.

To my fellow authors, I'm so proud to be a part of your community. Your constant inspiration and support is treasured.

To my readers, you are the best. Simply, THANK YOU. Your support and encouragement means the world.

Last but by no means least, thank you, my family and friends. I'll keep the mushy stuff for in person, but I love you all and am so blessed.

Milton Keynes UK
Ingram Content Group UK Ltd.
UKHW040940250823
427470UK00004B/161

9 781915 433190